ON STRIKE FOR CHRISTMAS

SHEILA ROBERTS

ISIS
LARGE
PRINT

First published in Great Britain 2014
by
Piatkus
An imprint of Little, Brown Book Group

First Isis Edition
published 2016
by arrangement with
Little, Brown Book Group

A catalogue record for this book is available
from the British Library.

ISBN 978–1–78541–139–5 (hb)
ISBN 978–1–78541–141–0 (pb)

Published by
F. A. Thorpe (Publishing)
Anstey, Leicestershire

Set by Words & Graphics Ltd.
Anstey, Leicestershire
Printed and bound in Great Britain by
T. J. International Ltd., Padstow, Cornwall

This book is printed on acid-free paper

ON STRIKE FOR CHRISTMAS

At Christmas time, it seems as though a woman's work is never done. Trimming the tree, mailing the cards, schlepping to the shops, the endless wrapping — bah humbug! So this year, Joy and Laura and the rest of their knitting group decide to go on strike. If their husbands and families want a nice holiday filled with parties, decorations and presents — well, they'll just have to do it themselves. The boycott soon takes on a life of its own when a reporter picks up the story and more women join in. But as Christmas Day approaches, Joy, Laura and their husbands confront larger issues in their marriages, and discover that a little holiday magic is exactly what they need to come together.

To Susan, Debbie, and Jill,
my three good fairies

Acknowledgements

I'd like to thank my friend Kema Bohn for helping me get my cancer facts straight. You beat the disease with grace and dignity — you're an inspiration. Thank you also to the Port Orchard Brain Trust: Lois Dyer, Rose Marie Harris, Patty Jough-Haan, Krysteen Seelen, Susan Plunkett, Kate Breslin, Susan Wiggs, and Anjalee Banerjee. Your insights were always appreciated. I also want to acknowledge my amazing agent, Paige Wheeler, and my wonderful editor, Rose Hilliard. Where would I be without you two? (I don't want to even try to imagine.) Thanks, too, to all those great cooks whose recipes have added richness to my life and pounds to my hips. Speaking of recipes, thanks, Marliss, for helping me make some of those old family recipes make sense. And last but not least, thanks to my long-suffering husband, Robert, who said to make sure I spelled his name right, for helping me with my football terminology. (So, did I get the name right?) Happy holidays to every one of you! May your stockings be filled with all the good things you deserve and may the Sugarplum Fairy make the calories vanish from every Christmas cookie you eat.

CHAPTER
ONE

We wish you a merry Christmas...

Glen Fredericks slapped the back of his last departing Thanksgiving dinner guest. "Good to see ya. Thanks for coming."

"Hey, man, great time," said the mooch. "Thanks for having me."

"No problem. We'll do it all again at Christmas," Glen promised.

Behind him, Glen's wife, Laura, suddenly envisioned herself going after her husband with the electric carving knife he'd used earlier on the turkey. "In your dreams," she growled. She stepped around Glen and shoved the front door shut. Having made contact with a hefty male hind end, it didn't shut easily, especially for a woman who was five feet two and a hundred and nineteen pounds, but she managed.

"Hey," Glen protested. "What was that all about?"

"You need to ask?" Laura gave her overchewed gum an angry snap. He did this to her every year, and every year he promised that next year things would be different. But they never were.

1

"Mama, Tyler's in the frigerator," called five-year-old Amy.

Laura marched toward the kitchen, Glen trotting after her. "Today might have been your idea of fun, but it sure wasn't mine."

No woman in her right mind would volunteer to have her house turned into the city dump by the invasion of family, friends, and Thanksgiving freeloaders her husband had invited into their home. Before the invasion, this room had looked great, decorated with little gourds, cute ceramic pumpkins, and her two prettiest vases filled with mums. Now everywhere she looked she saw a mess. CDs lay scattered on the floor in front of the entertainment center. Her new leather couch was littered with a plastic football, Glen's socks, magazines, and an open can of nuts (half-spilled). Glasses and bottles were strewn every which way across her coffee table. The little hand-painted, wooden Pilgrim couple that she'd set out on the sofa table now lay on their sides as if taking a nap, not that you could really see them anyway in the litter of napkins and appetizer plates and other party leftovers. And it was hard to ignore the towel on the carpet, evidence of an earlier wine spill mop-up.

People said you shouldn't have cream-colored carpet when you had little kids. Well, people were wrong. She managed to keep the carpet clean just fine with two kids. It was Glen's moocher co-worker who was the problem. And, of course, Glen had been too busy

2

yukking it up to tell her about the spill. She discovered it only when she stepped on it in her stockinged feet.

"Come on, babe," he protested. "It's the holidays, and it only comes once a year."

"It's a good thing because it takes me a whole year to recover. In case you didn't notice, Glen, we've got two children, a big house that *I* clean, and I work thirty hours a week." Before Glen could reply they heard the distinctive crash of a dish breaking followed by a startled cry. "Oh, great. Now what?" Laura muttered, and picked up speed.

She found Amy hovering near the doorway, a golden-haired cherub. "I told him not to," Amy said, already the bossy older sister.

Behind her, by the fridge, stood two-and-a-half-year-old Tyler — nickname, Tyler the Terrible — whimpering.

At his feet lay a fluffy pile of whipped cream fruit salad, broken shards of ceramic bowl sticking up through it like mountain peaks through the clouds.

Laura walked over to where her son stood and surveyed the damage. "Mess, Mama," Tyler told her.

She had been going nonstop since six in the morning and it was now eight at night. She sat down on the floor behind her son and began to cry. That set Tyler off, and he started wailing. She pulled him to her and they both went at it.

"It's okay, baby," Glen said and knelt beside her. He was a big, kindhearted, teddy bear of a man. Most days. Today, he was just a big pain in the butt.

He reached out to put a beefy arm around her and she gave him a shove. "Bite me. Do you have any idea what this day has been like for me, Glen? Do you even have a clue?"

"You made a great dinner," he tried.

"Yes, *I* made the dinner. No one brought anything except your mother, and all she brought was soggy pumpkin pies. I stuffed and baked the turkey, I made the fruit salad, the candied yams, the smelly rutabagas your lazy cousin loves, the green bean casserole, the mashed potatoes and gravy, and the dinner rolls from your mother's recipe. Why can't she make her own damn rolls?"

From the other side of the kitchen, Amy gasped. "Mama said damn."

"Mamas can do that on Thanksgiving," Glen said, thinking quickly.

Yeah, he had a comeback for a five-year-old, but he couldn't think of anything to say to his wife. What could he say, the big turkey? "I cleaned and decorated the house, set the table, and made the whole effing dinner. And, while you and your family and those freeloaders that you call friends all sat around afterward like beached whales and watched the football game, your mother and I got to clean up the big, effing mess you left. I don't care how much football you played in high school and college. You could miss fifteen minutes of one game to help."

He frowned. "Hey, I was watching the kids."

"Yeah, right. When, during the beer commercials? Tyler ate almost an entire candy bowl of M&M's. It's a wonder he hasn't thrown up yet. And if he does, guess who's dealing with it."

Glen held up a hand to cut her off. "I will, don't worry. But you know it's not entirely fair to say I did nothing. I helped."

She glared at him. "Oh, yeah, you put the extra leaf in the table and brought up the folding chairs. Real big of you." She got up and steamed out of the kitchen, calling over her shoulder, "I'm taking a bath. After that, I'm going to bed with my mystery novel. I don't want to see you or anyone for the rest of the evening."

Glen's voice followed her. "That's a good idea, babe. Take a break. You deserve it."

That was an understatement, Laura decided, looking at her reflection in the bathroom mirror. The makeup that hadn't worn off was now smudged and runny from her crying jag, and her hair was a mess. She looked like blond roadkill. She felt like it, too. The labors of Thanksgiving had almost crushed her.

And in just four weeks her husband expected her to do this all again. Four weeks? Who was she kidding? It would all start this weekend with cleaning up the mess Hurricane Glen had left in his wake. (Naturally, he'd help . . . for about two minutes until he got distracted horsing around with the kids or finding a football game to watch.) Then they'd start hauling out the Christmas decorations and begin the Christmas shopping. The day after Thanksgiving, the biggest shopping day of the year — she couldn't face it. Maybe she'd just stay in the tub until she turned into the world's largest prune. Or until Glen got a clue.

Except Glen was terminally clueless, so she'd never leave the tub again. If only his brain size matched the

5

size of his heart. Maybe he needed glasses. He obviously couldn't see how much extra work he dumped on her this time of year.

She dropped her gum in the garbage and turned on the bathwater, running it as hot as she could and pouring in an extra packet of bubbles. Sighing, she slipped into the steaming bath.

Okay, that was better. The scented water began to soothe away her anger. She really shouldn't have lost it with Glen. After all, it wasn't entirely his fault. She'd agreed to this insanity. But only after he'd promised to help her.

Her mind drifted back to the days when she enjoyed parties as much as Glen. Boy, that felt like ancient history. In those days she didn't have kids and a large house to keep up and a job, and a lot of the partying happened at restaurants and clubs and other people's places. Those days had sure vanished. Somewhere along the way her house had become Party Central, and she had become everyone's maid. Someone had tipped the scales, leaving her to do all the work while Glen did all the playing.

She'd tried to explain to him how hard he made it for her when he invited the world over. He always promised he'd do more to help, but then company would show up and he'd be useless. Or one of his buddies would call him to come play some flag football and the honey-do list would get completely forgotten. He loved people, and he loved the holidays. No matter what, Glen always managed to have a merry Christmas. In fact, his Christmases were getting merrier every year, while hers were getting more and more stressful. And she was sure she was getting TMJ. She'd quit smoking years ago and taken up chewing gum in its place, but lately it seemed she didn't so much chew as grind her molars in anger and frustration.

She frowned at the frothy pile of bubbles around her, poked one with her finger and watched it pop. There was definitely something wrong with the Fredrickses' holiday picture these days, but if she was going to keep her sanity, she'd have to find a way to fix it. Before Christmas came.

Joy Robertson could feel it even before she turned and saw the long-suffering expression on her husband's face. They'd been at her brother's house for nearly three hours and he'd had enough. It was time to leave.

Sometimes she wished she didn't have that mental connection forged over twenty-four years of marriage. Then she could just stay and party on until she dropped.

She set the second piece of pumpkin pie she'd been enjoying on the counter and said to her sister-in-law, "I guess we should get going."

Lonnie shot a look to where Bob stood in the kitchen doorway. He was a nice-looking middle-aged man. So far Father Time had been good to Bob, leaving him with a full head of sandy-colored hair, barely sprinkled with gray. He had a disgustingly great metabolism and was still as slim as the day they married.

"It won't kill Bob to wait while you finish your pie," Lonnie said with a grin.

Bob tried to look like he didn't mind if Joy lingered over her pie, but he was a very bad actor. The pleading was plain to see in those brown eyes of his.

"I don't know," Joy said, eyeing him. "It might."

"You can have another piece, too, while you're waiting," Lonnie told Bob. "Heck, as skinny as you are, have two." Good, old Lonnie; she was twelve years older than Joy and Bob, with a big heart and waistline to match, more a mother figure than a sister, and she was very much used to being in charge.

"No, thanks. I've had enough," Bob replied.

Obviously. When Bob was ready to leave, his adult body channeled an unhappy seven-year-old who followed Joy around and psychically whined, "Can we go now?" When the psychic whine didn't work he resorted to head nods in the direction of the door. And rather than argue, she always acquiesced.

Why should she always have to give in and make him happy? Bob knew how much holiday gatherings meant to her, especially these times with her family. Lucky for him she hadn't realized back when they were young and crazy in love that he was the world's biggest party pooper.

She sighed mentally. Oh, well. Something was better than nothing. "I don't need the extra calories anyway," she told Lonnie. Thanks to shifting middle-age hormones she was now carrying thirty more pounds than she wanted, pounds that kept sneaking up on her when she wasn't looking and attaching themselves to her hips.

Still, a woman only got to eat pumpkin pie once a year. And now that she was Menopause Mama, coping with hot flashes and mood swings, she ought to be allowed a few small pleasures. Anyway, she didn't look all that bad naked. So that meant it had to be the clothes that were making her look fat. *Note to self: Find some nonbulky winter sweaters.*

She picked up the plate again. "One more bite for the road," she decided and forked up another mouthful.

"Why not?" Lonnie agreed. "You've got a designated driver."

The designated driver gave his wife another pleading look.

Joy took one last quick bite. Rushing through pumpkin pie — it was a crime. She set down her plate, then brushed past Bob and went downstairs to the split-level's lower floor, dubbed the party room.

The two long tables that had held their Thanksgiving feast had been removed, and now her nephews and several of their children were busy with the annual Thanksgiving leg-wrestling contest. The spectators were coupled up, women standing with their husband's arms draped over their shoulders, all laughing, enjoying themselves. They looked like they could be posing for Norman Rockwell.

Joy felt a wistful tug on her heart. Over the years Bob had edged closer and closer to the outside of the extended family circle. Now, although they came to the celebration in the same car, they weren't really a couple. They were two people engaged in a holiday tug-of-war, each one pulling from opposite ends of a crowded house.

Their daughter, Melia, was holding eight-month-old Sarah, Joy's first grandchild, and standing at the edge of the circle next to her husband, Cam.

"We're leaving," Joy announced.

Melia's eyebrows shot up. "Already?"

"It's been almost three hours." That was Bob's limit.

Melia checked her watch. "It's only been two. What's Daddy's problem?"

"Too much of a good thing." Joy kissed her grandbaby, hugged her daughter and her son-in-law, and then started to make the rounds.

"Sorry you have to rush off," said her other sister-in-law, Susan.

Lonnie was with them now. "Well, Suki, if you weren't still holding that whipped-cream can maybe poor Bob could bring himself to stay. But he's been looking nervous ever since you started chasing people with it."

"Wait a minute. Let's set the record straight," said Susan. "It was Joy who started chasing people with the whipped cream."

Joy held up empty hands. "Do you see any whipped cream on me anywhere?"

Susan grinned. "No. It looks like you got it all out of your hair." She looked across the room and said, "Anyway, I'd never hurt Bob. He ought to know that after all these years."

10

Joy looked to see that Bob had changed doorways. Now he was hovering at the party room entrance like the Grim Reaper.

"Well, here," said Susan, holding up the can. "Open up and I'll give you a shot for the road."

Joy obliged and Susan gave her a whipped cream fill-up. She wished she had the rest of that piece of pie to go with it. She ought to have finished it. It wouldn't have done her steadily widening hips any good, but it might have made her feel better about leaving before she was ready.

She hugged her mother and Lonnie's mother, and all the little great-nieces and nephews, waved good-bye to the wrestlers, and, finally, hugged her big brother, Al, who was getting ready to referee a new wrestling match.

Now the gray-haired patriarch of the family, Al had been hosting the festivities ever since he and Lonnie married, and no one ever considered going anywhere else. Who would want to? Their house was always decorated to the hilt and filled with laughter. It was the quintessential holiday house.

"Glad you came, kiddo," Al said, and kissed the top of Joy's head. Kiddo. She was a middle-aged, overweight woman whose brown hair color now had to come from a bottle, and her brother still called her kiddo. She loved it.

"Me, too," she said, and thought, and sorry I'm leaving. The last to arrive, the first to leave. What else was new?

If only she could take some DNA from her neighbor Laura's husband and inject it into Bob. Knowing Bob he'd only morph into a two-hundred-pound hermit.

They retrieved their coats from the pile on the bed in the guest bedroom in silence, Bob's relieved, hers slightly miffed. Lonnie met them at the front door with Joy's bowls and platters, now empty and clean. "Thanks for bringing all the goodies," she said. "It pays to have a caterer in the family." Lonnie hugged her, then Bob. "Good to see you Bob," she said. "See you at Christmas."

"I'm afraid so," Bob muttered as he and Joy went down the front walk toward their car.

Joy pretended not to have heard. Oh, well, she told herself, you did have a wonderful time; be thankful for that. Pollyanna, playing the glad game, sneered the Joy who was miffed.

They got into the car. The good Joy ignored the miffed Joy and attempted to get Bob to join her in the game. "That was fun," she announced, forcing good humor into her voice.

As soon as the words were out of her mouth she realized this was as much a holiday tradition as anything that happened at her brother's house. Every year she tried to convince her husband that he really loved these holiday traditions. And every year he said something rude, like . . .

"Well, it was typical, I'll say that."

"What's that supposed to mean?" As if she didn't know.

Sure enough. "It's the same every year: same people, same jokes, same pranks. Someone always sticks their finger in the whipped cream on someone else's pumpkin pie; someone always gets in a fight with the whipped cream cans. Boring and juvenile."

"My family is not boring."

Where did Bob get off, anyway? Her husband, the brilliant mystery writer, superior to the rest of the world — bah, humbug. Her family could hold their own against anyone, even a writer. It ran the gamut from car mechanics to law students, with interests ranging from sports to travel. Surely somewhere in that mix of people her husband could find something or someone to interest him. She knew what the deal was. He was secretly jealous because her family was close, caring, and exciting — while his was distant and dull. They didn't even want to live near one another. Now, that said a lot.

"It's like a bad movie that gets replayed every year," Bob continued as they drove down the street. "And every year it gets bigger."

"Well, what do you expect? The family is growing."

"Like mold. I can only imagine what it will be like in another five years."

That did it. "If my family's holiday celebration is so unsatisfactory, why don't you ever do something to make it interesting? All you do at the holidays is complain."

"Maybe I wouldn't complain if you didn't have to turn these gatherings into a marathon. Geez, Joy, considering how much I hate them, I'd think you'd be glad I at least show up."

He showed up all right. And grumbled all the way there. And, as if that wasn't bad enough, now that the kids were grown he even complained in front of them, poisoning the well of family solidarity.

But he didn't stop with complaining about being with her family. He grumped his way through all the season's activities. The annual neighborhood Christmas party, New Year's Eve — whatever it was, if it involved a group of people and a good time Bob approached it like a man headed for the electric chair.

"Show up?" she retorted. "You're a ghost. You may as well not be there."

"So does that mean I don't have to go back at Christmas?" he cracked.

"Very funny." Joy frowned and looked out the window as they made their way through downtown Holly back to their house on the other side of town. It was dark now, and icy rain sliced through the streetlight beams, falling into puddles on the asphalt. The downtown stores were closed and, in spite of their holiday decorations, wore a deserted, sad look.

Joy sighed. Would Bob even have a life if he hadn't married her? What would his Christmases have looked like without her and the kids? *You've really had a wonderful life, Bob*. But he didn't realize it, and that was his problem.

"You should thank me," she informed him. "If it wasn't for me hauling you out to things like this your life would be so dull." He'd be as mummified as his

14

parents, who were spending their retirement in solitary in Yuma.

Bob smiled. "Sounds good to me. All that chaos and noise, who needs it?"

"Everyone. People need to feel connected, feel like they matter. The holidays make life special. They lift people out of their humdrum, everyday existence and remind them that it's good to be alive."

"Well, maybe people need to improve their humdrum, everyday existence. Then they'd be glad to be alive and we could avoid all this."

Joy frowned and shook her head at him. "You are so lucky I don't have a whipped-cream can in my hand."

What had happened to the man who, when they were first married, helped her trim the tree and sat next to her on the couch in her brother's living room and sang Christmas carols? He'd disappeared like the Ghost of Christmas Past. And, somewhere along the way, this soured version of Bob had moved in and taken over.

When had Bob's Christmas disconnect started? Maybe it was when the kids stopped believing in Santa. Maybe Bob had decided if they could stop pretending, so could he. And now Joy was the only one left pretending. But Winter Wonderland was meant to be shared. Bob's attitude made her feel like he had let go of her hand and was leaving her to walk on alone.

Now that they were empty nesters, was he figuring to pull farther back until he edged himself completely out of the picture? If he did, what would Christmas Future look like?

Joy remembered Mrs. Anderson, the mother of her best friend in grade school and junior high. Mrs. Anderson and her husband pretty much lived separate lives. Mrs. Anderson had come alone to everything from school concerts to parties while Mr. Anderson stayed home in his easy chair and watched TV. The Andersons had sometimes seemed more an oddity than a couple. Would that be Joy and Bob in a few more years?

She got a sudden vision of herself and her husband drifting slowly apart until they could only experience life's important moments from opposite sides of a great chasm. What a terrible thought! She couldn't let that happen.

He shot her an apologetic look. "Come on, hon, you know it's not that I don't like your family. It's just that, well, they go overboard on these occasions. Things don't always have to be done the way the Johnsons do them."

"My family knows how to make the holidays great," Joy retorted. "And, in case you haven't noticed, I do a lot of the same things they do, things you'd miss if I didn't do them."

"Wait a minute," Bob said. "Now we've moved from your family to you. Not a good idea."

"I am my family," Joy said. "And, unlike *some* people, who should be glad they married me —"

"They? Do you have more husbands hidden somewhere I don't know about?" interrupted the smart-mouth sitting behind the wheel.

She frowned at him. "Are you trying to tick me off?"

He reached a hand over and patted her leg. "I *am* glad I married you. Very glad."

"Are you?" she asked, arching an eyebrow. "Sometimes I wonder."

He looked shocked. "Of course I am. I couldn't imagine my life without you."

"Same here," Joy said, softening.

Her husband was a good man, loyal and dependable. He still had a great smile and a great sense of humor to match.

But sometimes the extreme differences in their personalities really bothered her. Her idea of a great life was good times with lots of people. Bob, on the other hand, was shy and hated big, noisy gatherings, and over the years she'd shrunk her social style to fit his. Except this time of year. Some things had to remain sacred. And she didn't think participating in a few celebrations at Christmas was too much to ask, considering how much she denied herself the rest of the year. She thought of those camping trips Bob dragged her on every summer — sleeping in the middle of nowhere in a tent with only mosquitoes for company. Ugh. And then there were the mini book tours and writers' conferences. Although she enjoyed attending those with him, she often sacrificed catering jobs and missed important social events. Last year they'd been gone on her mother's birthday.

"But just because we love each other, it doesn't mean I have to like everything you do, does it?" Bob said, hauling out one of his favorite arguments.

It was the opening salvo for a fresh verbal battle and they started in again. Finally Joy said in a huff, "You don't have a clue how to celebrate Christmas." Although God knew she'd tried hard enough to teach him over the years.

"There's no secret to celebrating Christmas. Any idiot can put up a tree and play some Christmas carols."

"Listen to you, Mr. Merry Christmas," Joy scoffed. "You don't realize that all the things you complain about are really what make the holidays memorable."

He shook his head. "Memorable by whose definition? If we're using yours, I'd as soon experience some memory loss."

"Oh, you don't mean that," Joy chided. "This is supposed to be a season of joy — the food, the decorations, the being together —"

"Is all a big pain in the neck. Ever hear of 'Silent Night'?"

"Ever hear of 'Joy to the World'?"

Bob gave a shrug. "We all experience that in different ways. And just once I wish the Grinch would steal Christmas."

Joy crossed her arms over her chest and fumed. Bob Robertson, direct descendant of Ebenezer Scrooge. It was a good thing he wasn't in charge of Christmas.

Wait a minute. What if he was? She studied him. Bob could plan the perfect murder, but could he solve the mystery of what made a happy holiday? What would he learn if he was given a George Bailey-like Christmas? What if he had to sample life as if he'd never been married, if he was given a taste of the holidays without all the traditions and festivities he enjoyed complaining about?

He couldn't read her mind, but he'd grown pretty good at reading her moods. They stopped for a red light and he turned to look suspiciously at her. "What?"

"I was just thinking."

Now he looked wary. "Uh-oh."

Uh-oh was right, because a plan was forming in Joy's mind. She grinned, feeling incredibly wicked. This could prove very interesting.

CHAPTER
TWO

Long after Bob was snoring, enjoying the blissful sleep of the ignorant, Joy lay awake, her own unique version of sugarplums dancing through her head in between hot flashes. She could already see it — Bob jumping out of bed Christmas morning like a reformed Scrooge, proclaiming himself a new man, then excitedly preparing to rush out and enjoy the day's festivities (after falling at her feet and thanking her for bringing him to his senses, of course). Oh, yes, she had been positively inspired.

The next morning Bob came into the kitchen in search of his morning coffee, which he would take with him to his computer.

Joy was busy frosting minicakes for a party she was catering the following night, and mentally fine-tuning her big announcement.

"I should be done in time for us to go see a matinee later if you want," he offered.

"Mmm," she said noncommittally.

Happily unaware of what was about to happen to him, he kissed her on the cheek and disappeared into the bonus room that served as his office.

She smiled as she piped frosting wreaths on the little cakes. *You might not have as much time as you think.*

She finished her decorating, then stored the cakes in the pantry. She checked the kitchen wall clock. Bob had been in his office almost an hour now and would be well into his story. He hated being interrupted when he wrote. Well, Scrooge hadn't thought he had time for all those ghosts, either. Sometimes, the vital intruded on the important.

He turned as she entered his office, looking slightly perturbed, and draped an arm over his chair. Except for the frown, he could have been posing for a publicity shot, wearing a turtleneck and jeans, his computer sitting behind him. His face was taking on that aura of maturity men got when they hit middle age. He looked oh so wise, but Mr. Know-it-all still had a lot to learn.

"Something wrong?" he asked.

"No, not at all. I just thought I'd better let you know about my new plans for the holidays."

His eyes shot heavenward. "Oh, no. What horrible torture have you planned for me now?"

"Absolutely nothing," she answered sweetly.

"I know you just said something in another language. How about a translation?"

"I've decided I'm going to give you nothing to complain about this year because we're going to have a very Bob kind of Christmas."

Bob's expression went from perturbed to relieved. And then it got suspicious. He pulled back like a man preparing for a slap in the face. "What do you mean?"

"I mean this is going to be a Bob Humbug holiday. I'm not doing anything."

He stared at her like she'd gone completely insane. "What?"

"You heard me."

"Hearing and understanding are two different things. Joy, you're not making any sense."

"Okay, let me clarify. I'm not doing any of it this year. No baking, no shopping, no present wrapping or stocking stuffing, no decorating, no cooking, and certainly no entertaining. You are going to get your wish for a non-Christmas."

Bob stared at her, at a loss for words. Bob caught without a clever comeback; now, there was a rare sight. Too bad she hadn't thought to record this moment for posterity.

"You can't do nothing, Joy," he finally said in a voice that showed he was already weary of the conversation and anxious to get back to his world of dismembered bodies. "In case you've forgotten, our son will be coming home in three weeks and he'll expect Christmas."

Bob Junior, whom they still called Bobby, her darling and his father's pride and joy, was a freshman this year, attending college two states away. He'd expect to see decorations up and old family friends and neighbors coming and going, and, of course, to find several batches of Joy's Christmas cookies waiting for him when he arrived.

She had a sudden vision of her son marching out the door, suitcase in hand, calling over his shoulder, "If this

22

is your idea of Christmas, I'm out of here." Okay, maybe this wasn't a good idea.

"Although if I had my way that's how it would be," Bob said.

There he went again, Mr. Sour Milk, spilling over everything. Well, you are going to get your way, Joy decided. She promised the angry son in her vision that she would make this up to him somehow. To Bob she said, "Guess we'll just have to tell Bobby that the Grinch hit town."

"Come on now, hon. You know you love this time of year," Bob reasoned.

"But you don't, so this is my present to you — a Christmas of nothing." And boy, she hoped he quickly came to see what she was really giving him. She thought of Clarence the angel in *It's a Wonderful Life*. *You've been given a great gift*. She turned and started back down the hall.

Bob followed her. "Okay, you can stop. I get your point. I'll go to your brother's on Christmas Eve without complaining."

"Too late," she said, waving away his plea bargain. "It's gone beyond that. I've had an epiphany and you're going to finally get your wish for a peaceful Christmas — no parties, no people, no hassles. This year you're going to be living in a holiday desert."

"That sounds more like an oasis to me," Bob retorted. "Most of that stuff is stupid and silly and has nothing to do with the meaning of Christmas. Anyway, in case you've forgotten, I've got a January thirty-first deadline on this book. I don't have time to play along with this little game."

What a crock! She knew he had only a couple chapters left to write. "Trust me, Bob. It's not a game. I'm not doing anything this year."

He trailed her all the way into the kitchen. "You can't just do nothing."

She went to work unloading the dishwasher. "Listen to you. I'm about to give you the kind of un-Christmas you've been dreaming about for years. I should think you'd be doing cartwheels about now."

"I'm only thinking about the kids. It makes no difference to me." He started helping, putting glasses in the cupboard every which way. After all these years, he still paid no attention to the well-planned order in her cupboards. It was her own fault; she'd trained him poorly.

For a moment Joy had a picture of her house all Bobbed up for Christmas, a holiday mausoleum with no tree, no happy guests, and no laughter. Her pretty, apple green kitchen, with its double oven and abundance of counter space, would sit useless, empty of the aroma of spices and baking chocolate. How badly did she want to make a point, anyway? She could see that holiday desert stretching before her and a weatherworn hand-painted sign that read TURN BACK. YOU'LL BE SOOOORY.

She averted her gaze and forged on. "I'm willing to live with whatever you're willing to do." And he'd have to do something.

24

"Hey, I'm willing to do nothing. I can live without all of it. Peace and quiet will be nice for a change."

And with that parting shot, he left, just as the cuckoo clock on the wall struck the hour. "Cuckoo," said the little bird, "Cuckoo, cuckoo, cuckoo . . ."

"Oh, shut up," Joy told it and started setting her cupboard to rights. What in the name of figgy pudding had she done? And, more to the point, how was she going to be able to stay strong and stick to the plan? *Note to self: Stock up on extra chocolate. You're going to need it.*

"What were you thinking?" she asked herself as she drove across town Saturday night, her car packed full of goodies for someone else's party. "What do you think you're going to accomplish, really? Bob's not going to change, not after all these years." And it was probably unfair to expect him to. They were opposites and that was that.

And most of the time their differences complemented each other. Bob brought order and security to her world, kept their finances humming along smoothly, and kept calm in the face of trouble. She gave him love and emotional support and put spice in his life.

Except this Christmas. There would be no spice. It would be like cookies without the salt. Yuck.

Frowning, she pulled up in front of a two-story tract mansion and opened her car trunk. Nestled inside it were Tupperware containers filled with bite-size wraps, chocolate-dipped fruit, white chocolate shortbread, the minicakes, and Joy's stuffing-filled phyllo appetizers, only needing a quick reheating. She never provided drinks, which was fine with the woman who had hired her. Julie's husband, Dave, had that under control.

Joy barely had her first container out of the trunk when the front door opened and Dave came bounding down the walk. "Hi, Joy," he called. "Let me help you."

A man eager to celebrate the season — what a stark contrast to Bob!

"Thanks for doing this," he said as they carried goodies up the front walk. "Julie told me you normally take December off."

"I do," Joy replied. Usually she was busy baking cookies for her own family and friends and neighbors, throwing and attending parties, and enjoying the season. With Bob in charge this year there might not be much to enjoy. She sighed inwardly.

"Well, I'm glad we got you," Dave said, ushering her up the front walk. "This is our first Christmas in the new house and we wanted to do it up right."

We. That was how celebrating the season should be done. Not as a me and a reluctant he.

They were in the house now. Dave set down his pile of containers on the kitchen's granite countertop and rubbed his hands together in anticipation. "Boy, I can hardly wait to try some of this."

His wife smiled indulgently. "How about first bringing in the rest of it for Joy?"

"I'm on it," he said, and bolted out of the room.

"He's so excited," Julie confided.

Joy felt a stab of jealousy. Bob had never gotten excited about a party, not in all the years they'd been married. Of course, he always had fun once the guests arrived. But excited? No.

Well, she reminded herself, he got excited about the things that mattered. The birth of their children, her first catering job. She still had the chef's apron he bought her for the occasion. And he always got excited when it was time to plan a vacation, throwing himself into the details of the planning. All she had to do was show up and have fun.

If only he would show up when she planned things for the holidays.

"Okay, that's the last of it," Dave announced, setting Joy's box of serving trays on the counter. "What else can I do?"

"Make us both a drink," his wife suggested. "How about a peppermint fizz?" she asked Joy.

"It's my own invention," Dave bragged.

"It's sounds lovely," Joy said, "but I never drink when I'm on duty."

"I'll have one," said Julie, and he brightened and hurried off to where he'd set up a bar in the living room.

"This is going to be wonderful," Julie predicted as Joy began pulling out trays of goodies.

Joy smiled. Even if her Christmas wasn't going to be much, she could at least make someone else's special.

Soon the house was full of guests, all talking and laughing, and raving over Joy's food. As she set out a tray of chocolate-dipped fruit she couldn't help noticing how Julie and her husband shot smiles back and forth across the room. Like Mr. Fezziwig and his wife, she thought.

There was a Mr. Fezziwig inside Bob somewhere, Joy just knew it. But he had no desire to get in touch with his inner Fezziwig. What would Charles Dickens do?

She had no idea. Bob was the writer.

Joy ran errands on Monday. Her first stop was the drugstore to take advantage of the in-store special and get some therapeutic chocolate. She was strongly tempted to buy one of the really cute rolls of wrapping paper she saw at the end of the Christmas aisle. But she resisted. She had some left from last year stored in the garage, and if Bob decided he wanted Christmas presents he could wrap them in that . . . if he could find it.

She went to the grocery store next, then stopped at Skeedaddles, her favorite gift shop, and bought a present for her knitting group's December gift exchange.

When she returned home Bob met her at the door, all smiles. "Did you change your mind and do some Christmas shopping?" he asked, pointing to her bags.

"No, I just picked up something for my knitting group's gift exchange. I'm not shopping this year. Remember? I'm not doing Christmas."

Bob frowned. "That again." He plopped on a chair and watched her hang up her coat. "So, what else did you do today?"

She shrugged. "Oh, just this and that. I must say it's rather nice not to have to worry about making the holidays merry."

"Joy, you can't ignore the season," Bob chided sweetly.

"Why not? If you can't share the Christmas spirit with me, there's no sense in doing any of it."

"I share it," he insisted.

You and Ebenezer Scrooge. "I really meant what I said, Bob. I'm not doing anything."

"Well, I don't have time," he said, the sugar coating slipping from his voice.

"Then I guess Christmas will be canceled for lack of interest this year," Joy said with a shrug.

Bob was looking very pouty now. "I have to get back to work," he said, and retreated to his office.

Joy just smiled and put away her groceries. She found a station playing Christmas music on the radio and turned the volume low — no sense letting Bob think she was getting in the mood to do something. Then she started a chicken stir-fry, humming as she worked.

At six she tapped on his office door. "Dinner."

"I need to keep writing," he called. "Go ahead without me. I'll eat later."

He was still pouting. She could hear it in his voice. *Very mature, Bob.*

"Suit yourself."

She dished up a plate for herself, then settled in front of the TV. Bob stayed away through the entire six o'clock news, and was still holding out when she left for her knitting group. She opened his office door and found him slumped at his desk, staring at the computer monitor. She noticed he had very few words on the screen. Poor Bob. Maybe his muse had left town for the holidays.

"You can come out and eat now. I'm leaving," she told him.

"Very funny," he replied, and started typing. Probably "the quick brown fox jumped over the fence."

She shut the door on him. It wasn't quite so easy to shut the door on the vision of herself all dressed up in an Elvis suit, singing, "Blue Christmas."

The Stitch In Time was a small shop in downtown Holly that sold yarn and fancy teas. Debbie, the shop's owner, taught several knitting classes, and she hung around after closing on Monday nights to help anyone who came in with a knitting crisis. Some of her students had gone on to form a knitting club, affectionately known as the Stitch 'N Bitch, and they'd been meeting at the shop every Monday night since August. It hadn't taken long for them to become good friends.

Debbie was still closing out the cash register when Joy walked in, but four other women were already seated around an old, oak table, cups of tea or coffee steaming in front of them. Someone had brought in the first Christmas cookies of the season and the plate sat in the middle of the table — easy access temptation. Well, calories only counted half as much when you ate them with friends.

"Hi, Joy," Debbie greeted her. "How was your Thanksgiving?"

"It was interesting," Joy replied as she set her project bag on the table.

"Sugar, from what I've heard of your family, I'm not surprised," drawled Sharon Benedict, a pretty, transplanted Texan in her late thirties.

Sharon never went anywhere without looking like she was interviewing for a job with Martha Stewart. Tonight she wore a beige turtleneck sweater over caramel-colored slacks. Her brown hair fell in one long, Texas-size wave and was tucked behind her ears to show off small, golden hoops. She was currently working on matching sweaters for her boys and using some of Debbie's most expensive yarn. "Nothing but the best for my boys," she always quipped. It hadn't taken the other women long to figure out that Sharon liked nothing but the best. Period.

"This Thanksgiving was more interesting than usual," Joy said. She poured herself a cup of coffee from the pot on a side table, then sat down and plucked a cookie off the plate.

Kay Carter, another knitter, had inherited children along with her husband and was a stepmother to a twelve-year-old and a fourteen-year-old. Her stepkids loved her and she still had a perfect figure, the best of both worlds, she claimed. Knitting was her second-favorite hobby. Spending money was her first, and she was famous for her after-work bargain hunting. Tonight she wore what looked like a new cashmere sweater — which she probably got for 50 percent off somewhere

— dark green to show off her auburn hair and green eyes.

She cocked an eyebrow at Joy. "So, what made this year so different?"

"I made an important decision Thanksgiving night," Joy informed her. "I'm not doing Christmas."

Every needle stopped, and four faces stared at Joy.

"Would y'all mind repeating that? I have to have misheard you," Sharon said.

"You heard right," Joy said and reached for another cookie to fortify herself. "I love these cookies with the Andes Mint frosting. Who made them?"

"Martha Stewart the Second," Kay said, pointing to Sharon, who smiled and tried to look modest.

"Joy, you can't do nothing," protested Jerri Rodriguez, putting the conversation back on track. She had reached the scarf stage in her battle against cancer, and tonight she was wearing a bright red one. With her round face and her big, brown eyes, she looked to Joy like Betty Boop dressed up as a Gypsy. "What would Dr. Phil say?" she chided.

"He'd say, 'How's that workin' for ya?'" Sharon answered. "I wish I could make it work for me. But I can just imagine what a disaster we'd have if I let Pete and the boys take over." She gave an elaborate shudder.

Carol White, the oldest in the group and a widow, looked shocked. "Joy, you love Christmas. You've been talking about your son coming home for the last two weeks and all the new recipes you want to try. How can you not do Christmas?"

"Um. I've delegated it."

"Delegated!" echoed Sharon. "To who?"

"To Bob."

"Bob!" Sharon made a face. "Honey, have you got elves in your attic? What can he do?"

"Probably nothing," Joy said. She took out the scarf she was knitting for Melia and began a row, trying to act as if it was no big deal that she had just sabotaged her Christmas.

Debbie had finished ringing up her last sale of the evening and came over to join them. "What's going on over here? It sounds like someone had a big announcement." She pulled out a half-finished cable-knit sweater and started on it, needles flying.

"Joy's not doing Christmas," explained Sharon.

"Oh." Debbie looked puzzled. "I never pegged you as one of those people who doesn't want to see a Christmas tree in the town square."

"I'm not," Joy said. "I love the holiday, and I think everyone can find something to celebrate in it."

"Everyone but you?" Debbie was still trying to follow.

"She's going on strike," Sharon cracked.

"On strike?" From the expression on Debbie's face, Sharon might just as well have announced that Joy was going to assassinate Santa Claus.

"I don't know what else to do," Joy explained. "Over the years my husband has evolved into a Grinch. He whines about my family traditions, balks at the Christmas parties, and basically complains his way through the holidays. I think it's time he saw what his life would be like without all the celebrating he claims to hate."

"Wow," breathed Debbie. "You're my hero."

"But what will your Christmas be like?" protested Jerri.

Jerri's question put Joy back in that holiday desert, surrounded by buzzards picking at empty gift boxes. She shook away the grim vision. "Probably pretty ugly, since I do it all."

"How does that make you any different from any other woman in America?" Sharon quipped.

"It probably doesn't, and that wouldn't matter if only I could get Bob to participate." Again Joy caught a vision of a Christmas Future where she moved through the holidays increasingly more alone. Joy Robertson, Christmas widow.

"It is an unfair division of labor," Kay pointed out.

"I didn't know that doing loving things for your family was a division of labor," Carol murmured.

"At least if I do everything it gets done right," Sharon said. "But I've got to admit I'm a little tired of having all my work go unappreciated. That man of mine has no idea how I work my fingers to the bone every holiday season," she added with a flick of a well-manicured hand.

"I don't think Bob realizes how much he really enjoys Christmas with all the trimmings," Joy said. Oh, how she hoped she was right! "Anyway, if he sees what it would be like without them then maybe it will cure him of his bad attitude."

Carol said nothing, just shrugged and went on knitting.

"Well, you go, girlfriend," said Sharon. "I think you're absolutely brilliant."

At that moment Joy's neighbor, Laura Fredericks, blew in. She was a tiny blonde who always managed to look great in spite of her perpetual harried state. Tonight she wore her favorite consignment-store leather jacket over jeans and a turtleneck.

"Hi, guys," she said, throwing her bag on the table. A tangle of yarn fell out.

"You look frazzled," Jerri observed.

Laura grimaced. "My usual condition." To Joy she said, "Sorry I couldn't car-pool with you tonight, but I had to work late. Then coming home and making dinner really put me behind. I left Glen a mountain of dishes."

"I think it would be fun to work at the Chamber of Commerce," said Jerri.

"Yeah, right. Today was a bundle of fun. We got back the brochures for the Hollydays Fair and the printer messed up on the dates. They all have to go back." Laura got her cup of tea and fell into her chair with a sigh. "I hate this time of year. Anybody want a used husband? I'll sell mine cheap."

"Not me. I've got enough trouble with the one I've got," said Kay.

"Sounds like you need chocolate therapy," Joy said, and passed the plate of cookies to Laura. "Save me and eat that last Andes Mint cookie before I do."

"No, thanks," said Laura.

"I guess I'll have to take it then," Joy decided. "It's the last of its kind. No sense letting it sit lonely on the plate." And this, said her diet conscience, is why Laura is a size Twiggy and you're a size . . . Never mind, she told it and turned her attention back to Laura. "What happened to you on Thanksgiving?"

"Just the usual invasion of the hungry hordes." Laura shook her head. "I love Glen, but sometimes I really hate him. You know?"

Joy nodded and Sharon said, "You're talkin' my language, darlin'."

Laura held up her tangled mess of yarn. "I need help."

Debbie took the tangle from her hands. "Well, you survived the invasion, and that's the main thing."

"The big turkey's going to do it all again to me on Christmas, I know it," Laura said. She dug in her purse and pulled out a package of gum, popped a piece in her mouth, and started chewing. "And God knows what he'll dump on me between now and then. Sometimes I wish my husband wasn't so social. He comes up with all these ideas for things to do, invites the whole world over, and then I'm the one who has to make it all happen."

"Y'all could do like Joy and go on strike," suggested Sharon, and Kay giggled.

Laura looked across the table at Joy. "You're going on strike?"

"I never thought of it that way, but I guess I am. I'm not doing anything."

"She's on strike for more appreciation," Sharon explained.

Laura stared at Joy. "I don't get it. How can you not do anything?"

"She can pretend she's a husband," Sharon said. "Do nothing all month, then just show up on Christmas Day. Of course, she'll show up to nothing."

"I hope not," Joy said. The mere thought was enough to drive her to the cookie plate for comfort. Except she'd just eaten the last one.

"Can you live with showing up to nothing?" asked Jerri, channeling Dr. Phil.

"Yes, I can," Joy said boldly. Even as she spoke, she was revisited by the image of a boring, Spartan holiday existence. A barren living room, no tree, no decorations, no goodies, no laughter. What had she done?

She tamped down her rising panic by assuring herself it was going to take that kind of radical bleakness to get through to Bob. And something had to get through to him. It was now or never.

"I think a strike is an awesome idea," Laura said. "So, give us details. How'd you pull it off?"

Joy hadn't meant to go public with this but, somehow, telling her friends felt good. It was obvious from the approving nods and the occasional snicker that the majority of the women present agreed with her in principle.

"A Christmas strike." Laura smiled. "I love it. I'm in. I'll go on strike with you, sister."

"You've got little kids," Joy protested. She could see it now. No Santa at Laura's house, no Christmas cookies, no stockings stuffed with goodies. And it would all be her fault.

"My kids have a father, and he's perfectly capable of doing something," Laura said with a snap of her gum. "In fact, since he's the one who loves all this so much, he can do it for a change."

"That's the Christmas spirit, honey," cracked Sharon. "And the more I think on it, the more I think I need to get Pete to stop sitting around like an old bull in a pasture while I do everything. Maybe I should join you."

"Jack's always complaining that I spend too much money. Maybe this would be a good year to stop," Kay mused. "You know, he doesn't even shop for his own kids. He leaves that for me to do. And, of course, I'm the one who does all the wrapping. I even sign the gift tags. If it weren't for me there wouldn't be anything under the tree when the kids come to visit. I think maybe Jack needs a wake-up call."

"You can't not get presents for your stepkids," Jerri protested, shocked. "They shouldn't have to pay because you're mad at their father."

"Yes, the poor kids," Carol agreed.

Laura gave a snort of disgust. "How sick is that? She says she's going to not shop for the presents and we're shocked. Jack should get his own kids' presents. Why should Kay have to?"

"Because she's the mom," Jerri argued, "the heart of the family, the designated love giver and holidaymaker.

And what if he blows it and doesn't get them anything? Or gets them something really dumb? They'll have to pay and that's not fair."

"I can always get something for them and hide it, or take them on an after-Christmas shopping binge," Kay said.

"That's sick," Jerri said flatly.

"No, that's brilliant," Laura corrected her. "I love it. Women of the world, unite."

Sharon snapped her fingers. "That's it!"

Laura looked at her, puzzled. "What's it?"

"We really do need to unite, organize," Sharon said. "That way we can help each other stay strong. And there's strength in numbers, so we should let other gals know. There might be a whole bunch who want to join us."

"She's right," said Kay. "Someone should call the paper."

"Ha! I'd love to see a picture of Glen trying to bake cookies plastered across the front page of the *Herald*," Laura crowed.

"I'd love to see all the men in this town trying to cope with Christmas shopping," said Kay. "They all wait till the last minute to buy for us. Imagine what it would be like for these guys if they had more than one person on their list."

"They couldn't do it," said Sharon.

"They'd go crazy trying," added Laura. Her grin was positively evil. "This is going to be great."

Little kids possibly missing out while women stopped the holiday machine all over town. Joy began to feel like

39

Dr. Frankenstein. She looked around the table. Sharon, Laura, and Kay were on a holiday high-jinks high and Debbie was nodding her support. Jerri was shaking her head while Carol was looking downright depressed.

Joy left the store later feeling a little depressed herself. Here it was, the season of giving, of happy holidays and peace on earth, and look what she'd started. And where. The good citizens of Holly tended to take the holiday season seriously. The whole downtown was already festooned with swags and giant candy canes, and every shop window boasted some kind of holiday display. The big sign outside the Town and Country grocery store had the dates posted for performances of *A Christmas Carol* by the Holly Players, and the paper had just announced its annual Christmas tree — decorating contest.

Joy had only wanted to help Bob see the light. She had never intended to bring other women on board. She should call this off before it got really ugly. Anyway, she'd made her point and Bob had gotten the message.

By the time she let herself into her house she had repented of her wicked ways and was ready to go to Bob and promise to do it all. Christmas was too important to be held hostage by a disgruntled wife.

Then she saw the mess in the living room and her remorse hardened into resolve.

There, in the middle of the room with its warm and inviting overstuffed sofa and chairs and lovely Sheridan end tables, sat their Christmas tree, a testimony to the power of passive-aggressive behavior. Christmas tree, what was she saying? This wasn't a Christmas tree, only a terrible parody of one. Bob hadn't even bothered to spread the branches out to make it look more natural when he set it up, so they all shot straight toward the ceiling in one big, fresh-out-of-the-box, ugly tower. He'd slapped on the lights unevenly, hadn't even bothered with the gold bead chains that had been her mother's, and had hung only a few ornaments. The poor angel dangled from the top at a drunken angle, ready to topple any minute. The whole thing looked like the work of a madman.

Rage welled up in Joy. She threw down her purse and knitting bag and marched across the room. She was going to pick up this tree and hit Bob over the head with it. Oh, how could he? How childish, how immature, how very Bob of him! She reached out to adjust the branches.

"Hi, hon. How was your meeting?"

She yanked her hands back. Of course, that was exactly what he wanted. He was goading her, trying to get her to cave.

She buried the anger, then turned and forced a smile for her husband, who was walking into the room looking very pleased with himself. "Great. I see you got the tree up," she added sarcastically.

He gave a faux-modest shrug. "I had a few minutes."

It looked more like a few seconds. "I suppose you think this is funny," she said.

He played dumb. "What?"

"Is this mess supposed to make me change my mind and rush to the rescue?"

He opened his eyes wide, the picture of middle-aged innocence. How had she managed to stay married to this man all these years without poisoning him?

"You know, you're really being immature about this," she said.

"Me? Who's the one who decided out of the blue that she wasn't going to do anything?"

"Not out of the blue. It's been building for a long time. This weekend was just the last straw."

He looked at her like she was a bratty little kid throwing a tantrum. Maybe she was, and maybe she shouldn't have snapped. Menopause was doing strange things to her. But his behavior . . . it was simply inexcusable.

He came up to her, wearing a reconciliation smile on that John Grisham look-alike face of his and put his arms around her. "Come on, hon. Let's forgive and forget and have a nice holiday. Okay? If you want, I'll even hang the outside lights tomorrow."

It was tempting. "Well."

He kissed her. "This was all ridiculous, and beneath you, anyway."

Her frustration over his abysmal, uncaring, antisocial attitude was ridiculous? No. Ridiculous was what he had done to a perfectly good tree.

She pulled away. "You just don't get it, do you? Your whole attitude about the things that are most important to me stinks and I'm sick of it. You really don't care, and this . . ." She waved her hands wildly. ". . . mess proves it." Her voice was rising with each word. She was out of control. It felt good.

He studied her. "Hon, are you about to have a hot flash?"

"Have all your brains fallen out?" she roared. "What kind of thing is that to say?" This man worked with words. He wrote about complex characters. He was supposed to understand people.

"Joy, this isn't you speaking. It's your hormones. Here. Why don't you sit down and I'll get you some eggnog."

"I'll get my own eggnog, thank you."

She left him in the living room with the disaster tree. Let it stay that way, she decided as she yanked the eggnog carton from the fridge. It could stand there all month, a testimony to her husband's disregard for both the season and his wife. She opened the carton with a savage pull. Let the strike continue.

CHAPTER
THREE

Carol tried to cheer herself up by humming holiday songs on her way home. It didn't work. She had only a five-minute walk from the Stitch In Time, and it just wasn't enough time for her to lift her sagging spirits.

Her condo was part of The Green, a charming shopping area at the heart of town that sported housing above boutiques, bakeries, and small businesses. During holidays like the Fourth of July, the annual Halloween Trick or Treat Walk, and the Hollydays Fair, those condos were the place to be. Residents got a bird's-eye view of the revelers and the concert bands that played in the bandstand down below on the actual green. It was handy to be close to shopping, and there was always something to do, someplace nearby where Carol could go and find people to hang out with.

Sometimes, the hanging out made her lonelier, though. Her only son, John, had been killed in a car accident when he was sixteen, and two years ago she'd lost Ray, her soul mate of thirty-six years. Both her parents were gone now, and her sister was getting ready to take a month-long cruise with husband number two.

Carol's nephews and nieces were all busy with their own lives, and she didn't want to impose herself on anyone, so this Christmas she had only . . .

She looked down at her cat, George, who had met her at the door and was now rubbing against her ankle. "You're happy to see me, aren't you?" she crooned, and picked him up.

He squirmed loose and jumped from her arms, trotting toward the kitchen, his signal that she was to follow him and give him his evening snack, which followed his after-dinner snack. George had been svelte and gorgeous like his namesake, George Clooney, when Carol first got him, but he was fast losing his trim physique, thanks to her overfeeding.

She followed him to the kitchen. It was much too big for one woman, with more cupboards than she could fill, counters too long to work at alone, and a breakfast bar it depressed her to sit at. When she and Ray had moved in, though, they'd planned to do a lot of entertaining. These days she only entertained George.

"What would the people at PAWS say if they saw you now?" she asked him. "They'd probably have me arrested for cat abuse."

George rubbed against her again, unconcerned with what PAWS thought about her cat-parenting skills. She knew from experience that he'd give her one more polite leg rub; then, if she didn't cough up the food, he'd nip her.

She sighed. "Either I've trained you badly or you've trained me well."

She dumped half a can of cat food in his bowl and crouched on the kitchen floor, watching him eat. "You and I are going to have to think up something to do with ourselves or this is going to be a very unmerry season," she informed him.

She replayed the conversation at the Stitch In Time in her head and sighed. Joy and Laura and the others — who would have pegged them for Grinchettes? All that complaining about their lives when they had their health and their families — it was like whining about inferior caviar while just outside your door people were starving.

Jerri, like her, had remained silent, and as they followed the other Stitch 'N Bitchers out of the shop, she'd asked Jerri what she thought of the strike.

Jerri had shaken her head and said, "I wish I had the energy to do all those things they're complaining about. They don't know how lucky they are."

Carol's sentiment exactly. Maybe they'd come to their senses once they got home.

Sharon arrived home to find Pete raiding the cookies. "Peter Timothy Benedict! I told you to stay out of those."

He stuffed one in his mouth before she could grab the Tupperware container. "Well, I don't see the point of you making them if we can't eat them," he said around a mouthful of cookie.

She put the lid on the container and stashed it in the top cupboard. "You know they're for special occasions."

"Since when is your knitting group a special occasion?"

There he stood in those stained, ripped jeans she kept trying to throw away and that grubby old, gray sweatshirt, his chin covered in so much five o'clock shadow he looked like a Chia plant. Even after almost thirteen years of husband training he still could be such a barbarian.

"Going someplace where people are dressed up and act civilized counts as a special occasion," she informed him. "And besides, it takes a long time to make those cookies, so I don't want you devouring them in one day like a big, old locust when I may need them for a church or school function." And since she was on strike, she couldn't be baking any more. What she had would have to last. Maybe she should hide them.

Pete made a face. "Oh, no. Yulezilla is back to take over the world."

That made her blood bubble. She put her hands on her hips and scowled at him. "You know I hate it when you call me that. It's rude and insulting."

"And true. And I can always tell when it's starting."

Sharon narrowed her eyes. "You have no idea what's about to start, mister."

"And just what is that supposed to mean?" he said with a smirk.

"It means I'm fixin' to give you a lesson on Christmas that you won't soon forget."

"You've been giving me lessons for years," Pete retorted. "How about just giving me a break?"

She shrugged and turned her back on him. "If that's what you'd like to call it. You're going to find out first-hand just how much I do for you every year because this year you'll be doing it. I'm on strike."

"On strike, huh?" he said.

She waited for him to come put his arms around her, plead with her to come to her senses and be his holiday slave. But instead he began to laugh.

She looked over her shoulder and frowned at him, but it didn't stop him from shouting, "Hallelujah," and raising both hands. "We'll finally get to enjoy the holidays," he crowed, and started doing the happy dance.

It made her want to pull a leftover turkey leg out of the refrigerator and smack him with it. But her mama raised her to be a lady, so instead she marched out of the kitchen, her heels tapping an angry staccato as she went.

He thought this was all one big joke, did he? Well, he wouldn't be laughing so hard when the cookie dough hit the fan. And first thing in the morning she was going to make a little ol' call to make sure that was exactly what happened.

The kids were in bed when Laura got home and Glen was camped in front of the TV, lounging on the sofa and laughing right along to the sitcom laugh track. He looked up at her and smiled. "Did they get your yarn unstuck?" She held up several neat rows of knitting and he nodded approvingly. "Lookin' good. So, who's getting that for Christmas?"

"Me," she said.

"You go for it, babe. You deserve it."

"Brown noser. You're just trying to butter me up for the next invasion."

He grinned and patted the sofa cushion, inviting her to join him.

She did, saying, "And speaking of the holidays, there's something you need to know."

Glen's attention was already drifting back to his program. "Hmmm," he said absently.

"I'm going on strike."

"Okay."

Obviously someone was not listening. Laura picked up the remote from the coffee table and muted the TV. "I said I'm going on strike."

"Isn't that a little extreme? I mean, things are always crazy at the Chamber this time of year."

"I'm not going on strike at the office. I'm going on strike here at home."

He shook his head, a quizzical smile on his face. "For what, more sex? No problem."

He reached for the remote and she held it away. "No, for some appreciation. All of us are. If you want to have a million people over for the holidays, you'll have to cook for them."

Glen sighed. "You're not making any sense, babe."

"Oh, I'm making perfect sense, believe me. I'm tired of doing everything and being taken for granted, so this year you get to do it, Glen. All of it."

He stared at her. "Is this some kind of joke?"

A corner of Laura's mouth lifted. "Yeah, babe, and it's on you."

He frowned. "What the hell happened down at that yarn shop?"

Laura gave a one-shouldered shrug. "We got to talking and realized that you guys don't get it."

Glen made a face. "Sounds kind of dumb if you ask me. I mean, what's to get?"

"The fact that you just asked that shows that you have no idea how much I do this time of year, and all with no help from you."

"Oh, not this again," Glen moaned, and slumped back against the sofa cushions, grabbing a sofa pillow and putting it over his face.

Laura moved onto his lap and pulled away the pillow. "Yes, this again, you big goof. I'm just giving you fair warning. I'm not doing anything."

"Okay, okay," he said, running his hand up her back. "Take Christmas off. I can handle it. No big deal."

"No big deal?" Laura echoed in disgust. He really didn't have any idea what all she did. He just walked through the holidays like an actor moving around a movie set. She shook her head at him. "You are so clueless."

He frowned, insulted. "So, clue me in. Make me a list of what you need done and I'll do it."

"Seriously?"

"Sure. I can handle it."

Like there was nothing to juggling Christmas on top of everything else. "Yeah?"

"Yeah, piece of cake. I mean, really, babe, I don't know what you're making such a big deal about."

Laura gave a snort of disgust. "Well, you're going to find out, because this year you're on your own. I'm going to be you. I'll invite people over whenever I feel like it, sit around and yak, and do nothing. Oh, except help you put an extra leaf in the table."

He frowned at her, snatched back the remote, and turned the volume back on. "You're a real crack-up. Just go make the list. I'll take care of it."

She did, and presented it to him as they climbed into bed.

He began to read. "Decorate house." He gave a disdainful snort. "There's ten minutes."

"Really?" She propped up her pillows and leaned against the headboard. "Well, read on."

"Get and decorate tree. How's that different from 'decorate house'?"

She looked at him in disgust. "The nativity set, the Christmas wall hanging, the lighted village, the wreath for the front door, the —"

"Okay, okay. I get it. And as for the tree, well, I already take you to get that, and I put up the thing for you. Another five minutes and it's trimmed."

Laura began to feel the slightest bit uneasy now. Five minutes to trim the tree? What kind of job would that be, especially with the kids helping him? "You have to watch the kids while you're doing this. I don't want all my ornaments broken." She'd better hide her most precious ones. No sense taking chances.

"No problem." He went back to the list. "Bake cookies, shop, get present for Amy's teacher. Amy's teacher?"

"You have to give a present to the teacher," said Laura.

"Okay," he said dubiously. "Take kids to get their picture taken with Santa, get Christmas outfits."

"Oh, you have to make sure you do that before you take them to see Santa."

Laura reached for the list so she could note that detail, but he held it out of reach, saying, "I can handle this. What do you think I am, a moron?"

She shrugged and let him continue.

"Make costumes for school holiday concert and Christmas pageant." He looked pained. "Make costumes. That's chick stuff."

"No, that's Christmas stuff," she corrected him.

"Two programs?"

She nodded.

He let out a long breath, then continued. "Do Christmas cards, wrap presents, get stocking stuffers, buy food for Christmas party." He scratched his head. "Can some of this be left off?"

"It's all the things you love every year, all those things that you say make the season."

"I say that, huh?"

"Yes, you do. And it's all the things I do every year without any help because someone around here drops the ball a lot."

He rolled his eyes and returned to the list. "Get Advent calendar and open with the kids every day." He set down the paper. "You know, I'm still stuck on the two-program thing. And what are these costumes?"

"Easy. Amy is an angel for the church Christmas pageant, and a tree for the school holiday concert."

"A tree, huh?"

"Her class is singing 'O, Christmas Tree.'"

"Mail packages by December fifteenth. What packages are those?"

"The presents for your sister and her family," Laura reminded him.

"Oh. Do we have those?"

"Not yet. You haven't bought them."

Glen suddenly looked slightly sick. "You haven't bought anything yet?"

"You said you're doing it this year," she hedged. She had bought some things, but nothing she couldn't use next year. Glen needed to have the full holiday experience.

He eyed the list again. "Buy food for Christmas dinner, clean house, set table." He looked up at her. "Somewhere in between all this I have to work, you know."

"Welcome to my world," Laura said with a smile.

"Okay, fine," he said, sounding like a football player in the locker room, getting pumped up for a game. "I can handle it. And you won't hear me complaining, either."

"Oh, I won't, huh?"

"No, you won't."

He made it sound like she was making a big deal out of nothing. Yeah, right. He'd see.

It was eight-thirty in the morning when Joy's bedside phone rang. "Tell 'em we're not interested," Bob mumbled, and rolled over.

Joy fumbled the receiver to her ear and said a sleepy hello.

"This is Rosemary Charles at the *Holly Herald*. Is this the Joy Robertson who's starting the Christmas strike?"

Joy was fully awake now. She looked over at Bob, who was back in dreamland. "Um, yes. How'd you get my name?" Sharon, of course.

"Your fellow striker, Sharon Benedict, called us. This is a great story, and I think a lot of our readers would like to know how you're doing this and where they can sign up. I'd like to come over and interview you."

Oh, boy. What to do? Joy looked to where Bob lay sleeping. Last night when she was mad it had sounded like a great idea to continue the strike. But now, with the prospect of her discontent becoming news . . . "Gosh, I don't know," she said.

Bob pulled his pillow over his head. "Hon, can you take it downstairs?"

Heaven forbid she should rob her husband of his sleep. When, exactly, had Bob become so self-centered? "I guess it would be fine," she decided, staying right where she was. "Anytime after nine-thirty."

"Great! I'd like to bring a photographer, too, and get a picture."

"All right."

"Joy." Bob moaned.

"What's your address?" asked Rosemary Charles.

Joy rattled off their street address. She was still talking when Bob shoved aside his pillow, threw off the covers, and stomped off to the bathroom, muttering, "I may as well get up now that I'm awake."

An hour, she thought as she hung up. She had an hour to get ready. The house was a mess. She was a mess. She jumped out of bed, grabbed her robe, and hurried down the hall to pick up in the living room. She had her arms full with Bob's loafers, her purse and knitting bag, and a dirty coffee mug when he came down the hall.

"What's going on?"

"I've got company coming," she said, and rushed past him to the kitchen.

"Company. When?"

"In an hour." She set the mug in the sink, then flew by him.

He followed her as she picked up more debris and headed to the bedroom. "Who the heck's coming to see you so early?"

"A reporter from the *Holly Herald*."

"The *Herald*!"

"They heard about the strike and they want to do an article on it." Joy had never seen her name in the paper for anything before. She was going to be famous!

"The strike? For a strike you need a lot of people. This is just you and me. Well, just you, really."

"Oh, yeah? Well, for your information, several other women are doing this, too." Joy dumped the debris and started to put the bed to rights.

Bob leaned against the doorjamb and crossed his arms. "Like who?"

"Like Sharon and Laura and Kay from the knitting group."

He threw up his hands. "This is insane."

"If it's so insane, how come it resonates with so many women?"

"You've incited a couple of malcontents from your knitting group to screw up their families' holidays and you call that resonating? Joy, I can't believe you're doing this. How many people's Christmases do you want to ruin?"

"How do you know I'm ruining anyone's Christmas? Where's your evidence, Mr. Mystery Writer?"

"I have enough evidence right here in my own home. At least I can make my own work schedule. A lot of men can't. They won't have time to fit in all that extra nonsense. Instead of peace and joy and Christmas spirit, this is going to inspire fights and stress. You're going to make every man in town look like a jerk."

"Not every man. Just the ones who are jerks already."

The significance of her reply was lost on Bob, who was still musing over the misery to come. "God knows how many marriages could break up over this."

"If a marriage can break up over this it's not very strong," Joy retorted.

Bob shook his head in disgust. "Okay, fine. Go ahead, make us look like fools. But don't expect me to come out and talk to that reporter. I am not available for comment. I have a book deadline."

56

"She doesn't want to talk to you, anyway." Joy went to the walk-in closet and started moving clothes around. What should a woman wear for a newspaper interview? Maybe her red blouse and black slacks.

Bob walked right in with her. "She?" he echoed. "Oh, yeah, let a woman write the piece. That will make it nice and unbiased," he said in disgust and stomped off. "You're going to be sorry you started this," he called over his shoulder.

Not as sorry as you are, Bob Humbug. Joy grabbed her red blouse and eyed it critically. Did she have time to iron?

CHAPTER
FOUR

Bob sat staring at his computer screen. Instead of helping his detective, Hawk Malone, unravel the clues to the mysterious poisoning of Arthur Blackwell, he kept turning his own situation over and over in his mind. How, exactly, had he gotten into this mess? Where had he gone wrong?

Nowhere. He didn't deserve this. What he deserved was a medal for accompanying Joy to her big, chaotic family gatherings every year. Year in, year out, he endured teasing about his writing . . . *So, who are you murdering now, Bob? Hey, I've got this boss . . .* and the helpful critiques . . . *I think you should have made the car mechanic the murderer. It seemed to me like he had the best motive, but no one would have suspected him. I mean, I didn't, and isn't it the person you least suspect who does the murder?* And then there was always someone who had a plan. *Bob, I've got a great idea for a book. You could write it and we could split the money.* That was easily shrugged off, and when you were a writer it pretty much went with the territory. And it was only a small part of a very long afternoon. It was the chaos that nearly short-circuited him every year. Kids running everywhere like so many accidents waiting to happen. No one watched their children at these things. He couldn't believe nobody had broken their arm or at least some valuable knickknack yet. As out of control as it all was, someone sure should have. And the noise level; every year it rose higher.

Joy's family seemed to thrive on that sort of thing. The wilder a party got, the more they liked it. From what he could tell, her house had had a revolving front door when she and her brothers were growing up — people always coming and going, tons of company, big, loud parties. It was a way of life for the Johnsons.

But it wasn't for his family. His house had been quiet. He couldn't remember his parents having much company, and his brother, the chess club king, didn't exactly throw wild parties. Bob had spent a lot of time in his room with his nose in a book or in front of the TV as a kid, and that had been fine with him. As a teenager, he and his two best friends mostly went hiking or cruised around in their cars, listening to music and trying to pick up girls. No big, wild parties, no chaos.

Christmas at his house had been pretty quiet, too — the ritual of present opening in the morning, a dinner with just the four of them, and maybe a pair of grandparents or a stray aunt and uncle, followed by a holiday movie like *White Christmas* on TV afterward. Then everyone scattered to do his own thing.

So far in his writing career Bob had solved fourteen mysteries. But the workings of his wife's mind and that of her family's remained the greatest unsolved mystery of all. Why did they think everyone should be like them? And why, after all these years, did it still bother Joy that he wasn't? She'd known what he was like when she married him.

And he'd known what she was like too, came the thought. He'd loved her sense of fun and her enthusiasm for life. But somehow, he'd concluded that when she chose him she chose his lifestyle, too. But she hadn't. Even though he'd gone along with all her ideas on just how Christmas should be done, it simply hadn't been enough for her. He wasn't enough for her.

He rubbed his aching forehead. Now she was making his shortcomings public. So far he'd enjoyed a fairly good relationship with the press: good reviews, some nice articles, friendly interviews with the local paper. His sales were gaining on the big boys like Tom Clancy and John Grisham, and his publicist billed him as the mild-mannered master of murder and mayhem. How was he going to be billed if news of his wife's Christmas strike got out? He'd be Bob Humbug, killer of Christmas. Would that boost sales? It sure wouldn't do much for public relations here where he lived, of that much he was certain.

The doorbell rang and he gave a start. Oh, no. The nightmare before Christmas was beginning.

A herd of demented Sugarplum Fairies started dancing in Joy's stomach as she went to answer the door. Maybe this was a bad idea.

But then she walked past her poor, handicapped tree and irritation took over, sending the fairies scampering. How many men all over this town, all over America even, needed to learn to become active participants in their families' lives rather than spectators who showed up on Christmas morning? This wasn't a strike, it was a cause.

By the time she got to the front door, her irritation had grown into righteous anger. She practically yanked the door open, making the man and woman on the front step jump.

The woman looked about Melia's age, somewhere in her twenties. Her chestnut hair sported the latest cut and her clothes looked *Vogue* hip. Everything about her said I'm young and I have time to work at looking this good because I'm free — no husband to dump the duties of Christmas on me. The man standing in back of her didn't look much older. He was dressed in jeans and a jacket, and was holding a camera.

Behind them, the sky provided a gray backdrop. It looked like the snow flurries the weatherman had predicted would be coming soon.

"I'm Rosemary Charles," said the young woman. "This is Rick Daniels, our photographer. Thanks for agreeing to see us."

"No problem," Joy said. She stepped aside and motioned them in.

They came into the front hall of Joy's Victorian, and their presence seemed to fill the house. What should she do now? She'd never entertained the media before.

"Would you like some coffee?" she asked as she hung their coats on the oak coat tree. Everything went better with coffee. Too bad she didn't have any home-baked cookies to offer them.

The photographer looked hopeful, but Rosemary Charles shook her head. "No, we're fine. But thanks."

"Well, come on into the living room," Joy said.

That might have been a mistake. "Whoa," said the photographer, gawking at her tree.

Rosemary Charles stopped short at the sight it. "I see you've already got your tree up," she said diplomatically.

Joy felt herself blushing. The tree looked worse than any Charlie Brown tree. It was an embarrassment to treehood. "My husband did it." She sounded like a tattletale. Great way to start an interview.

Rosemary perched on the edge of Joy's sofa and whipped out a small tablet. "So, you're on strike and he's doing everything?"

"Something like that," Joy said.

"And how did this come about?" Rosemary Charles wanted to know.

Joy looked at the tree and squirmed. There it stood, the symbol of her and Bob on display for the whole world to see, everything connected but not quite right. "Are you sure I can't get you something to drink?" She could sure use a drink, preferably one that was spiked.

"Oh, no. We're fine," said Rosemary Charles. She sat watching Joy, pen poised.

Joy cleared her throat. "Well, my friends and I got talking about how women do most of the work to make the holidays happen." So far so good, but now she wasn't sure what to say next.

Rosemary Charles nodded encouragingly as she wrote.

Joy eased further into the conversation, like a nervous ice skater entering the rink. "And sometimes the men in our lives don't really appreciate what we do. They don't see the importance of it. They just sort of take it all for granted. They take us for granted." She stopped her sentence, but in her head, she was on a roll. *They think it's a waste of time and they don't want to be bothered, which translates into not wanting to be bothered with us. They don't value what we value. They complain or belittle it. They don't care, and that translates into not caring about us.*

That was it in a nutshell, she realized. Bob didn't care enough to really make an effort for her. Oh, he came to the annual family holiday gatherings, but just once she'd like him to make an effort and really be there, participate instead of sitting on the outside looking in with an impatient frown.

"Your husband, he's Bob Robertson the mystery writer, right?" asked Rosemary Charles.

Joy nodded. Here was the part Bob had dreaded. For just a moment she couldn't help wondering if publicly pillorying him was going to make him any fonder of the holiday festivities.

"And what does he think of this?"

Now Joy was really stumped. Part of her wanted to blurt, "He's a Grinch. What do you think he thinks?" But she didn't. Bob could be a turkey this time of year, but he was her turkey and she didn't want to roast him too badly. "I guess you'd have to ask him."

That response might have been a mistake. Rosemary Charles suddenly looked like a puppy that had been promised an entire bag of doggy treats. "Is he home? Can we talk to him?"

As if on cue, Bob came sauntering into the living room. How convenient. He had to have been lurking just down the hall, eavesdropping.

"Mr. Robertson?" The young reporter stood and moved to shake hands with Bob. "I'm a big fan of yours. In fact, I was at your last book signing."

Bob hated book signings. All that schmoozing with the public was painful for him, and Joy usually attended the events with him, chatting with readers and running interference between him and his most ardent fans.

But he was great one-on-one. He also knew how to put up a friendly facade. He smiled for the reporter. "Did you enjoy the book?"

"Oh, yes, it was great. Um, do you mind giving us a statement for this article?"

"No, I guess not."

Joy stared at him, shocked. What happened to not talking to the press?

"What do you think of your wife's strike?"

"It could be worse. She could be on strike for higher wages."

Bob Humbug does Bob Hope. Ha, ha, ha.

"What do you think about your wife's theory that women do it all this time of year and the men do nothing?"

Had she said that exactly? What had she said? And, more important, what was this article going to say?

"I can only speak for my own household," Bob said diplomatically. "My wife does a lot."

Well, that was very kind. Joy waited to see if he'd add, "Who needs it?" He didn't, the big coward.

"So are you going to pick up the slack while she's on strike, and do you think you'll be able to do everything she does?" asked Rosemary Charles, scribbling in her pad.

"Not everything," Bob said. "Christmas will probably look a little different this year."

Yeah, bleak.

"But I'm not sure that's a bad thing," Bob continued. "I think most men would appreciate seeing the holiday simplified."

"So, if all the wives in Holly went on strike, how do you think the men would do?" Rosemary asked.

"I think they'd do fine."

"You're a real sport, Mr. Robertson," said Rosemary Charles. "Especially considering the fact that your wife is going to probably be the hero of every woman in town."

If Joy was the hero, that left only one person for the villain. Bob's polite smile did a slow fade.

"Well, then," said Rosemary Charles briskly. "How about a picture of you two in front of the tree? Could we do that?"

This disaster of a tree would be in the paper? Joy looked at the reporter in horror.

Bob surveyed his masterpiece of mess, and then a sly grin grew on his face. Joy could see the wheels turning. Here was petty revenge served up on a platter, and an unwritten message to any potential strikers. *Go ahead, strike. But this is what your Christmas will look like.*

"Okay. Come on, hon." He held out a hand to her. He was enjoying this, the sicko! They got in front of the tree and he pulled her close to his side.

"Maybe we should each stand on one side of the tree," Joy said, pulling away. "So you can see it better."

"Oh, good idea," agreed the reporter.

"Yeah, that works," said Rick, the photographer. Joy and Bob posed on opposite sides of the tree and he aimed the camera and snapped.

"Well, thanks. I guess that does it," Rosemary Charles said when Rick had finished. "And who else is involved in this strike besides . . ." She consulted her tablet. "Sharon Benedict?"

Joy gave her Laura's and Kay's names and numbers; then Rosemary and the photographer collected their coats and departed.

As soon as the door was shut, Joy turned to Bob. "I thought you weren't available for comment."

"I decided I'd better come out and defend myself. Things get twisted when you only hear one side of a story."

"And speaking of twisted." She pointed to the tree. "That monster you created is going to be in the paper."

"I created it, huh? Well, maybe it will inspire some of the guys who read the article."

She narrowed her eyes. "Cute, Bob. I know what you're up to. If your wife tries to pull anything just sabotage her with an ugly tree, and God knows what else. That's the plan, isn't it?"

Another shrug. "It's done, isn't it? And it's not all that bad. Not how you'd do it, maybe, but you abdicated so I'm afraid you have to take what you get."

This was like an old *I Love Lucy* show where Lucy set out to teach Ricky a lesson and Ricky countered with his own strategy. Only this was real life and Joy was not laughing.

She folded her arms across her chest. "So, this is the best you can do. This is how Christmas will look with Bob in charge? That's your reputation on the line, your work on display in the paper for everyone in town to see."

He eyed the tree. "And I stand by my work," he said, giving her a playful grin and putting his arms around her. "Come on, hon," he coaxed, "give up. You know you enjoy doing all this stuff. Why deprive yourself of the fun?"

"You won't find doing things by myself and dragging my husband through the holidays listed under fun in my dictionary," Joy informed him. "I swear, you've got Grinch blood running through your veins."

"Maybe I do, but don't be surprised when all the men here in Whoville put up a statue in my honor."

Joy shook her head at him. "Okay, fine. Be that way. This is war now."

He gave her his little-boy-in-trouble look, the one with the downturned mouth and sad puppy eyes that almost always got him off the hook. "I'd rather make love than war. Can't we sign a peace treaty?"

"No peace for you this season," she said sternly. "But I tell you what. We'll make the bedroom neutral territory. What do you say to that idea?"

Bob grinned. "God bless us, every one." He waggled his eyebrows at her. "How about a quick trip to the DMZ?"

The phone rang and Joy picked it up, saying, "Sorry, this could be a call from one of my generals. I'll have to take it."

The look on Bob's face told her what he thought of her priorities. "Bah, humbug," he muttered and left for his office, probably to plan some strategy of his own.

"Merry Christmas," Joy sang into the phone just to irritate him.

"Same to you, sugar," said Sharon. "I'm not getting you in the middle of anything, am I?"

In another couple of minutes she would have been. "No. I can talk."

"I just called to warn you that you're about to become famous. I hope you don't mind, but I went ahead and called the newspaper like we talked about doing the other night."

"Actually, the reporter and photographer were just here," Joy said.

Sharon let out a low whistle. "They sure didn't let any grass grow under their feet, did they? How'd it go?"

"Let's just say that a line has been drawn in the snow," said Joy.

"That doesn't sound good. I guess I should have checked with you first, but, honestly, I was so mad at Pete I couldn't see straight, and when I'm riled up I

68

just have to do something. Let me tell you, when I meet with that reporter she's going to get an earful."

Oh, dear. "So, how did Pete react? Was he mad?"

"Worse than that. He laughed at me. He was actually glad I'm not doing anything. Let me tell you, that boy is so deep in the doghouse even the fleas can't find him."

"Why are men so difficult?" Joy said with a sigh.

"Because they're men, honey."

Joy could hear little boys whooping in the background.

"You boys stop that right now," Sharon scolded. "Someone's going to get hurt."

Joy heard another whoop, followed by a wail.

"Pete Junior, I told you to stop. Now, you tell Tommy Joe you're sorry." Sharon came back to Joy. "Three boys. What was I thinking? Mama told me girls don't run in our family and I should quit trying, but did I listen? James, you stop that right now! I've got to go," she decided. "Y'all stay strong. We're counting on you as our fearless leader."

Fearless leader? Joy thought as she hung up the phone. As Laura would say, Yeah, right. She wasn't really the leader type. And she was already contemplating retreat. *Note to self: Next time you come up with a brilliant idea, don't tell anyone.*

Laura called an hour later. "Guess what I'm doing."

After talking with Sharon, Joy was almost afraid to ask.

Laura didn't give her a chance anyway. "I'm here at work bragging to everyone about the easy, relaxed

Christmas I'm going to have. Glen and I had a little talk, and he's doing everything this year."

At least someone was having success. "That's great," Joy said.

"So let me take you out to lunch to thank you for being so brilliant."

"Sure," Joy said and tried not to think about the conversation she'd just had with Sharon. If this all backfired would she have any friends left?

CHAPTER
FIVE

Rosemary Charles had just finished her interviews with Sharon Benedict and Kay Carter. They had met at the Java Hut after Kay got off work from her job as a school secretary. Since Rosemary figured there'd be no good pictures to be had at a coffee shop, she had dropped Rick at his favorite fast-food burger place before going to the interview. She'd been right about the pictures, but what the interview lacked in picture potential it more than made up for in copy. Boy, had she gotten an earful!

Now she couldn't help thinking about her own mom and all the things she'd done to make the holidays special when Rosemary was growing up. She and her brother had taken it all for granted, just like these women's families. But Rosemary's mom would never have resorted to such drastic measures to get help or recognition. Maybe she should have.

"So, off the record, you're not afraid this is going to cause problems in your marriages?" Rosemary asked as they prepared to leave.

Kay Carter gave her hand-knit green scarf a flip over one shoulder. "No. It's going to cure the problem in my marriage: my husband's disease."

"Disease?" Was there something she'd missed?

"Yeah, Penny-Pinchitis, also known as cheap," Kay explained.

Rosemary smiled and nodded. Kay Carter was a pretty funny woman. Would her husband see the humor in this? "Well, thanks. I may want to write a follow-up piece. Would you two be okay with that?"

Sharon Benedict's eyes narrowed and her chin jutted out. "That'd be just fine and dandy with me."

Looking at her, Rosemary almost felt sorry for her poor husband. This woman, with her perfect outfit, her expensive haircut and color job, and her big frown, looked like Martha Stewart ready to come after the gardener. Pete Benedict would be lucky to make it to New Year's without bruises.

"Me, too," Kay said.

Rosemary felt almost giddy as she got in her car. She was going to get a lot more than just a follow-up piece out of this. She was going to get a whole series. Once the first article ran in Sunday's paper everyone would be talking about this strike.

She pulled up outside of Beefy Boy Burgers and saw Rick sitting by a window, slurping something supersize. He caught sight of her and crumpled the bag and hamburger wrapper in front of him, then stood up. A minute later he was at the car.

"What are these chicks' gripes?" he asked as he got in.

"They do it all."

72

Rick made a face. "I think we've got a theme going here. I hope you've got several ways to spin this, because that chorus could get real old after a while."

"Well, Kay's funny. And Sharon's pretty out there. I think I can do something with her. You know what her husband calls her?"

"Nuts?"

"Yulezilla."

"Oh, sorry I missed meeting her. What is she, Martha Stewart on steroids?"

"How did you guess?"

"I'm just a genius," Rick said, and shot a grin at Rosemary. "What about the other one? What makes her special?"

"Her husband's a cheapo."

Rick shook his head. "Let me guess. He doesn't spend enough on her at Christmas."

"He doesn't spend on anybody, from the sound of it," Rosemary said. "She gets stuck buying everything. She even gets the presents for her stepkids."

"So, she's a mean, ugly stepmother who doesn't want to buy anything for her husband's kids for Christmas. Is that it?"

Rick was being deliberately irritating. "Never mind," Rosemary said in disgust, and turned the car toward their last destination, the home of Laura and Glen Fredericks.

It was after five now, and the Christmas lights on the houses they passed twinkled in the winter darkness like fat jewels.

"Looks like the guys have already been out and done their part," Rick observed.

"One afternoon with the ladder," Rosemary mused. "It doesn't seem like much."

"Yeah? You try getting out there and freezing your butt off for a day and then we'll see what you have to say."

"Whoa," Rosemary teased. "Does seeing the Christmas lights bring back bad childhood memories?"

"Let's just say if I ever want lights outside at my place I'm paying someone else to put them up. Are we there yet?" he added.

Rosemary shook her head at him. "I'll bet you were fun on road trips."

"Still am."

She checked the address on her tablet. "I think it's one more block."

"I can hardly wait to hear what this one has to say," Rick muttered.

Five minutes later they walked into the Frederickses' living room. The room could have been in a magazine with its carefully grouped new furniture and the vase with the Christmas floral arrangement on the sofa table. There was only one drawback: The entire floor was a holiday explosion of boxes of ornaments, tissue, tinsel, and tree lights.

"My husband and the kids went to get a tree," Laura Fredericks explained. "He took off work early hoping he'd be able to get it up before you got here."

"So, your husband is doing everything?" Rosemary asked.

Laura Fredericks nodded.

If this mess was any indication of how her husband operated, Laura Fredericks was in trouble. Rosemary wisely kept the thought to herself. Instead, she asked, "And how does he feel about that?"

Laura smiled like she was remembering a really good joke. "He thinks he's got it all under control. Doing Christmas is a piece of cake."

Rosemary wrote fast. "Really." This should prove interesting.

"We have small children," Laura continued, "and I work. It's just too much for me to do everything myself, especially since my husband likes to entertain a lot. He doesn't know how much work goes into making the holidays happen." The woman's smile became positively devilish as she added, "But he will."

"So, what all will he be doing?" Rosemary asked.

Laura began ticking off chores on her fingers. "Putting up the tree and decorating, baking, doing the Christmas cards, cooking Christmas dinner."

Next to Rosemary, Rick's mouth fell open.

"Shopping, wrapping presents," Laura continued. "Oh, and he needs to make the costumes for the kids' holiday performances."

"Costumes?" Rick squeaked.

Laura just shrugged. "That's the deal. I'm not doing any of it. My husband wants to experience firsthand everything I do every year."

Rick looked disgusted.

"Well, I'm sorry he doesn't have the tree up," said Rosemary, "but this would actually make a pretty cool picture. Don't you think, Rick?" She didn't give Rick time to answer. Instead, she said to the woman, "How about we move that easy chair over by the boxes and put you in it, say, relaxing with a mug of coffee?"

Laura grinned. "Works for me."

"Rick, could you get the chair?" Rosemary commanded.

He obliged, and in another couple of minutes Laura was curled up in it, posing with a mug and a magazine.

"Would you be open to us following your family through the season?" Rosemary asked after they'd finished the interview.

"You mean like a reality show?" asked Laura.

"Yeah, only in print."

"Sure."

"Great," said Rosemary. "I'll talk to my editor and get back to you. We'll want an exclusive, of course." She'd have to remember to talk to Joy Robertson about that, too.

"Okay."

Rosemary beamed. "People are going to love this."

The new star of her series grinned.

"I'll be in touch," Rosemary promised as she and Rick walked out the door. "Good luck."

"Thanks. I think my husband will need it."

Rosemary was practically chortling as she and Rick walked back to her car. "Let's see," she said, flipping through her notes, "I've got the woman who's married to the Scrooge. Her main thing is no shopping. Then I've got Sharon Benedict."

"Yulezilla," Rick interjected.

Rosemary ignored him. "And I've got Laura Fredericks and Joy Robertson. This is going to be awesome."

Rick shook his head. "This is all dumb, if you ask me."

"Well, no one asked you," Rosemary said. Then she couldn't resist adding, "But let's pretend someone did. What's your problem, anyway?"

He shrugged. "I don't know. It's just dumb. These woman are making a big deal out of all this, threatening to do nothing, like the guys care."

"What's that supposed to mean?"

"Guys don't."

"Of course they do," Rosemary insisted.

Rick shook his head. "Most don't. At least not the way women do. Yeah, we'll eat the cookies and stuff, but if it was up to guys we wouldn't do all that other crap. I mean, how many men do you know who send out Christmas cards? And you won't see a bunch of angels and Santas sitting around my place."

"Don't tell me you don't like getting presents."

Rick shook his head as if over the folly of it all. "Do you know how out of hand that gets? A guy buys the wrong thing for his woman and he's in deep shit. He doesn't get something big and cool enough for his mom, she looks all disappointed. He's got to fight all those crowds on Christmas Eve —"

"He wouldn't have to do that if he shopped before Christmas Eve."

The only answer Rick had for that was another shake of the head.

"Don't you like to give your friends presents?"

"No. I'd rather just take 'em to a ball game."

"You are not normal," Rosemary decided. He looked normal enough — average height, nice, buff body, cute smile, brown eyes. But beneath that normal guy facade lurked a real Scrooge.

"I think I am," Rick insisted. "Most guys don't want hassle. Christmas with the chicks in charge usually means hassle. That's all I'm saying. Most of these guys will be perfectly happy if the women don't do anything."

"Yeah?"

"Trust me. I know what I'm talking about."

Was Rick typical? Rosemary got a sudden image of all the hungry guys swarming her three-layer bean dip and Martha the food editor's red velvet cake at the newspaper's annual Christmas party. And they sure fought over the presents when it was time to play that white elephant gift-stealing game. Of course, they expected the women to organize the party.

Now, was that fair? It wasn't like the women didn't work the same number of hours as the men. When did it become an unwritten rule that the guys did nothing while the women brought in the holiday eats and organized the party?

Maybe the *Holly Herald* needed a strike, too.

"You just missed the reporter," Laura informed Glen as he wrestled the Christmas tree through the door.

His eyes shot to the mess in the living room. That was supposed to have been gone and he was going to

78

have the tree set up and looking good. "Aw, crap," he muttered.

"What took you so long, anyway? What happened?"

"What didn't? I lost Tyler in the trees. Then Amy had to go potty. Then . . ." Someone was being a very poor sport here. He pointed a finger at his wife. "Hey, what are you laughing about?"

Laura sobered. "Sorry, nothing."

"You know, you never have to go to the tree lot alone. I go with you. It wasn't exactly playing fair making me do it all by myself."

"I had to stay here in case the reporters came," Laura said.

Glen looked at her suspiciously. Was she jerking his chain?

"Okay, so you want me to help you with the tree?" she offered.

He stuck out his chin. "No, I can handle it without any help. Piece of cake. Right, kids?"

"Right, Daddy," Amy chirped.

"Well, okay then, let's get going," he said, rubbing his hands together. He went to the entertainment center and put on a Christmas CD.

"I'll just sit here and watch," Laura said, sauntering over to the couch. Translation: And give you a bad time.

"Oh, no you won't," Glen said.

She shrugged. "Fine. I'll go start dinner."

"Don't bother. We got Monster Meals at Burger Land."

She nodded sagely. "That would take some time."

"Why don't you go watch a chick flick or something," Glen said irritably.

"I think I'll go over to Joy's."

"Good idea." He didn't need any witnesses.

She left him alone with the tree, the ornaments, and the kids and suddenly he wished he hadn't told her to go. *Don't be stupid*, he told himself. *You can handle this.*

But he soon felt like he was in a chick flick as he wrestled with the tree and tried to keep an eye on the kids at the same time. He didn't even have the thing secure in the tree stand before Amy was trying to put on ornaments.

"Not yet, baby girl," he grunted, wobbling the trunk into place. "We've got to put the lights on first." Maybe Laura was right. They should get one of those fake trees that came with the lights already on. He gave this one another tweak. It wiggled and he suddenly heard a gasp from Amy and a soft plop that sounded like an ornament falling on the carpet. Great. All he needed was to break a bunch of Laura's good ornaments. "Amy, wait," he commanded.

"It's okay, Daddy. It didn't break. Tyler, look out. Tyler, no."

Glen heard a crunch. Looking from under the branches, he saw that Tyler had crushed something on his way to the ornament box. "You guys, stay out of those."

"Tyler, Daddy said no."

This was followed by a wail of protest and the stamping of feet.

Glen gave the tree one final adjustment, then scooted out. "Okay, you two. You have to wait till I get the lights on. If you don't wait, you can't help. Got it?"

Tyler stopped his stamping and they both looked at him. Amy nodded solemnly.

Okay, that was settled. He opened the carton with the Christmas lights and pulled out a string. Lifting it carefully, he went to a back branch and set it in place. Then he started, very carefully, winding it around the tree. All right. Lookin' good. Laura made such a big deal out of this, but it wasn't that hard. He was almost to the back of the tree again when he felt a tug on the light string like someone had found an end and was playing tug-of-war. What the heck?

"Tyler," Amy scolded. "Daddy, Tyler's caught in the lights. Tyler!"

Glen looked around the tree just in time to see his son with his foot in the string of lights, stumbling backward. Now both feet were caught. The light string went taut and the tree began to tip right along with Tyler.

There went the tree, there went his kid. Which to grab? Glen opted for the tree, figuring Tyler's fall would be a lot less painful if he didn't have a six-foot Douglas fir on top of him.

Tyler landed with a yelp, managing to push Amy backward in the process. She landed in the box of ornaments, creating a chorus of crunches.

Shit. Glen leapt from around the tree, hauled up Tyler, then pulled a crying Amy out of the box.

"He pushed me," she sobbed.

"He didn't mean to," Glen said. He lifted the tissue padding and peered into the box. The whole top layer of ornaments was a flattened mess of shattered pieces. Thank God Laura was out of the house. Glen picked up the box and took it to the kitchen, the kids trailing behind him.

"What are you doing, Daddy?" asked Amy.

"Destroying the evidence," Glen muttered. "We're just going to get rid of these broken pieces," he told her, "so nobody gets hurt." He shook out the broken shards into the garbage, then went back into the living room, the kids skipping along behind. He set down the now half-full box and pointed to the couch. "Okay, you two. You sit there until I tell you that you can move. Got it?"

"But we want to help," Amy protested.

"You can. As soon as the lights are up."

Glen went back to the tree and raced around it with the remaining tree lights. This was always a time-consuming production when Laura was involved. She liked the lights strung just so, so that they had a nice balance of color all around the tree. Well, this year Glen was more concerned with keeping the tree itself balanced and off the kids. He plugged in the lights and stepped back to survey his work. Not bad, actually.

"Okay, guys. Time for the ornaments. Now you can get up."

The kids were off the couch and to the tree in about one second, and digging through the box, sending tissue paper everywhere.

82

Glen had a vision of more broken decorations. "Take it easy. We've got lots of time." He pulled an ornament out of the box, put a hook on it, and handed it to Tyler. "Okay, big guy. Put that up."

"I'm hanging up my special ornament," Amy announced, putting up a Disney princess.

"Good job," Glen said, and felt himself relax. Okay, they were going to make it through this just fine now.

Five minutes later, he wasn't so sure. He was just trying to decide when, in this process, he was supposed to hang the tinsel garland when Amy cried, "Tyler!" then burst into tears as Tyler ran off with something in his mouth.

Oh, no! Glen caught him in two steps and found he was munching on what looked like a gingerbread boy.

"My ornament," Amy sobbed.

"It looks like a cookie," Glen said, thoroughly confused. And then he remembered Laura and Amy making some useless dough you couldn't eat last Christmas and baking up a batch of stuff to hang on the tree.

"Mommy and I made that!" Amy was practically going ballistic now.

Glen took the ornament from Tyler. "Hey, guy, you can't eat this. It'll make you sick."

Tyler let out a howl of protest and now Glen had two of them crying. "Okay, okay, let's take a break. Who wants eggnog?"

Amy's cry settled down to a whimper. "Can we have the Christmas mugs?"

"Sure, sure." *Anything*. "Um. Where are the Christmas mugs?"

Amy pointed to the buffet in the dining room. The buffet. That was total woman territory. Glen never got into it, never went near it. It was filled with Laura's fanciest dishes and crystal and decorations. He hesitated, undecided.

Amy, however, had no reservations. She scampered over to the buffet and opened the bottom door, then started pulling stuff out. It was bad enough they'd broken ornaments, but if any of that broke, Glen could just start planning his funeral.

He jumped into action and raced over to the buffet. "Here, let Daddy do it."

Getting the mugs felt like disarming a bomb. There were any number of delicate plates and dishes he had to move. *Oh, God, please don't let me break anything. Please, please, please.*

His prayers were answered, and he made it out with two Christmas mugs. He breathed a sigh of relief, then went to the kitchen where he poured the eggnog. "Okay," he said, "back to the tree."

And back at the tree, Tyler dropped his mug. It hit the carpet with a sick thud, making Glen's heart stop in the process. The mug looked like it survived in one piece, but he now had an eggnog lake on the carpet.

The music from the CD filled the room, mocking him. "Deck the halls with boughs of holly . . . 'tis the season to be jolly."

In what universe?

CHAPTER
SIX

Wednesday morning a fresh pang of regret struck Joy when Melia called to find out when they were going to make their traditional Christmas bonbons. She and her daughter had been making the candies together ever since Melia was in grade school. They had started out giving the bonbons as gifts for the kids' teachers; then, after Melia got older, she gave them to the aunts and uncles and her best girlfriend. Joy had tired of the candy making, but her daughter still enjoyed it and she enjoyed being with her daughter.

So, what to say? "Um."

"We are making them, aren't we?" Melia's tone of voice betrayed a sudden suspicion of unpleasant news.

"I can't make the bonbons this year," said Joy, feeling like a rat.

Suddenly, she needed chocolate. She pulled open the junk drawer where she had half a bag of Hershey's Kisses stashed. Nothing. Bob must have found them and polished them off.

"Why?" asked Melia. She sounded hurt.

"I'm taking Christmas off," Joy said, keeping her voice light. Phone to her ear, she hurried to the dining room and opened the top drawer of the buffet, her favorite chocolate hiding place. Thank God. Three little Dove dark chocolates winked at her. She took two.

"So, what does that mean? Are you, like, taking off for Hawaii or something?"

And miss Christmas Eve with her family and Christmas Day with her children and her new grandbaby? Not unless she'd been drugged and kidnapped. She already had presents she'd bought months ago stashed away to give the kids at Al's on Christmas Eve, just in case Bob failed to find any Christmas spirit.

"No." She walked back to the kitchen, unwrapping her chocolate as she went. "I'm just not doing anything. I'm leaving it all up to your father, and that includes all the Christmas baking and candy making."

"Mom, no offense or anything, but are you out of your mind? All Daddy can make is toast, and he usually burns that."

"It's time he learned how to burn something else. If anything happened to me he'd be helpless," Joy said, and popped the chocolate in her mouth.

"I don't understand why you have to have him learn at Christmas. And why can't you do this one thing? Let Daddy do everything else."

"I can't because I'm kind of on strike. Making bonbons would be cheating and if I cheated it would end up in the paper."

"Oh, my gosh! You're in the paper?"

"I'm going to be. A reporter from the *Herald* is following the whole thing."

"Wow, Mom. You're a mover and shaker."

"It's not just me. Some of my friends are doing this, too."

"But why? You love doing all this stuff. And we always make the bonbons, together," Melia added, coming full circle to her initial disappointment.

Joy's skin was beginning to sizzle. Was it menopause or guilt? She opened the back door and stepped outside. That was better, like standing in front of the fridge on a hot, summer day.

The cool air got her brain cells working again, and she came up with an idea. "Well, why don't you come over and teach your father how to make them and I'll keep you company and feed you," she suggested.

"Okay, that works," Melia said, satisfied with the compromise.

"But you have to make sure he does everything I normally do."

"That means he has to buy the ingredients," Melia said doubtfully.

"He can handle it."

"Okay." She still sounded doubtful.

"This will be good for him," Joy told her.

"Yeah, but will it be good for the bonbons? I give these to people. Remember?"

Joy chuckled. "Trust me. It will be fine." *I hope.*

"I guess," Melia said. "I still don't understand why you're doing this strike thing, though."

"I'm doing this because your father and I . . ." *need to reconnect.* She couldn't say that to her daughter. That would sound like their marriage was in trouble, which wasn't really the case. There was a difference between a marriage being in trouble and a husband being in trouble. Wasn't there? Joy popped another chocolate. "We just need to learn how to celebrate the holidays as empty nesters and I want to establish some new ground rules. That's all."

"Well, okay," Melia said dubiously. "So, when should I come over?"

"How about one day next week? Friday looks clear. You and Cam can both come for dinner if you want; then he can take Sarah home and put her to bed and you and Daddy can do your Candy Land thing."

"Hmmm, a free meal and a free evening. Twist my arm."

They chatted a few more minutes, then Melia hung up and Joy put Bob's candy-making date on the calendar. *Melia and Bob: bonbons.* It should have been her doing this with her daughter. What was this proving, anyway?

Bob sauntered into the kitchen in search of coffee. "Who was that on the phone?"

"Melia."

"Oh? What did she want?"

"To know when we're going to make the Christmas bonbons."

"You're going to do that?" He asked the question casually, but she could hear the hope hiding in his voice.

"Not this year. That's going to be your job." She smiled sweetly at him.

He didn't smile sweetly back. "What if I don't want to?"

Joy shrugged. "Then you can tell your daughter that Christmas bonbons are just, let's see, how did you put it? Oh, yes, a big 'pain in the neck' and that you don't want to do it with her." Like that would ever happen. She had him trapped.

He paled. "Those candies take hours."

"You're right. Who needs them anyway? I'm sure Melia will understand."

He capitulated with a sigh. "When's she coming over?"

"Friday evening," Joy said, careful not to gloat over her victory.

"Can't we do this a different time? You know I like to relax on Friday nights."

True. Friday was always their night to sack out side by side on the couch and watch a DVD.

"I guess you can call her and reschedule," Joy suggested.

"Never mind," he said grumpily. Then, after a minute, "So, how's that going to work? She's going to buy the ingredients?"

"You're going to get the ingredients and then you'll both make them together."

"I guess I can handle it," he said. "I managed the tree just fine."

It was a veiled threat and they both knew it. Score another point for Bob Humbug.

"Cute," Joy said, and went to retrieve the last chocolate from the buffet.

Carol met Sharon at the Java Hut after Sharon got off work from her part-time job at Finest Floral. An instrumental jazz version of "Have Yourself a Merry Little Christmas" greeted her as she walked in the door, and the smell of freshly ground coffee made her mouth water. The place was all done up with tinsel and multicolored lights, with potted poinsettias in the windows. It felt cozy and Christmasy, unlike her own place, which was hanging in holiday limbo.

Limbo was fine with Carol. The last thing she wanted was to haul out all the favorite, old decorations and infect the condo with bittersweet memories. Anyway, she got a big enough taste of the season every time she went out, she told herself, and ordered a Super Grande eggnog latte to prove it.

Sharon came in just as Carol was taking her drink off the counter.

"What are you having? It looks good."

Carol told her and she nodded. "I'll take one, too," she told the barista. "Make it a double. I've got a powerful thirst."

They were barely settled in a couple of overstuffed chairs in a quiet corner when Sharon launched into a report on how the interview with the reporter had gone. "When Santa reads that article the best Pete Benedict can hope for is a lump of coal in his stocking. Serves him right, too," she concluded with a sneer. "This year Pete's going to learn firsthand what it feels like to do things and have no one appreciate them."

90

Carol looked at her with concern. "Are you sure you want to do this?"

Sharon found a stray crumb on the table and brushed it away. "That sounds suspiciously like something my mama would say."

"Sorry," Carol said.

"Whose side are you on, anyway?"

"Yours, of course. I just hate to see you make yourself and your family miserable. Why are you doing this, really?"

"Now you sound like Jerri playing Dr. Phil," Sharon said, and frowned. "Come to think of it, maybe I should write Dr. Phil about our strike. He'd have a thing or two to say to that man of mine. I'm busier than a one-armed paperhanger this time of year, but does Pete care?"

What to say to that? Carol studied the contents of her coffee mug. No answer there.

"Okay, spit it out," Sharon commanded.

"What?"

"How sick and wrong we all are. I know you think it so you might as well get it out of your craw."

Carol gave an apologetic half-shrug. "It just seems like such a waste of energy when you all have such nice husbands. At least they all sound nice."

Sharon took a sip of her drink. "I never said Pete wasn't nice, but that doesn't mean he couldn't use some improving. He's no help at all this time of year, and the boys take their cue from him. And it doesn't exactly help that he calls me Yulezilla."

"Are you?"

"No. I just try to make things nice."

"Maybe things don't have to be so nice," Carol suggested.

"Well, they won't be this year. And that's exactly what it's going to take for me to finally get some respect and cooperation."

"R-e-s-p-e-c-t?" Carol's tone of voice was judgmental. She knew it. But, somehow, she couldn't help it.

"That's right," Sharon snapped. "Find out what it means to me." An uncomfortable silence slipped in between them. "I know I sound a little hot under the collar," Sharon said at last, "but I've had it up to here. I truly have. Maybe your relationship with your man was perfect, or maybe you've just forgotten all the things he did to irritate you. But I'm telling you how it is at my house, okay? Things need improving."

Carol sighed and shoved aside her empty mug. "I'm sorry." She wasn't sure whether she was sorry for what she'd said or sorry for Sharon's situation. Maybe she was just sorry she'd agreed to meet Sharon at all. "Good luck in your mission." That had sounded insincere. Sharon was frowning. "I'd better get going," Carol decided.

Sharon didn't beg her to stay, and she left the coffee shop feeling thoroughly depressed. Why were husbands and children wasted on women who didn't appreciate them? It seemed so unfair.

Of course, not everyone had a husband as wonderful as hers had been. He hadn't been perfect and they'd had their disagreements, but they'd respected each other. And she would never have dreamed of pulling this kind of silly stunt. How did that help anything, really?

Decorations were going up all over town, but it didn't feel like Christmas to her. Maybe it never would again.

Her second Christmas alone — what was she going to do to make it meaningful? She knew she couldn't sit around moping all month, but, honestly, Ray's death had left such a big hole in her life she still didn't have the foggiest idea how to fill it, at least not this time of year.

Maybe it was time to go back to work. She enjoyed real estate, loved matching up families with the perfect house. Families, houses — the thought made her eyes tear up. She wasn't ready yet. Maybe after the holidays. Things were slow in the market right now, anyway.

She turned on the car radio to her favorite talk station. "Corey Carlson and Flo are still at Toy Town, taking donations for our Santa Surprise program," said the afternoon drive guy. "How's it going over there, Corey?"

"We're doing great, Don. Lots of generous folks out today. And it's still not too late if you want to come by. I'll be here with Flo until seven."

"Well," Carol told herself, "it's a start." She turned at the traffic signal and headed for the toy store.

The parking lot wasn't as full as she'd anticipated, and she decided it was probably because the main toy purchasers were all busy plunging into after-school activities with their kids. Inside, the store wore the deserted look a store gets in between shopping rushes.

Carol looked to her left and saw the radio station had set up a donation booth just past the checkout registers, complete with cookies and coffee. And there stood the morning traffic lady along with Corey Carlson, the morning drive personality.

A tall, slim man with salt-and-pepper hair and a face that should have gone into television, he was talking to a couple of middle-aged women. Actually, flirting would have been a better word. And they were certainly holding up their end of the deal. She couldn't blame them. He was a hunk.

Carol felt suddenly conscious of the way she'd let herself go. She'd lost weight and turned herself into a stick. What she'd lost in weight she'd more than made up for in new wrinkles, and her blond hair was now shot with gray. After Ray's death there had seemed no point in bleaching it anymore.

She started down the first aisle, which was dedicated to games. It took less than a minute for her to find the perfect gift. Clue. How she'd loved playing that classic mystery game herself as a kid. She picked one off the shelf. That should do it. Oh, but there was Chutes and Ladders. She'd played that with John when he was little. She shied away from the vision of a little boy with a sweet face and strawberry blond curls, instead forcing her mind to stay with the business at hand, and piled that game on top of the other. Look at all these aisles, she thought. So many toys. What else did they have that might tempt her?

They had plenty, and before she knew it Carol had a teetering pile of goodies in addition to her two board games: a puzzle, a doll, a baseball and mitt, and a kit for growing sea monkeys. Okay, enough already.

She paid for her treasures, then went to the booth where Corey Carlson and Flo the traffic girl stood exchanging chitchat. The other women had left and the two were alone now.

The gaze Corey ran over Carol proclaimed him a connoisseur of women. By his age he'd probably had a few, so it was no surprise that he'd look. What surprised Carol was that the look seemed to hold some measure of appreciation.

"Here comes another Santa's helper," he said jovially as she stepped up to the booth. "That looks like a pretty generous donation."

"It's for a good cause."

"You're right there."

"Can we give you a cookie in exchange?" Flo offered.

Corey Carlson wasn't wearing a wedding ring. Carol took a cookie and wished she could remember how to flirt. She took the wish back instantly. What a disloyal thought!

"How about a cup of coffee to go with that?" he offered.

Coffee would keep her up all night, and she hated being awake and alone in the long, dark hours.

She shook her head. "No, thanks."

"It's Starbucks, only the best for our listeners. You are a listener, aren't you?" he added with a grin.

"Yes, and if you're fishing for compliments, I'll be happy to give you one. I love your show."

His grin widened. "Glad to hear it." He leaned his elbows on the counter. "Tell me more."

"Well, I've actually learned a lot about politics. And I like the way you treat your listeners when they call in. You're not rude like some talk show hosts. I've never heard you cut someone off or call anyone a name."

"I try not to. Have I ever talked to you? What's your name?"

"Carol."

"Christmas Carol," he quipped.

Was he flirting with her? Yes, that was definitely the smile of a man who was flirting.

Carol felt suddenly flattered, nervous, and guilty. She realized she was fingering the gold band she had finally transferred to her right hand. "Well, merry Christmas," she said quickly, and started for the door.

"What's your hurry?" he called after her.

"I have to get home," she called back. *My cat is waiting for dinner.*

She kicked herself all the way to her car. She'd just had an opportunity to rejoin the human race and she'd tossed away the application. She unlocked her car and got in, heart pounding fast. She wasn't ready yet. Miserable as she was, she just wasn't ready. Maybe she never would be.

She flipped down her visor and looked at her reflection. What could that man have possibly seen in her? She looked old, and tired, like a woman who had run a race that turned out to be much too long and hard. She burst into tears. She hated her life, and right now she hated Christmas.

CHAPTER
SEVEN

On Thursday, December 1, Whit Walters, the editor of the *Holly Herald*, called Rosemary Charles into his office. "This," he said, tapping the screen on his computer monitor, "is good stuff."

She couldn't help preening a little. She sashayed over to the old leather chair opposite his desk and slid into it. "I know. I'm brilliant."

He ignored the opportunity to agree with her, instead turning back to his copy on the screen and saying, "I've got a nose for hot stories." It was the only thing he had a nose for — he never seemed to notice that his office smelled like male sweat, farts, and old cigars. "And this is hot. It's so dumb, so battle of the sexes — we are going to sell a lot of papers."

"So I guess I can safely assume you liked my idea about doing a whole series, following some of these couples clear through to Christmas?"

Whit was a large man with white hair, which was getting a little sparse on top. For just a minute, the way he smiled made Rosemary think of Santa contemplating a relaxing, postholiday evening with Mrs. Claus. He rubbed his stubbled chin, then nodded. "Oh, yeah. We're going to have letters to the editor on this one coming out our ears. Good work, kid," he added, and picked up a well-chewed, smoking cigar from the ashtray on his desk.

"Thanks," she said. She started to get up, anxious to leave before she began smelling like the inside of a cigar box. Did newspaper editors all belong to some secret society that demanded they smoke those stinky things?

"Oh, before you go," Whit said, "we should talk about the office party. You and Martha got it covered?"

Rosemary regarded him playfully. "Actually, no."

Whit's eyebrows took a dip, taking away the Santa resemblance. "No?"

"I think, in the spirit of these articles, we're going to go on strike, too."

Now the eyebrows shot up toward Whit's vanishing hairline. "What?"

Rosemary shrugged. "It's not that hard to plan an office party. Call a restaurant, reserve a room."

"A restaurant won't have that cake Martha always makes. And who's going to plan the gift exchange?"

"Whit, there's nothing to plan. Everybody just brings something stupid all wrapped up like always. You put numbers in a hat and draw. You guys can handle it."

Whit was frowning. "You know, it's all well and good to write about this, but that doesn't mean you need to join it."

"I'm not at home. Just here."

"Well, that's the dumbest thing I ever heard," Whit blustered.

"Don't you think it's a little sexist to make the women do all the holiday things around here?"

98

"You women like that kind of thing."

"That's because we've had the pleasure of getting to do it." She sauntered toward the door. "And this year I think you guys should have a chance to experience that same pleasure."

"You're not forgetting who works for whom around here, are you?"

Rosemary smiled at him over her shoulder. "Of course not, boss. But party planning is not in my job description."

"Should be." He pointed his cigar at her. "I spoiled you. That's the problem."

She just smiled and shut the door on him.

Glen's day at the office had been the pits, with one fire after another to put out. He almost wished he hadn't taken that new position. Sure, the money was good, and he liked his job. He especially liked the nice, big office that went with it. But he wasn't sure he liked the headaches that accompanied moving up the old ladder of success. It demanded a lot of mental toughness for a guy to keep his game sharp, and that drained a lot of energy.

He heaved a sigh of relief as he pulled up in front of his house. Home, sweet home, his two-story Craftsman-style castle with the front porch and the big columns, and the thirty-year mortgage, his sanctuary from the hassles of the office rat race. This was why he went to work every day, so he could return home to Laura and the kids and a good meal and a relaxing evening where the hassles of the office melted off him. The air had a nip to it, which made the thought of relaxing inside his nice, warm house all the more appealing. Unless a guy was doing something important, like playing football, who wanted to be out in the cold?

As he walked up the front walk he could see the Christmas tree sitting by the living room bay window, glowing in silent testimony to his first task successfully completed. And he'd celebrated his success by reaching for a bottle of Excedrin.

Thank God there was nothing on for tonight. He'd kick back and pull out a DVD, some good guy flick with lots of things blowing up.

He barely had the door open before Amy was bouncing up and down in front of him, eagerly asking, "Did you get it, Daddy?"

He swung her up in his arms and carried her into the living room. "Get what, baby girl?" Now Tyler was running toward him, Laura following behind. Glen rumpled Tyler's hair and leaned over to kiss his wife.

"The Advent calendar," Amy said.

Advent calendar, Christmas to-do list. A sinking uh-oh feeling slugged Glen in the gut.

Laura must have caught a flash of panic in his eyes because now she was smirking.

Never let 'em see you sweat. He put on a jovial smile and stalled for time. "Hi, babe."

"How was your day?" she asked.

Here was his excuse. "Insane. Crazy."

"Guess we both had one of those days," Laura said. "It was a zoo at the Chamber."

Now Amy was tugging on his pant leg. "Where is it, Daddy? This is December first. We get to open the first window."

December first. What a smart kid. How did she know that?

Take a wild guess. He looked at his wife. Still smirking.

Shit. Shit. Shit.

This was like the domestic version of a football game — the Christmas Bowl — and while he may have just lost some yardage, he would not lose the ball. He thought fast, adjusting his game plan on the fly.

Inspiration came like a gift from the Magi. "You know what?" he said to his daughter.

Amy was jumping up and down again. "What?"

"We're going to go out and get it tonight, right after dinner." Back out into the cold.

"Yay," Amy whooped, and began to skip in a circle around him.

"Yay," echoed Tyler, following her.

Where the hell was he going to find an Advent calendar? Time for a quarterback sneak. "Hey, hon. Want to come with us?"

"In your dreams," she said as she turned back toward the kitchen. "I just started a great book. I'm going to curl up on the couch and read."

Curl up on the couch. Glen thought longingly about his movie plans for the night. Things blowing up. Yeah, right. The only thing that would be blowing up tonight was the relaxing evening at home. But how long could it take to run out and buy an Advent calendar? He should be able to get that done and still get home in time to kick back with a movie.

Not wanting to waste any time in getting his mission completed, they were barely done with dinner when he said, "Okay, team. Let's go get ourselves a calendar. Get your coats." The kids dashed off with squeals of excitement and he turned to Laura. "So where do I get one of these things?"

"You should be able to find one at the book store, if they haven't run out. I always get mine before the first."

"Oh, thanks. Way to set a guy up for failure. You know, it would have been nice if you told me when you gave me that stadium-size honey-do list."

She smiled and kissed him on the cheek. "I guess I just thought a smart guy like you would have no trouble figuring that out."

What the hell was that supposed to mean? "Are you being a smart-ass?"

"Moi?" She put a hand to her heart in a Miss Piggy gesture.

Glen pointed a finger at her. "Hey, I can do this."

"Piece of cake," she mocked, turning him toward the door and giving him a little shove. "Now, get going. I had a rough day at work today, too, and I want to relax."

"Okay, fine," Glen grumbled. At least she only had to work part-time. He had to work full-time and come home to this nonsense.

The cold air hit him like a slap in the face as he walked the kids to the minivan. He told himself it was

102

no big deal. He'd be done in no time. No, make that record time.

Laura popped a fresh stick of gum in her mouth and savored it as she watched the minivan pull away. Poor Glen. He'd put in a busy day at work and now he had to go back out into the cold and complete another one of the tasks that she did every year and he took for granted. Chances are this errand would eat up his whole evening. She smiled. *Welcome to my world.*

Learning that the bookstore was out of Advent calendars didn't improve Glen's mood. *Fumble at the fifty-yard line.*

"Where are we going now, Daddy?" Amy asked as they left the store.

"We're going to go to another store."

"And get an Advent calendar," Amy added with the same firm belief she showed when talking about Santa.

"Yep," Glen agreed. The game wasn't over yet.

He tried a gift card store next. And, lo and behold, it looked like they had an Advent calendar sitting in the window. *Ha! Fumble recovery. First down and ten.* He hustled the kids inside. The store was packed with chicks, and the smell of twenty different perfumes made him sneeze. Finding the spot empty where only moments before he'd seen the elusive calendar made him grind his molars. The sales clerk looked at him pityingly and informed him that they'd just sold their last calendar. *Second down and ten.*

He drove to Hollyworld, the nearest thing Holly had to a discount superstore. Housed in an old warehouse on the edge of town, it was now a popular shopping destination for the thrifty and, in Glen's case, the desperate. If any store would have an Advent calendar, this one would, Glen assured himself. They probably had tons.

At least he hoped they did. He was running out of ideas. If he didn't succeed here . . . Don't even go there, he told himself. *You will not disappoint your kids. And you can't come home an empty-handed loser.*

As it turned out, Hollyworld had one. Just one. Keeping his eye on the goal, Glen dodged crying kids and stressed-out parents, wheeling his shopping cart toward it at breakneck speed. If he didn't get that calendar there would be two more crying kids and one more stressed parent on this aisle.

He was almost to the prize when suddenly a woman blocked him with a cart piled high with clothes, potato chips, and wrapping paper, and snagged it.

Glen had played football. He understood the importance of mental toughness. *Never give up. Never give in.*

"Hey, how bad do you need that?" he asked her.

She looked at him like he'd just asked where she kept the key to her front door.

"I'll buy it from you," he offered, digging for his wallet.

"I haven't even bought it yet," she protested.

"I'll give you five bucks if you let me have it."

She looked at him suspiciously.

"I mean it." Glen nodded down at his two children. Both kids were looking up at him with big, blue, trusting eyes. He couldn't disappoint them. "I promised my kids."

"Sorry. I promised mine, too," she said, and started to wheel away.

"Ten bucks," he said, following her. "I'll give you ten bucks."

"Sorry," she said, and picked up her pace.

"Twenty!" He was racing after her now, Amy running to keep up and Tyler in the cart crying, "Whee!"

"Go away," she called over her shoulder.

A pot-bellied security guard appeared out of nowhere. "Is there a problem, sir?"

The woman hurried off, like a deer escaping the hunter's gun. "That woman took the last Advent calendar," Glen tattled.

The guy shrugged. "It happens."

"I promised my kids." Glen knew he sounded desperate. But this guy was older. He probably had kids, maybe even grandkids. He'd understand.

"It looks like you'll have to go somewhere else," the guy said.

"Hey, they don't have any more in the back somewhere, do they? Can somebody find out for me?"

"Fella. You think they ain't gonna put out all the calendars they got? They're out. Those things go fast. Usually people buy them before the first, you know."

"So I hear," Glen said grumpily. *Third down and ten*.

Now Amy was beginning to look worried. "Are we going to get an Advent calendar, Daddy?"

"You bet we are," he said. "Just not at this store. In fact, we probably won't shop at this store ever again," he added, for the benefit of the uncooperative security guard.

"Suit yourself," the guy said as he turned and walked away. "It's not like they need the business."

Glen glared at his retreating back. *Okay, shake it off.* Maybe he could still find that woman. Catch her in the parking lot. She'd part with the calendar if the price was right.

He caught sight of her just leaving the checkout. "Come on, guys," he said, hauling Tyler out of the cart.

Amy was now squatting in front of a display of wild-colored nail polish. "Look Daddy. Nail polish. Can we get some?"

"Not now," Glen said, taking her arm. "We've got to get our calendar. And it's getting away."

He tried to make a dash, Tyler in one arm and Amy holding his hand, but quickly realized that his daughter wasn't going to be able to keep up. He tucked her under his arm like a football and ran for all he was worth, dodging shoppers like a quarterback escaping a blitz.

But it did no good. By the time they hit the parking lot, there was no sign of the woman in the crowd of cars and shoppers. It was dark and beginning to sleet. Glen felt ready to punch something, but the kids were with him, so he settled for a growl and a few choice words muttered under his breath.

"When are we going to get our calendar?" Amy asked.

Never, because this was Christmas purgatory. "Soon," Glen lied. Now it was fourth down and ten at the fifty-yard line and he didn't know whether to attempt a field goal, punt, or kill himself.

Two hours later he finally found the coveted calendar at their neighborhood drugstore. It was way past Tyler's bedtime, and even Amy was getting whiny. Glen couldn't say he blamed her. He felt damned whiny himself. But at least he'd scored an Advent calendar. *Touchdown, at long last.*

They got back home and hung their prize with much ceremony. Glen felt warm all over, looking at his daughter's glowing face. This was one small thing on a big list, but it had made the kids happy, and that made him feel like a real superhero. He smiled as he watched Amy reach up and open the first window. He'd been missing out on a real Hallmark high leaving Laura to do this kind of thing without him.

"There it is," he said proudly. "December first."

"Where's the candy?" Amy asked.

"Candy?"

"It's s'posed to have candy in it." Her lower lip started trembling and the Hallmark high began to melt into a bad trip.

"Oh. Well, this one has this cool picture," Glen said, pointing.

Amy began to sniff — little sobby sniffs that heralded a tear storm.

Oh, no, not that. Glen knelt in front of her. "I tell you what. I'll get you some special candies tomorrow and every day you can open the calendar and have one."

She was still looking at him with sad eyes, but she sniffed again and nodded.

"Now, go find Mommy and tell her you're ready for bed." He'd done his part for the night. Laura could put 'em to bed.

"But I want a candy," Amy protested.

Obviously, they had a lack of communication here. "Daddy still has to get the candy," Glen explained.

"I want candy," Tyler whined, and Amy began to sniff again.

"Okay, tell you what. Tomorrow you can both have two candies. How's that? Two honkin' big candies," he added, stretching his arms wide for effect.

That seemed to be okay. "All right," said Amy with a smile.

"Okay. Give me five."

Both kids giggled and slapped his open palm.

"Now, how about a kiss?"

Amy obliged and he hugged her. He hugged Tyler next and sent him off after his sister. Then he let out a sigh and went in search of more Excedrin. Lord. How did his wife go through this every year?

Bob woke up on Friday morning with the uncomfortable feeling that something unpleasant was hanging over his head. *The bonbons.*

He moaned and rolled over in bed, pulling the covers tightly around him. What had he been thinking when he let Joy dare him into making candy?

He'd been thinking of his daughter, of course. She'd have been hurt if he'd said he didn't want to do this.

And then there was Joy. If he'd refused to be a sport he would have found himself labeled as the world's biggest villain. Would have? Who was he kidding? It seemed like he was always doing something to tick his wife off these days. It had to be those hormonally induced mood swings, because sometimes she seemed to be mad at him for simply breathing. How long did menopause last, anyway? Well, it wouldn't be over by tonight, so he might as well get up and get to the store to find the ingredients.

Joy was already gone. She'd said something the day before about errands and meeting someone for lunch, which had been fine with him. He never minded when she left him to go do things. He always figured that the more she went out with her friends, the less she'd want to import a crowd into their house.

For years they'd argued and negotiated the size of her guest list every time she felt the need for a party. It always wound up fewer people than she wanted and more than he liked. Lots more. Just once he'd like to have the number of guests in his house that he felt comfortable with.

The happy realization dawned on him that since Joy was on strike this Christmas he didn't have to have any party. The thought cheered him, and he was smiling when he entered the kitchen in search of morning coffee.

Next to the coffeemaker sat the bonbon recipe and a short note. "Happy shopping. See you later."

Shopping for ingredients to make something he could just go to the store and buy — what a waste of time! Bob downed a bowl of Joy's homemade granola, then showered and made his trek to the store.

Shopping basket in hand, he studied the ingredients listed on the recipe and realized his wife knew a foreign language, one he had never had to learn. What on earth was "pwd. sug"? "Choc chips" was easy to figure, so he got those. He couldn't find the brand specified on the recipe, but chocolate chips were chocolate chips so he just grabbed a couple of bags and dropped them into the basket. "Marg." Marg? He stood a moment, scowling at the list. "Swt. condensed milk." The only milk Bob knew about came in cartons or jugs. And that was the kind of thing he was used to getting sent to the store for: milk, eggs, lettuce. When it came to baking, Joy's specialty, she preferred to handle those necessities herself. But now here he was being Joy, handling it all, and all without having the necessary information downloaded into his brain. It could take him hours to figure out the shorthand on this recipe card. He needed to find a translator.

He heard the sound of an approaching grocery cart and looked up hopefully. Another man, probably no help there. His fellow shopper came down the aisle and Bob turned to study the raisins, keeping his shopping basket in front of him so the other guy couldn't see into

110

it. Somehow, chocolate chips didn't seem like a manly sort of thing to be carrying around, and Bob felt a little like he'd been caught browsing in the feminine protection aisle.

"S'cuze me," said the other guy as he leaned past Bob and took a box of raisins off the shelf.

Bob felt his face heating. He nodded and turned, hiding his chocolate chips.

The man wheeled off down the aisle, and Bob looked again at the Greek on the recipe card, willing his brain to understand it.

And then deliverance rounded the corner, a middle-aged woman pushing a half-full shopping cart. Bob flagged her down.

"My wife sent me to the store to get some items for her candy recipe, but I'm not sure what some of the things on her list mean," Bob confessed, feeling like an idiot. It was awkward to have to ask a stranger for help, like stopping and asking for directions in the days before GPS. He had to remind himself he'd feel like a bigger idiot if he failed in his quest for candy makings.

"Could you help me?" He held out the recipe card.

"Sure," she said, smiling sympathetically at him. "What exactly don't you understand?"

He pointed to the undecipherable shorthand. "I'm not sure what this 'pwd. sug.' is."

"Oh, that's powdered sugar. Let's see, you need three boxes." She pulled three blue and white boxes off the shelf and dropped them into his basket.

"And 'swt. condensed milk'?" he asked.

"Sweetened condensed milk. Over here." He trailed her down the aisle and watched while she scooped a little can off the shelf. "And do you have the paraffin wax at home?" she asked.

He had no idea. And why that was even included in this list of ingredients was way beyond him. They were making candy, not candles. What on earth did they need wax for?

His translator found that, too, and added it to his basket. "Now you just need your flavorings and you're about done."

"What about this 'marg.'?"

"That's probably margarine."

"Oh." Bob nodded.

"And the extracts you want are right down there," she added, pointing to the end of the aisle.

"Great," he said. "Thanks."

"You're welcome," she said, then wheeled away down the aisle, leaving Bob feeling like he'd just been rescued by the female counterpart to the Lone Ranger. *Who was that masked woman?*

His elation was short-lived. He reached the extract shelf and was almost overwhelmed by the variety of flavorings available. Joy's recipe didn't specify what kind to get. It just said flavorings. After several minutes of careful study, he decided to take a bottle of each. Okay, that should do it.

Back home he proudly set all his purchases on the counter. Poor Joy. Her plan to shame and manipulate him into becoming a good little boy for the holidays

112

was completely backfiring. He outsmarted her at every turn. *Elementary, my dear Watson.*

He chuckled and sauntered down the hall to his office, back to his computer, where words made sense.

He was long done with lunch and had just finished proofing his pages for the day when she finally came home.

He could hear her moving around in the kitchen and went out to find her putting away groceries. She'd gone to the store? Bob felt slightly had. Why couldn't she have gone ahead and gotten the bonbon makings when she was going to be at the store anyway?

She smiled at him over her shoulder. "I see you got the ingredients for the candy."

"I did, but if I'd known you were going to the store I'd have had you pick them up and saved myself a trip."

"Oh, but if I'd done that I would have been crossing the picket line. By the way, you'll have to go back. You forgot one."

"No, I didn't." Bob went over to the counter to examine his purchases.

"You didn't get the margarine."

The marg. He'd gotten sidetracked with the extracts and forgotten. "Don't we have any? You always stock up on extra groceries."

"Sorry, we're out."

She'd probably hidden it. "Fine," he said shortly. "I'll take care of it."

"I'm sure you will."

And he did. He sneaked off to his office and called Melia and asked her to bring the marg. When he hung up, he was grinning like the Grinch. Ha! Score a point for Bob Humbug.

"So, you ready?" Melia asked him later that evening as they stood in the kitchen.

Ready to shoot down an entire evening? His daughter was oozing anticipation. This was obviously important to her. "Absolutely," Bob lied.

"Okay. Here, put this on." She held out an old apron of Joy's to him. It had pink rosebuds on it. She actually expected him to wear this?

"Then wash your hands," she instructed, "and I'll start heating the milk."

It looked like she really did expect him to wear the apron. Bob took it and tied it on. At least he wouldn't have to worry about following the recipe instructions. His daughter seemed to have that well in hand.

"Oh," she said.

It wasn't the kind of "oh" that meant something good. "What?" Bob asked.

"These aren't the brand of chocolate chips we usually use."

"I couldn't find those," he said. *Please don't send me back to the store.*

She gnawed on her lip as she considered what to do, a habit she'd gotten from her mother.

With her hazel eyes and brown hair, she looked a lot like Joy had when they were first married. She even had Joy's dimples when she smiled. When they were first married it seemed Joy was always smiling, always

114

laughing. Somewhere along the way she'd stopped laughing as much. Come to think of it, so had he.

"Oh, well. I think we can make this work," Melia decided. "We should be okay if we add a little more wax."

"To the chocolate?" All the years he'd been enjoying those candies he'd been eating wax? That was just too gross.

"It helps them set up," Melia explained.

What was it doing to his arteries? He vowed to eat no bonbons this year, or ever again, for that matter. None, nada, zip.

He watched as his daughter deftly mixed the candy filling and added extract, sampling little pinches until she had it just right. He looked over his shoulder a couple of times, worried that Joy would come into the kitchen and make him do the mixing. It looked like a delicate process, not one he wanted to try.

After a few minutes Melia set a bowl containing a mountain of candy filling in front of him. "Okay, Daddy. You're going to roll this into little balls," she instructed.

That should be fun. Bob broke off a hunk of filling and started rolling.

"Only not that big." His daughter took the ball away from him and broke off half. "This size."

He looked at the little ball in his hand, then at the giant mound of filling in his bowl. At this rate he'd be doing this all night. He thought of Sisyphus, the poor mythical king forced to spend eternity rolling a boulder uphill that always rolled back down on him. "This is going to take forever," he complained.

"It takes about three hours to do these."

He was going to stand around in the kitchen and roll little balls for three hours. He'd lose his mind.

Melia grinned at him. "Don't worry. It'll be fun."

For whom?

CHAPTER
EIGHT

Joy sat in the living room pretending to read her December issue of *Bon Appétit*, smiling as she listened to Bob and Melia out in the kitchen singing old Sting songs together. Good. Things were going well. Maybe it would whet his appetite for more holiday experiences.

Suddenly she heard her husband yelp and went to the kitchen to investigate. She found Bob shaking his hand like he'd scalded it while Melia fished a candy out of the double boiler.

"He dropped the filling into the hot chocolate and spattered himself," Melia explained.

"This is dangerous work," Bob said.

"Only if you dive-bomb the melted chocolate," Melia told him. "You don't want to drop it from so high up. It splatters."

Bob had his hand under the faucet now, and was running cold water on his wrist. "Somebody should have warned me."

"Well, other than burning yourself, Emeril, are you having fun?" Joy asked.

"Oh, yes," he said diplomatically.

"He's doing a really good job," Melia said. She looked adoringly at her father, like it had been all his idea to make the candy with her.

Did Bob have any idea what a favor Joy had done him? Knowing Bob, probably not. "Well, you can be proud of yourself," she said encouragingly. "And when you deliver those to the neighbors you can brag that you made them all by yourself. With a little help from your daughter."

Bob didn't say anything, but from the mulish slant of his jaw, she could tell the neighbors probably wouldn't be getting any bonbons this year.

"Okay, Daddy," Melia said. "Get right back on the horse. Let's see if you can do a better job of dunking the filling this time."

Bob didn't look thrilled about getting back on the horse, but he took his position again in front of the tray of rounded balls on the counter next to the stove.

"Now just lower it in at the side of the pan," Melia instructed.

Joy couldn't help smiling. He looked so cute standing there by the stove wearing her old apron, his head bent next to their daughter's. Joy dashed to the den and grabbed the digital camera, then sneaked back. "Say cheese."

She caught Bob looking over his shoulder, half-shocked, half-fearful, and Melia grinning impishly.

"Must you do that?" he complained.

"For posterity," she said. "To prove that once upon a time literary great Bob Robertson actually did something in the kitchen besides make coffee. Maybe you can use it to promote the next book."

"The apron will be a nice touch," he grumbled.

"You do look pretty in pink," Joy teased. She took a pinch of candy filling and a pinch of Bob's cute, skinny behind, then left the kitchen, her daughter's mock scold of "Mother!" ushering her out.

An hour later Melia took off and Bob collapsed on the couch next to Joy. "That was exhausting."

"But well worth the effort," Joy said and popped a mint bonbon in her mouth.

She offered the container to Bob and he grimaced, saying, "I'm never eating another one of those as long as I live. All these years you've been feeding me wax."

"It helps the chocolate set up."

"So I hear. It probably helps my arteries set up, too." He smiled and leaned his head back on the couch cushions. "You know, we've got a great daughter."

Joy smiled. "I know."

Glen had had a busy evening decorating the house. He'd scampered around hanging stockings, setting out candles, and putting ceramic angels on guard over small, lighted villages trimmed with lots of doodads and little cords running every which way that made him feel like he had ten thumbs. It had been yet another time-consuming pain in the butt that had kept him from the relaxing evening in front of the TV that he'd envisioned.

But Laura had just made it all up to him, and now he was spooned up against her in bed, happily drifting off for the night.

And then an awful thing happened. She sighed sleepily and said, "So I guess you're getting the kids' outfits tomorrow morning before they have their pictures taken with Santa."

Glen's eyes popped open. "What?"

"Night," she murmured.

"Oh, no. You can't just drop that bomb on me and go to sleep," he protested. "I mean, what if I had plans for tomorrow?"

She rolled over in bed to face him. "Did you?"

Maybe this wasn't the best time to tell her. He could feel the wifely inquisitor stare boring into him. *Confess.*

"Well, some of the guys were coming over to watch the game." Even in the dark he could see her frown. "Don't worry," he said quickly. "I wasn't gonna ask you to feed them. Everybody's bringing beer and chips."

"And who's cleaning up the mess afterward?"

"Uh. I am?"

"Good guess. And you still have to take the kids to see Santa before you party."

"It's barely December. Why do they have to go see Santa so early?"

"Because we get extra pictures and stick them in a lot of the Christmas cards, which, by the way, need to get done next weekend."

Glen swore. "Are you trying to kill me? I work, you know."

She rolled back over, turning her back to him. "So do I. Then I come home and work some more on top of that. You're only doing Christmas stuff, Glen. I have to do that on top of taking care of the kids and the house. I've been trying to finish the same book for three months and I'm still working on the same scarf I started in September. I can't remember the last time I made it to the gym. In fact, it's a good day when I can find time to go to the bathroom."

Glen decided it was time to drop the subject. "Okay, okay, I get the idea," he said, cutting her off.

She sighed. "I guess I made my point. If you can't handle it I'll end the strike."

Right. Like he was going to throw in the towel after that little speech she just made. It would be Super Babe kayos Weinie Man in the first round. "Hey, I can handle it."

"Are you sure?"

"Yeah, I'm sure." He should have kept his big mouth shut.

"Okay. Good night," she said sweetly. "Pleasant dreams."

Dreams? He was going to be awake for hours thinking about all he had to do. Kickoff was at two. Would he make it back in time? Don't even go there, he told himself.

As it turned out, he did get to sleep, but once there he found a nightmare waiting for him. It was Saturday, ten minutes until kickoff, and he still had to drive to the mall and get his kids their outfits, then take them to see Santa. But he was having trouble even getting to the minivan. It was like he was trapped in invisible quicksand and no matter how hard he forced his muscles, every part of his body moved in cartoon slow motion. He finally wound up crawling on his hands and knees. Then, suddenly, he was at the mall with his buddies and they were all yelling at him because they were missing the kickoff. And he'd lost the kids. Santa drove by in his sleigh, right down the center of the mall with the kids sitting on top of a huge sack of presents, waving at him. Santa pointed at Glen and laughed, and it wasn't his usual ho, ho, ho. It was a nasty, mocking cackle. "You're gonna miss the game, fool," Santa called. "You're gonna miss everything."

Glen's eyes popped open. He spread out his hands and felt firm mattress beneath him and let out a sigh of relief. Okay, it was just a bad dream, his id or something acting up.

He went downstairs and found Laura in the utility room, putting in a load of laundry. He gave her a kiss, then asked, "How soon does the mall open?"

"Ten."

Glen nodded. "Good." They'd be there when the doors opened. It shouldn't take more than fifteen minutes to grab some clothes for the kids. Santa was probably camped out right in the middle of the mall. Half an hour for that, tops. They'd be back home in plenty of time.

He found the kids at the tiled oak table in the kitchen nook, finishing up breakfast. "Okay, team," he said, clapping his hands like a football coach about to make a locker room speech. "Everybody ready to go see Santa?"

"Santa!" cried Amy, scooting out of her chair.

"Santa!" echoed Tyler, mirroring the action.

"First Daddy's going to take you to get new clothes for your Christmas pictures," Laura said from behind him. "So be good and help him pick out something pretty."

Amy nodded enthusiastically. "We will."

To Glen she added, "Get her a dress, something red. And Tyler just needs a little red bow tie to go with his slacks and shirt."

"Hey, I can handle it, okay?" Glen said, irritated. What kind of bozo did she think he was, anyway?

"Okay," she said. She cocked her head and examined her daughter.

Glen looked, too. Amy's hair was sticking out in several directions. "You better go brush your hair," he told her. "You want to look nice for your picture."

"Mommy always fixes it special," Amy said.

Uh-oh. But he was already doing so much. She wouldn't throw him a curve like that.

She would. "Daddy's going to fix your hair this year."

"Oh, come on, Laura. What do I know about fixing girls' hair?"

"About as much as you know about what I do around here at the holidays. All you have to do is brush it and put it in a ponytail. But if you think you can't handle it . . ."

He held up a hand, stopping her in midsentence. "I can handle it."

Well, sort of. Just like with the Christmas decorations, his big hands proved ill equipped for the challenge. He finally got the hair band wrapped around most of her hair. It stuck straight up like Pebbles in the Flintstones and was slightly off center. But it looked cute, trendy even.

Amy studied her reflection in the bathroom mirror, brows knit. Not a good sign.

Glen spied some sort of fuzzy pink hair clip on the counter. He handed it to her. "Here. Put this in your hair."

She obliged then smiled, content with the fix.

"Okay. Get your coat and let's go," Glen said.

"What are you going to do all day?" he asked Laura as they headed for the door. She gave Amy's hair a quick tweak, then opened it for them, snapping her gum and smirking. All she needed was a red tail and a pitchfork. "Don't tell me, let me guess," he said bitterly. "You're gonna read, knit, and sit on the pot."

Amy cracked up over that. "Mommy's going to sit on the pot."

Not to be left out, Tyler started laughing, too, bobbing from side to side chanting, "Pot, pot, pot."

"For your information, smart guy, I'm going to start another load of laundry, clean the kitchen, and then get my hair done." She bent over and kissed both kids. "Be good for Daddy."

"We will," Amy promised, then skipped out the door with Tyler bouncing after her.

124

"Have fun," Laura cooed to Glen.

"Don't worry," he snapped. "We will. Piece of cake."

The mall was already crowded and Glen had to park at the farthest end. He'd forgotten to put the stroller in the minivan, so he had to carry Tyler. Oh, well. He could handle it. He didn't go to the gym for nothing.

By the time they reached the mall entrance he was convinced Laura had smuggled rocks into their kid's diaper. Why else would he be so damned heavy? Glen put Tyler down and he immediately took off toward the play area after his sister.

"We're not playing today," Glen called and chased after them.

An hour later they left the play area and went on the hunt for clothes.

"Look, Daddy. Deer ears," Amy said, pointing to a headband sporting a goofy pair of brown felt antlers. "Can I have some?"

"Me want ears," said Tyler.

"Okay. Sure." Glen paid for two sets of antlers and settled them on the kid's heads. "Now, we've got to find something to put you in for your pictures." They were in the girls' department, surrounded by racks of pants, tops, pajamas, and dresses of all kinds and colors. Glen blinked, overwhelmed with the choices. *Dress, red dress.* He started for the rack with the dresses.

Amy hopped over to the pajamas. "Daddy, I want princess jammies," she called, holding out a flannel pant leg stamped with Disney princesses.

Glen scratched his head. Could a kid wear pajamas to see Santa? Laura had said get a red dress. "We better look at dresses," he said.

"But I want princess jammies," Amy pleaded, her voice sounding teary. She started to do the sobby sniff thing.

Oh, no. No crying. This department was full of women. They'd look at him like he was some kind of child abuser. "Okay, princess jammies it is," he decided, and yanked a pair off the rack. Kids in pajamas were cute. He held them up to Amy. The pajamas seemed to keep going long after her feet stopped. Hmmm. "I think we better find another size."

Naturally, there weren't any damn princess jammies in a smaller size. "It looks like we're gonna have to bag the jammies," Glen said.

"No, Daddy. You promised."

Oh, geez, she was gearing up for a tear storm again. "Okay, okay. We'll get these. You'll have room to grow."

She rewarded him with an ecstatic smile. He had to be the world's biggest pushover.

"Let's find jammies for Tyler, too," she suggested.

Why not? That way, they could match. Both the kids in matching jammies. That'd look cute. Anyway, Glen had no idea where to find a little kid bow tie. The search could take hours.

They got Sponge Bob Square Pants pajamas for Tyler; then Glen took the kids back to the minivan and changed them into their new duds. Of course, the tags were stuck on with those stupid plastic doohickeys that even Superman couldn't break. After putting a hole in

126

the armpit of Tyler's pajamas yanking one off, Glen finally gave up and stuck the tags inside the necks. Then he put the kids in their coats again and trotted them back to see Santa.

The line stretched halfway to South America. Glen checked his watch. Nearly noon. Well, it would probably move fast.

Forty-five minutes later they were up to the fake snow lawn and one kid away from entering the red plywood shack to see Santa, and Tyler smelled funny.

"Tyler smells poopy," Amy announced.

Great. Just one kid away and Tyler had to drop a bomb in his pants. If they left the line to change him they'd have to start all over again and no way was Glen going to do that. He considered changing Tyler right on the spot and decided against it. Laura was the kid expert, but even Glen knew that was a social no-no.

"He'll be okay until we get home," Glen decided. He took off the kids' coats so they'd be ready for the big moment and studied them. There they stood, Amy wearing jammies that flopped over her feet and Tyler with a load in his diaper. Well, what could Laura expect? She was on strike and he was a scab. You had to take what you got when the scabs were on the job.

Santa got done ho-ho-ho-ing a kid who looked like she should be on a magazine cover and held out his arms to Tyler and Amy. Amy walked obediently up to him, flopping her way around her too-long pant legs, but Tyler suddenly got alarmed. He started to cry and turned to bolt.

"It's okay," Glen told him, picking him up. "It's Santa. He's going to bring you cool stuff for Christmas."

Glen tried to set Tyler on Santa's lap and Tyler's howl got louder. His feet began to pump and he tried to wiggle free. His deer antlers slipped sideways. Tyler wasn't crying in last year's Santa pictures. What had Laura done to make him stop? Drugged him?

"Come on, Tyler," Amy said encouragingly, and perched on Santa.

Glen tried again. Tyler let Glen set him down, but he kept on crying. He looked like a kid who'd just had his candy cane stolen.

"It's okay, sweetie," cooed a female elf with a camera. "What's this I've got?" She squeezed a squeaky toy duck at Tyler.

Tyler kept wailing.

"Can you smile for Santa?" she suggested.

She said it just as Santa made a face.

Glen couldn't blame him. Tyler smelled pretty ripe.

"Whoa there," said Santa. "Somebody needs a clean diaper for Christmas."

"Yeah, well. We're gonna take care of that," Glen said.

The look Santa gave him promised Glen a lump of something in his stocking on a par with what was in Tyler's diaper.

The elf snapped away while Tyler cried and wiggled, popping loose the stuck-down tag from the neck of his pajamas. At least Amy smiled. She looked like a little angel . . . with no feet who was having a bad hair day.

128

(The ponytail was mostly out now, and her antlers weren't exactly front and center, either.) And Santa kept trying to smile but mostly looked like he'd just been fed a lemon.

Somehow, Glen couldn't imagine Laura wanting to stick very many of these pictures in their Christmas cards.

As soon as the elf was done, Santa removed Tyler from his lap. "Whoa," he said, fanning out his pant leg. "Next time bring your Mommy, kids."

"Very funny," said Glen.

"Not from where I'm sitting," Santa retorted.

The minute they were away from Santa, Tyler stopped yelling. Glen noticed that the woman behind him was bringing up a couple of kids who looked like they'd been dressed by a fashion designer. Of course, that was the look Laura would have wanted for the kids.

Glen paid the hefty picture price and gave the Santa rip-off company the necessary address for sending the pics, then got out of there. He'd thought they'd have a computer set up that would give him a chance to see some proofs and pick the least awful one like the photographers did over at the place where Laura often took the kids for portraits, but no such luck. Maybe it was just as well, because Glen knew he'd never be able to find any picture his wife would approve.

By the time he got the kids home he was completely wrung out.

Laura was back, looking totally hot with a new hair-style. "How'd it go?" she asked. She was watching him like she was half afraid to hear.

No sense ruining her day. "Piece of cake. Here," he said, handing Tyler over to her. "He needs changing."

She looked from one child to the other. "What's with the pajamas?"

"We went with a 'Night Before Christmas theme'," Glen said. "Now, if you're done torturing me for the day, I'd like to go back to being myself."

She looked at him innocently, like she wasn't enjoying every moment of his misery, and said, "Sure."

The sad thing was, Glen never completely got back to being himself. He was tired when the guys came, and wished he hadn't invited anyone over. And it ticked him off that they moved his decorations off the coffee table to make room for the chips and salsa. Then, when Roger and Mac started throwing the football around at halftime, he snapped, "Don't be throwing that in the house. You'll knock over my lighted village."

Rog stopped, his arm in midair. Three pairs of jaws dropped open and the only sound in the room was the TV blatting out a beer commercial.

Mac was the first to speak. "Dude. What is wrong with you? You sound like Martha Stewart."

Glen suddenly felt like he was going to puke. *Oh, God. What's happening to me?*

CHAPTER
NINE

The article about the strike appeared in Sunday's paper. The picture of his wife reclining amid the mess of ornament boxes didn't bother Glen, but what she said in the article sure did.

He gave the paper a disgusted thump. "You make me look like a jerk."

Laura took it away from him and studied her picture. "I'm donating those pants to the Goodwill. They definitely make me look fat."

"Never mind the pants. What about me and how I look?"

She peered at him over the top of the paper, both eye-brows raised. "All I did was tell the reporter how it is around here every Christmas, babe. How does that make you look like a jerk?"

He was about to step into some kind of verbal trap. He could sense it the way an animal could smell trouble on the wind. He decided to try a different strategy. "You could have said something good about me, you know."

She gave him that sexy grin of hers and moved from her side of the kitchen table to sit on his lap, twining her arms around his neck. "Now, you know they can't print that kind of stuff in the paper."

"What stuff?" Amy asked, looking up from her bowl of Tootie Fruities.

Laura left Glen's lap — darn — and started clearing the breakfast dishes. "Never mind. Finish your cereal. We have to get out the door."

The last thing Glen wanted to do now was go to Mass. As of this morning, everyone in the entire parish knew that he was the holiday version of Mr. Mom. He had to have been out of his mind to go along with this. Either that or Laura was slipping drugs into his food.

That last thought gave him an idea. "I don't think I'll go today." He rubbed his gut for effect. "I think I'm coming down with something."

Laura looked over her shoulder at him. "Yeah? A case of *chicken* pox?" She started to cluck under her breath.

He scowled, sitting up a little straighter and pushing out his chest. "No. I just —"

"You're just chicken," she taunted.

Amy, sensing a good joke, echoed, "You're a chicken, Daddy."

He launched himself from his chair and growled, "Never mind. I'll go."

Laura chuckled as he pushed past her to go brush his teeth. The woman would have made a good Spanish Inquisitor.

He'd been right about what it would be like at church. All through Father Thomas's homily Glen could feel curious stares burning into his back. They were barely out of the sanctuary when Derrick

132

Matthews gave him a playful punch in the arm and said, "Hey, how's the cookie baking going, Mrs. Claus?"

"That's real funny," Glen said with a frown.

Roger was with them now, and studying Glen with narrowed eyes. "Does that article have something to do with you weirding out over the lighted village yesterday? He was all worried about us knocking it over with the football," Rog explained to Derrick.

"Whoa. So, what are you asking for this Christmas, a new vacuum?" Derrick teased.

Glen leaned over and lowered his voice. "One more word and you're black and blue for Christmas. Got it?"

Derrick took a step back and held up his hands, a joking smile on his face. "Hey, pal. Take some Midol."

That was it. Glen was going to take him out right here in front of God and everyone. He pushed up his shirtsleeves and started for Derrick the dickhead.

The only thing that saved the guy was his wife, Gina, coming up to them. She wiggled in front of Derrick and looked up at Glen like he was Superman. "Glen, this is so cool. You're really doing everything?"

"It wasn't my idea," Glen said sullenly. He'd been tricked. Or hypnotized. Or something.

"Well, I think it's awesome," Gina gushed. She gave Derrick a look that said his turn was coming, and Derrick's smile slipped off, making Glen feel much better.

"Yeah, well, any man can handle that Christmas stuff if he puts his mind to it," Glen said, making himself

133

sound like a candidate for an upcoming season of *Survivor*.

Another husband walked past as this conversation was taking place. "Thanks a lot," he said to Glen. "My wife ragged on me all the way here. Now I'm stuck with doing the Christmas cards."

"Glen can't help it if he's whipped," said another. The moron was doing a pretty good job of gloating until his wife came and told him it was time to get over to her mother's for lunch.

Glen couldn't help gloating a little himself. These clowns put up great facades, but when it came right down to it, they were all whipped. Women just had a way of taking a guy's life and turning it upside down.

Laura broke away from the group of women she'd been talking to and started toward him, Tyler in her arms, Amy skipping beside her. Watching them, he felt the familiar swell of love and pride rise in his chest and he had to shake his head and smile. Being whipped wasn't all that bad.

He changed his mind once they got home, though. He was just about to turn on the TV for the pregame show when Laura said, "Christmas cards need to get done today, remember."

"The game's about to start," Glen protested.

"So, address envelopes while you watch it. Multitask. That's what I do."

Only a woman would suggest such a dumb thing.

Laura flipped on the radio and a cheery chorus came over the stereo system, telling him that he needed a

134

little Christmas. Yeah, right. What he needed was a break from Christmas.

After lunch Laura put Tyler down for a nap. Then, while Glen sat in front of the TV swearing over the Christmas cards, she and Amy snuggled under the down comforter on Glen's and her king-size bed and read storybooks together. It felt great to spend a Sunday afternoon just relaxing with her daughter. Last year she hadn't had time for this sort of thing, hadn't even had a minute for herself because of everything she'd wound up doing. And there had been Glen, the Christmas drone, just relaxing and inviting company over at the drop of a hat, while she ran in circles. It felt good not to run. In fact, it felt so good that she knew she would never do it again. She and Glen would either be entering into some serious negotiations at the end of the strike or he'd be living at the North Pole.

At one point Glen called up the stairs, "I have to get something. I'll be back," then she heard the front door slam. Poor Glen, he was probably going out to buy more Excedrin.

She finished the last page of *The Night Before Christmas* and shut the book.

"I like that book," Amy said.

Laura kissed the top of her head. "I know you do."

"Does Daddy want to come and read stories with us?"

"Oh, honey, I'm afraid Daddy's going to be busy for a while," Laura said with a wicked grin. What a brilliant idea this strike was. Joy had been positively inspired when she came up with it.

The phone wouldn't stop ringing. It seemed to Bob that every woman Joy had ever known felt the need to call and talk about the strike. And that included his mother-in-law. Pretty soon Joy was dishing out advice like she was Dr. Phil in drag. By late afternoon Bob had to get out of the house.

He got some pop at the grocery store, then went to Hollywood Heaven for an order of escapism. That was where he ran into Karen Doolittle, their most obnoxious neighbor. Just hearing her bullhorn voice call hello from the other side of the store was enough to convince him it was time to sign up for Netflix. Of course he couldn't pretend he hadn't heard her. The whole store had heard her. He gave her a wave, hoping that would be enough, and turned back to the shelf of foreign films he'd been perusing.

Of course, it wasn't enough. Next thing he knew she was next to him, telling him and everyone in the place who wasn't deaf that she'd read all about him in the paper. "So does that mean you're in charge of fun and games for Christmas?" she asked in an attempt to be coy.

"It looks that way," Bob agreed. Then added, "Which means we'll be having a nice, quiet Christmas. Guess you'll have to do the neighborhood party this year." Like that would ever happen. Karen's husband was the cheapest bum on the block.

136

She looked at him like he'd just told her that Santa would be passing her house without stopping.

"Merry Christmas," he said, and pulled a DVD off the shelf.

"Same to you," she said in a tone of voice that wished him a lump of coal up his butt.

He couldn't help smiling as he walked away. For the first time since he'd gotten married, his wife wasn't running the holiday show. He could do anything he wanted. Anything. The holiday was his. He was writing the scenario this year.

He practically skipped to the comedy section and randomly picked something. Then he stopped by the action/adventure shelf and got an old Arnold Schwarzenegger movie, *The Terminator*. Bob felt a little bit like a terminator, himself — the Christmas Terminator, wiping out irritating, invasive traditions wherever he went. Ho, ho, ho and blast away. This really was going to be a great holiday. No neighborhood Christmas party at his house, no herds of chattering women traipsing through his living room and kitchen for teas and cookie exchanges. Just the peace and silence of a brave, new world.

On the way home, the Christmas Terminator made one more stop, and pulled his car into the parking lot of Hank's Hardware.

Hank's sat squarely in the middle of town, a good, strong dose of testosterone to balance the kitchen shops, women's clothing boutiques, toy stores, and other female-friendly stores that dominated downtown Holly. Hank didn't bother to cater to women. Shoppers would find no wind chimes, no picnic doodads, no cutesy gardening utensils or little stone frogs for the front yard in his place. The few small appliances he stocked were cool guy toys, like the George Foreman Lean Mean Grilling Machine. Hank's was Man Land, packed full of saws and hammers and nails, wheelbarrows, levels, screwdrivers, bits, and anything else a man could want, including male conversation. His only concession to the holidays was a limited selection of outdoor lights — no garlands or tinsel or lighted villages. In short, nothing to tempt the women of Holly to invade his territory. Bob always liked wandering around in there and seeing what was new.

He walked in to find a couple of men leaning on the front counter, talking to Hank and watching the last of the game playing on the TV mounted on the wall behind him. The big, beefy one Bob recognized right away as his neighbor, Glen Fredericks. Bob didn't recognize the man next to him. He was shorter, with the sinewy build of a runner, and was wearing a baseball cap on his head. It was obvious he'd taken the day off from shaving.

Hank, a grizzled, old bachelor, spat a streak of tobacco into the old-fashioned spittoon he kept by the cash register and said, "The problem with you morons is you've forgotten how to be men. Christmas cards," he said in disgust, and spat again. And then he saw Bob. "Well, speak of the devil."

The other two men turned to look in Bob's direction; then both frowned.

138

Bob nodded politely and scurried down the aisle with the flashlights. What was that all about? Of course, the article in the newspaper. But why give him the stink eye? Fredericks's wife was in this clear up to her pretty, blond curls.

Bob selected a flashlight and some batteries, then walked up to the counter, steeling himself for attack.

"My wife's trying to kill me," Fredericks greeted him. "I just spent an hour doing Christmas cards and I'm still not done. The only way I could watch the game in peace was to come here."

"I hear this was all your wife's idea," the other guy accused Bob.

"This is Pete," Glen began. "What'd you say your last name was?"

"Benedict." The man was frowning like he wanted to punch Bob's lights out. Writing and an occasional round of golf hadn't exactly kept Bob in top fighting condition. The guy would have no problem.

Lucky for Bob, Pete took his proffered hand and shook it. "My wife joined that strike your wife started, and now, instead of driving me crazy making everything perfect, she's driving me crazy telling me that nothing's perfect."

Glen shook his head. "So far this game is going to the women."

"You should've stayed single," Hank told him.

"So, did you do that tree in the picture in the paper?" Pete asked Bob.

Bob shrugged. "Just a little sabotage."

Glen gave Bob a thumbs-up, but Pete let out a snort. "Passive-aggressive stuff doesn't work. It just makes 'em madder."

"Well, I thought it was worth a try," Bob said.

"Nothing works when they've made up their minds about something," Fredericks said.

"Sick," Hank muttered, and let fly with another stream of tobacco juice.

"The best we can do is stay strong," Bob said. "Don't let them think they're getting to us."

"Hey, I'm not letting this get to me," Fredericks insisted. "I can take anything she can dish out."

"Which is why you're down here," said Hank.

Another man came up to the counter now. Around the pipe in his mouth, he asked, "You talking about the strike?" They nodded and he frowned. "If I get my hands on the wimp who let his wife start this . . ." The other two closed ranks to protect Bob, and the newcomer's eyes narrowed. "Wait a minute."

"It's not his fault," Glen said. "The women all got together. None of us had any control over this."

The man looked at them all in disgust. "Well, your wives convinced mine that I have to go Christmas shopping."

"Don't tell me, let me guess," said Glen. "Jack Carter the Scrooge."

"I'm not a Scrooge," Jack snarled.

Now another man had joined them. "Hey, you think shopping is bad — my wife is making me cook a turkey. What do I look like, anyway, Chef Boyardee? I don't have a clue how to do that."

140

"You don't," Bob told him. "You order one precooked from Town and Country."

The guy nodded thoughtfully. "Good idea."

"We don't have to do everything the women do," Bob added.

Fredericks puffed out his massive chest. "Yeah, we're men."

"Yeah," the others chorused.

"So, does anybody know how to make cookies?" Pete asked.

Silence fell on Hank's Hardware.

"I've gotta get home," Glen finally said.

"Me, too," said Pete.

"Henpecked," said Hank in disgust.

Not me, Bob told himself as he drove away. These poor slobs needed help. They needed the Christmas Terminator.

He came home to find his wife waiting for him on the living room sofa, cupping a steaming mug of tea and wearing a melancholy expression. He felt his cloud of euphoria begin to dissolve around the edges. "What's wrong?"

"I've already had two people ask me if we're going to have our annual Christmas party."

Uh-oh. The Christmas Terminator started to fall apart and the ground under Bob's feet suddenly felt unstable. "What did you tell them?"

"That I'm not in charge this year." She said it like it was his fault she'd abdicated her position as ruler of the holidays. She took a sip from her mug and watched him over the rim.

The Christmas Terminator was crumbling into a useless pile of nuts and bolts and melting steel. This was how she always got him, with guilt.

But not this time, Bob told himself firmly. Joy was on strike and Bob was the new ruler. The queen was picketing; long live the king.

He willed the Terminator back together and said, "Good girl." No parties this year, thank God. He handed over the DVDs. "What do you want to watch?"

Arnold, of course, did not get first pick. Neither did the foreign film. She picked the comedy. Bob realized he should have paid closer attention to what he was grabbing. The movie with Will Smith had been a tactical error. It was all about a date doctor who advised men to do anything for the woman they wanted — a bad message for a man who was trying to gain some measure of control over his own existence.

Just pretend you don't get the message, he told himself as they headed for the TV room.

"So I guess we're not having a party this Christmas," Joy said from behind him.

She was trying to sound casual, but he could hear the hope hiding in her voice. He smiled grimly. It had been easy enough to announce she was going on strike, talk a big talk to the newspaper reporter, but she wasn't finding her strike so much fun when faced with the reality of losing control. Well, now she knew how he felt.

"Are you ending your strike?" he countered.

It took her a minute to answer. "No."

"Then I guess we're not."

142

"Fine," she said, miserable resignation tainting every particle of breath. She was Joan of Arc, waiting for the bonfire. He could see their quiet evening together vanishing quicker than a plate of Christmas cookies. Who was he kidding? Her unhappiness would spread out far beyond this evening.

"You're the one who wanted me to see how miserable I'd be if we did things my way," he reminded her. "Don't you want to give me a chance to be miserable?"

That coaxed a reluctant smile from her. "Hurry up and get miserable, will you?"

He put in the DVD and settled on the love seat, patting the cushion next to him. "Come on. Let's enjoy the movie."

She snuggled in next to him and he put an arm around her, deep contentment settling over him. He loved times like this when it was just the two of them enjoying something together. Who needed a party?

Joy had trouble paying attention to the movie. Her thoughts kept drifting to the bleak Bob Humbug Christmas that lay ahead of her. She felt like Mrs. Claus stuck in a tug-of-war with the Grinch. At the rate they were going there was only one thing that was going to save her. *Note to self: Buy more chocolate.*

After the ribbing he'd taken at church, Glen entered the office on Monday like a soldier preparing to cross territory riddled with land mines. Mitzi, the receptionist, greeted him with a glare. He wasn't sure, but he thought she growled.

"Don't believe everything you read in the paper," he told her, and pressed on.

One of the guys called from his desk, "Hey, man, saw the article. Hang in there," and that made Glen feel better.

His secretary, Kathleen, shook her head at him as he tried to slip past her desk. She hung up her phone and said, "I told you it would all catch up with you someday. You'd better pray your wife doesn't decide to have a party."

Like it was his fault Christmas came every year? Like it was his fault they had family and friends who wanted to come over? Like he couldn't handle this? He was doing fine.

He spread out his arms, briefcase dangling from one hand. "So, let her. Game on."

Kathleen was ten years older than he was. She seemed to think it gave her the right to act like his mother and dish out advice and make ominous predictions. Oh, and dish out superior looks like the one she was giving him now.

He decided to ignore it. "Hold my calls," he said. "I've got some work to do."

He locked his office door, then went to his desk, opened his briefcase, and took out a fat pile of Christmas cards to address.

Laura was restocking the brochure rack with the reprinted Hollydays brochures when the call came in to the Chamber of Commerce. It was Kathleen, Glen's secretary.

"I thought you might like to know your husband informed me this morning that he's perfectly capable of throwing a Christmas party."

Laura gave a snort of disgust. "Yeah, right. And who does he think is going to get all the food for it and serve it and clean up the mess afterward?" Just the thought of the work that came along with any pairing of the words "Glen" and "party" made her start snapping her gum.

"He claims he's up to the challenge."

"That'll be a first," Laura said. "I can just see Glen in charge of a party."

"Sounds like fun. Can I come?"

Glen having to deal with the kind of instant invasion he dumped on her. That should be interesting. Give the boy some circles to run in. "Yeah, the more the merrier. In fact, why don't you invite the whole office? I'll call some of our friends."

"Okay. When?"

"This Friday," Laura decided. "He can get ready for it in between addressing Christmas cards and baking cookies."

"Are we going to have to eat them?" Kathleen asked, obviously horrified.

"Afraid so."

"Great. Then I'm bringing a giant bottle of Tums for a hostess gift."

CHAPTER
TEN

Carol had been in a relatively good mood before coming to volunteer at the food bank on Monday, but seeing Sunday's paper with the article on the strike sitting on the little house's kitchen counter had made her grumpy. Now the Christmas music playing on the small, portable radio in the reception area sawed on her nerves with every tinny note. Who had brought that article in, anyway?

She managed to ignore it while she bagged food requests and started to fill a pot with chopped vegetables for soup. But every time she had a temporary lull in customers the darned thing drew her attention.

She leaned on the formica counter and studied the shot of Bob and Joy and their terrifying tree. Why had Joy pulled this stunt? It didn't seem like her. And surely, after all the years she'd been married, she and Bob had established the rules of give and take for their marriage. Was everything okay with them?

Carol turned her attention to the picture of Laura, stretched out in a chair, sipping something from a big mug, while behind her chaos bloomed. She was obviously enjoying this.

So were the others. They wore their various states of discontent like new fashion finds.

They should all be ashamed of themselves. They had so much and they appreciated it so little. They should each have to spend a few days here at Helping Hands, talking with people who were homeless, unemployed, or suddenly divorced and struggling desperately to make ends meet, or try rattling around a house with only memories for company. Maybe then they'd appreciate what they had.

"Ho, ho, ho!"

The deep voice behind Carol made her jump. She turned to see Darren Matthews entering the small, utilitarian kitchen, grinning at her.

Darren was divorced, in his early sixties, and recently retired. He was also a recent recruit, eager to make meaningful use of his newfound spare time. Every Monday he went to Holly's two grocery stores and picked up food contributions.

He was a big, husky man, and the clothes he was wearing made him look even huskier. It wasn't the usual slacks and shirt outfit that he wore to make his collection rounds. Today he was in old jeans and work boots, with a plaid flannel shirt under an Eddie Bauer vest. This Paul Bunyan look was accessorized by the leather work gloves he carried in one hand.

Darren wasn't the most handsome man Carol had ever seen, but he certainly made the top ten list for most appealing. With his burly frame and round, Germanic face, he always made her think of Santa. Right now she looked at him and thought not of Santa, but of hard muscle hiding beneath soft flannel. He smelled good, too, a winning combination of fresh air and aftershave. All in all he was an appealing package . . . for some woman.

"Think you'd have any customers for a Christmas tree?" he asked.

"A Christmas tree?"

"I've got some out in my truck."

"The grocery stores donated Christmas trees?" Here was a first.

"No. I've got a friend who lives on a tree farm. He let me cut a dozen down yesterday. I know we give away other things besides food here, and I thought we could use some trees."

"They'll be gone by tomorrow," Carol predicted.

She stuck her head out the kitchen door and called over to Gert, the food bank's oldest volunteer, who was busily writing at her tinsel-swagged desk, "Guess what we got."

Gert pulled off her bifocals and looked up expectantly.

"Darren brought us some Christmas trees."

Gert craned her head. "Some what?"

"Trees," Carol repeated.

"Trees!" That got Gert up and hobbling over to the kitchen as fast as her bad hip would let her.

"I've got a dozen out in my truck," Darren said. "Where should I set them up?"

"Oh, my stars!" declared Gert. "Well, let's just prop them along the front porch where people can see them when they come up the walk."

148

Darren nodded and started for the back door.

"I'll help you," Carol offered.

"It's okay, I've got it," he called over his shoulder. "Anyway, you'll get your hands all cut up."

"This is so exciting," Carol said to Gert. "I can think of several people who will be thrilled."

"A wonderful idea," Gert agreed. She gave Carol a nudge. "That Darren is quite a find."

"We're lucky to have him," Carol said, playing dumb.

"I wasn't talking about Helping Hands," Gert said, and arched an eyebrow.

Carol knew where this conversation was going. She gave Gert a look that made her shrug and return to her desk.

But not without getting in the last word. "He's interested in you. I can tell."

"Thanks for sharing," Carol said, then turned to check on her soup. He wasn't interested, he was just being nice. And that was all Carol wanted him to be. Anything else she simply couldn't deal with.

She was fine-tuning the seasoning in her soup when Darren returned to the kitchen. "There's one left in my truck, and it's a beauty. Noble fir. Got a tree yet?"

"Oh, that's sweet of you," Carol said. "But I'm not doing a tree this year."

"Not having a tree at Christmas? I can't believe it. I'm an old bachelor and even I put up a tree."

"Maybe next year. Meanwhile, I know we'll have lots of people who will want to stake a claim to that noble fir."

"Okay," Darren said, resigned. "But let me know if you change your mind. I'm sure I could get another. And I'd help you put it up, too."

His friendly promise turned Carol's throat tight and started images from the past swirling around her like snow in a globe. She saw her young son, clapping chubby hands at the sight of the tree on Christmas morning, her husband kissing her after they put up the last ornament, the three of them sitting beneath the tree, opening presents.

She blinked hard to hold back the tears and, unable to speak, nodded her thanks to Darren.

"I guess I'll put that last one out with the others," he said, suddenly awkward. "Then I'm off to Town and Country for food."

Carol nodded again and he left. She listened to the sound of his boots clumping out of the room and sighed.

Maybe she should have taken him up on his offer, but somehow it seemed disloyal to her husband's memory, frivolous even. She'd felt that way after their son died, too, and Ray had finally insisted they try to find their way back to normal and put up a tree. It hadn't taken them back to normal then. It wouldn't take her there now. Anyway, trees were a bother, and live ones shed their needles and made such a mess.

The kitchen was filling up with the aroma of garlic and bay leaves now. Soon it would waft through the building, sending a subliminal message of comfort. Carol turned the burner to Simmer and started cutting up French bread. The food bank always had plenty of

150

customers for lunch. Men looking to pick up odd jobs fortified themselves with whatever the volunteers concocted from the pantry, and women with hungry children always sat down for a quick meal.

While Carol was cutting she looked up and saw a young mother approaching the order window with her list of needs, a two-year-old girl on her hip, and two preschoolers in tow. Good. Customers. Carol set some of the bread on a plate and smiled a greeting.

The food bank supplied its customers with a sort of grocery list that itemized what was available. Their customers checked what they needed and volunteers went to the pantry and filled grocery bags according the list.

Carol knew this woman. Her name was Ariel, and she was on her own. The father of her two-year-old girl was no longer in the picture. Ariel was starting school in January to become a dental hygienist. Meanwhile, she did child care for friends and supplemented that sketchy income with occasional checks from her mother, who lived in another state. Ariel was a pencil-thin, thrift-store fashion model, always wearing a determined smile. And it was that smile that tugged at Carol's heart every time she saw the girl.

"Need a Christmas tree?" she asked Ariel.

The girl's eyes lit up. "Those ones out in front? Are they free?"

Carol nodded.

Ariel's forehead wrinkled as she thought. Then her eyes dimmed and she shook her head. "I don't think any of those would fit on the roof of my car."

"I think I know someone who might be willing to make a delivery," Carol said, and added, "You've got to have a place for Santa to leave his presents."

"Santa's coming to our house this year," announced one of the preschoolers in Ariel's care.

Carol smiled down at her. "So, you've been good?"

The child nodded.

"Then I'm sure he'll come."

Ariel looked at her own child, a little doll with huge, brown eyes and hair that was a cascade of black ringlets. "A tree would be nice."

"Leave me your address and I'll have our tree guy bring it over later," Carol promised.

Ariel nodded. "Wow, that's awesome. Thanks."

"Our pleasure," said Carol. And it was. Every child should have a tree at Christmas.

Ariel handed over her request list and Carol went to fill it.

The pantry was a huge storeroom with rows of shelves marching across its rough, hardwood floor. It held everything from diapers to dog food. And off that room was a smaller room with a huge chest freezer stocked with meats. Soon they would be getting frozen turkeys and holiday hams.

Carol had never had to wonder where her next meal would come from. She'd never needed to worry about how to pay for groceries, or to humble herself to go to some charitable organization and ask for food. As she pulled canned goods off a shelf she tried to imagine herself in Ariel's shoes, but quickly gave up. The bottom line was, she didn't want to. At least Ariel had a

152

child. Having a child made all the difference. A woman could face anything as long as her child was with her, safe and well.

Children, there was another road she was not going to let her thoughts wander down. She pulled the last of the requested canned goods from the shelves and went to get bread and milk.

By the time she returned with the groceries, Ariel had gotten the kids settled at a little table in one corner of the reception area and they were happily munching on gingerbread boys donated by the local bakery.

"Do I have some customers for vegetable soup?" Carol asked.

"Oh, yeah," Ariel said.

The smell of soup had permeated the reception area now, and Carol hoped it gave the little house a homey smell. She ladled it into bowls, then set them on the counter. "So, how's it going?" she asked.

Ariel shrugged. "Okay, I guess. But maybe I won't take that tree after all."

"Why not?" It really wasn't any of her business. She probably wasn't supposed to ask. On the other hand, no one had told her when she went through her volunteer training that she couldn't show an interest in someone's life.

"I don't have any ornaments," Ariel confessed. "Well, I have a few, but not enough for one of those monsters."

Carol could see the disappointment in the girl's face. It wasn't right to not have a tree for a child at Christmas. She had three huge boxes filled with tissue-wrapped ornaments and enough lights for two trees just collecting dust on a shelf in her basement.

"You know. I think we've got that covered."

Ariel looked at Carol as if she'd just promised a trip to Tahiti. "Really?"

Carol nodded. "So, write down your address and phone number."

Ariel was grinning as she wrote.

And Carol was still grinning when Darren returned an hour later with his grocery store finds. "Are you up for making a Christmas tree delivery?" she asked him.

He smiled like a guy who had just gotten a date for the prom. "Change your mind?"

"This isn't for me, it's for one of our single moms. But we do have to swing by my house to get some ornaments."

"Works for me."

"I'm done in an hour."

"That works for me, too. I'll be back," he said and sauntered out of the kitchen.

"Now you're getting smart," Gert murmured from her post at the desk.

Carol sighed. The last thing she wanted was to give Darren the idea she was interested. She should have handled that differently — she should have just sent him to deliver the tree. She could have gone home, gotten the ornaments, and dropped them by later, after he was gone. Actually, she could still do that.

She scrawled Ariel's address on a fresh piece of paper, then hurried outside to catch Darren before he drove off.

154

He was just about to back his big, manly-man pickup out of its parking slot when she called his name. He rolled down the window and stuck out his head, an expectant smile on his face.

Now that she had his attention she wasn't sure what to say. As she ran up to the cab she dug around in the corner of her mind where she kept polite refusals. It wasn't all that well stocked, at least not for things to say to a man who was interested in her. Too many years of married life honesty.

"You know, I was thinking," she began.

"Yeah?"

Great. Now he probably thought she was going to throw in dinner at her place. Oh, Lord, this was awkward. "I think, if you don't mind, I'll just have you go on over to Ariel's."

His smile fell as he took the slip of paper with the address. It was a quick fall because male pride demanded he instantly cover the hurt feelings he'd just betrayed. He picked up the corners of his mouth and looked questioningly at her.

She should have been honest, just blurt out that she was depressed and scared and bad company and not even remotely interested in getting involved with anyone. But that would have been even more awkward. After all, he hadn't exactly asked her out. And maybe his Christmas tree offer earlier was simply kindness. Then she'd look egotistical and make them both feel like fools.

So, of course, that left only one option. Lie. "I forgot I've got a commitment later. If you can just tell Ariel I'll be by with the ornaments that would be great." Carol started backing away from the truck, still talking so he couldn't edge in any awkward questions or offers to go at a different time. "Thanks so much for doing this. I know she'll really appreciate it."

Now he was making a frown that could have meant puzzlement or disappointment or just plain irritation. She didn't want to stick around to find out what, exactly, it did mean, so she turned tail and ran back into the building.

Her heart was dancing like the little drummer boy on speed by the time she got back inside the food bank. Then she had a new thought. What if he followed her? He didn't seem like the kind of guy to get pushy, but you never knew. She went into the bathroom and locked herself in. Then she leaned against the sink and let out a sigh.

"Oh, Ray," she whispered. "Look what you've done. You died and I'm in hell."

A knock on the bathroom door made her jump. "Are you okay, dear?" came Gert's voice.

Carol gave herself a mental shake. "I'm fine. I'll be right out."

Fine, what a lie. But whether you were in heaven or hell, life went on. She looked in the mirror and gave her wilted reflection a pull-it-together look, then came out and went back to work. And prayed that Darren wouldn't show up again before her shift was over.

Fortunately, he didn't. She took Ariel's phone number home with her and called the girl later in the afternoon. "Did your tree arrive?"

156

"Oh, yeah," Ariel said. "He even put it up for me."

"So, are you ready for some ornaments?"

"Are you sure?"

"Heavens yes. I've got tons, and I'm not doing a tree this year."

"You're not?" The girl sounded shocked.

"Too much mess." *Too much everything.*

"Oh."

Carol could tell by the sound of the girl's voice that she couldn't imagine letting such a flimsy excuse keep someone from putting up a tree. "So, is your tree delivery guy gone?" She sure wasn't coming over until he was.

"He left a couple hours ago."

Perfect. "Is this a good time for me to come over?"

"Oh, yeah."

Just hearing the excitement in the girl's voice made Carol feel good. This was going to be fun.

And it was. Ariel insisted Carol stay and help trim the tree. Her little girl, Chloe, timidly helped hang ornaments, and when it was all done and lit, the child stood staring at it, an expression of wonder on her face.

Looking at the little girl, Carol felt a swirl of emotion — sorrow, self-pity, but also a small glow of satisfaction for having helped someone in need, and pleasure in seeing a child so happy.

"Would you like to stay for dinner?" Ariel offered.

She couldn't. This girl was surviving on food bank offerings.

"I've got mac and cheese. And we can bake up that brownie mix I got today."

Carol realized her would-be hostess wasn't just being polite. Ariel really wanted her to stay. She probably missed her own mom, who was far away. "Well, who can resist brownies and macaroni and cheese?" Carol said with a smile.

Ariel smiled, too. She looked down at her daughter. "Want to make some brownies?"

Chloe nodded, smiling.

So they made brownies, and ate macaroni and cheese and drank Kool-Aid. It was the best meal Carol had eaten in months. "So," she said as she prepared to leave for her knitting group, "you guys will have to come to my house for a meal."

They had talked about Ariel's rat boyfriend, about her money struggles and about how much she missed her family. Ariel had openly envied Carol's good life and Carol had shared a little of the not-so-good parts. But now Ariel seemed almost shy, as if they were strangers once more. Ariel looked pointedly at Carol's gray wool slacks and her black cashmere sweater. "I don't think I have the right clothes to wear."

"Since when is friendship about clothes?" Carol countered. Ariel still hesitated, so Carol pulled out her trump card. "We can make some Christmas cookies and have hamburgers."

"Hangubers!" cried Chloe, jumping up and down, clapping her hands.

"I guess we'll come," Ariel said.

Carol nodded. "Good. How about Friday? Will that work for you?"

158

"Let me check my calendar," Ariel said. She cocked her head and put a finger to her chin. "What a surprise. It's clear."

"Good. I'll call you. Bye, Chloe. See you soon."

Chloe, suddenly shy, clung to her mom's leg.

"Thanks," Ariel said as Carol turned toward the door. "For . . . everything."

"My pleasure," Carol said, and meant it. She smiled as she went down the walk, a new emotion pushing away all the others: happiness, pure happiness.

CHAPTER
ELEVEN

"Glen's doing our Christmas party," Laura told Joy as they drove to the Stitch In Time for their weekly Monday night knitting session. "Want to come?"

"I'd come in a heartbeat, but with Bob in charge of our social calendar, don't hold your breath waiting for us to show up on your doorstep."

Laura gave her a sympathetic look. "Poor Joy."

Joy shrugged, like missing out on all the fun was no big deal. "What can I say? I'm married to Herman the Hermit."

Laura turned sideways and studied her. "You two are so different. How'd you ever get together, anyway?"

"Opposites attract. One of nature's little jokes." Only these days she wasn't laughing.

"Tell me about it," Laura said as Joy stopped the car for a light.

"You two aren't really that opposite, are you?" Joy asked.

Laura rolled her eyes. "One of us is a grown-up and one of us is a big kid. I'd say that's pretty opposite."

"Well, other than the obvious."

"Oh, I guess not. We both like to have a good time. What I don't like is to have to do all the work while he

160

does all the playing. And he is a slob, which makes even more work." She smiled over at Joy. "But I'm betting by the end of the strike he'll be a changed man."

The way things were going with Bob, Joy wasn't making any bets.

The light turned green and they drove into downtown Holly. With its festive decorations, it looked like a scene out of *It's a Wonderful Life*. How Joy hoped this strike would wind up with her George Bailey appreciating what he had!

They parked the car and walked into the knitting shop to find it abuzz with excited voices.

Debbie waved to them from the cash register and called, "Saw you in the paper. I saved you a copy."

"Thanks," Joy said, trying to sound appreciative. The last thing she wanted was another copy of that picture of Bob and herself and the Bob Humbug tree. She caught a whiff of cinnamon and cloves and hot apple juice. Mulled cider. Good. She needed a stiff drink.

"Hey, there, fellow strikers," Sharon greeted them. She looked like Christmas in her red sweater with its appliquéd snowmen. "How're y'all doin'?"

"Life at my house is good," Laura bragged. She dropped her knitting on the table and made a beeline for the pot. "All right, cider!"

"Deb knows how to keep up our morale," Kay said.

"How are things going at your place?" Laura asked her.

"It's going. You should have seen Jack's eyes bug out when he read my name in the paper. Of course, he had a rude remark to make," she added in disgust.

"What did he say?" asked Laura.

"He said we'd probably save a ton of money because I wouldn't be out buying decorations we don't need."

"What a weasel," Sharon said.

Kay's lips thinned. She looked like a general in the war room. "That's a polite way of describing him," she said, and dipped into the little bowl of holiday Hershey's Kisses that Sharon had brought. "What about Pete? What was his reaction?"

Sharon scowled. "Not the right one, I can tell you. He thinks he's doing fine and he's one happy camper. And if he calls me Yulezilla one more time he'll be pushin' up daisies."

Joy wasn't surprised by Pete's nickname for his wife. No matter what the weather, Sharon's car remained shiny and clean, and she, herself, always looked like she'd just had an Oprah makeover. Joy could easily imagine Sharon's house looking like something right out of *Southern Living*, and at Christmas it would, of course, have to be perfect.

"According to Pete I go overboard every year and drive them all insane," Sharon continued. "Just because I like to have the tree look a certain way and the house decorated nice."

"How do you like the tree to look?" Laura asked.

Sharon's cheeks bloomed pink, but she raised her chin and said, "I always coordinate the ornaments and the wrapping paper, and I like to put the breakable and

162

smaller ornaments up on the top with the larger ones on the bottom, and the tinsel hung, not just thrown."

"Who bothers with tinsel?" Laura said.

Carol smiled and gave a knowing nod. "Boys like to throw." Her eyes turned misty. "My son was a thrower."

An awkward silence settled over the women. Joy knew it had been nearly fifteen years since Carol's son died, but losing a child wasn't something from which a woman ever recovered. She reached over and patted Carol's arm.

"It's okay," Carol said, pulling herself together. Then to Sharon, "They grow up so fast. Having a messy tree can be kind of fun."

Sharon frowned. "I guess. Anyway, Pete claims he and the boys are doing it this year and they're going to show me how to do it right. They'll probably break half my ornaments."

"Hide the ones you really want," Laura advised. "That's what I did."

"So, how's Glen doing?" Sharon asked. "I'll bet reading your interview in the paper went over about as well as a flannel nightgown on a wedding night."

A corner of Laura's lip lifted. "He said it made him look like a jerk. Imagine that."

"Him and every other husband represented here, bless their hearts," said Sharon. "I swear, this is the first time in years I've read an unbiased news story."

"I've got to admit, he's being a sport," Laura said. "So far he's decorated the tree, gotten the Advent calendar, and taken the kids to see Santa. And he's started on the Christmas cards. Oh, and he's already gone through half a bottle of Excedrin," she added, making her fellow strikers snicker.

"How about our fearless leader?" Sharon asked. "How's Bob doing?"

Too well. "So far this isn't working out like I'd imagined," Joy confessed. "Someone could make a movie about us and call it *Scrooge Wins*." She sighed. "I think I need some chocolate therapy. Somebody pass me that candy."

Jerri shook her head like a frustrated Dr. Phil as she passed the bowl to Joy, and Carol said, "Some things play out better in our heads than in real life."

"Hey, this is playing out just fine for me," Laura said with a snap of her gum.

"And me," Sharon agreed. "My Pete's going to find out it's not so easy to pull off Christmas."

Kay maintained a thoughtful silence.

"Kay?" Joy prodded.

She gave a little shrug. "I'm just wondering how I wound up with such a tightwad."

Joy sensed her friend paddling from the burbling waters of playful retribution toward more dangerous currents. In an attempt to turn Kay back from the looming waterfall, she said, "Most men are budget-conscious."

Kay looked her straight in the face. "This is more than that. If he had to choose between me and his savings account, I think he'd pick savings."

"Oh, don't be silly," Carol chided. "Of course he'd pick you."

"Maybe," Kay said, and rubbed a finger over the modest diamond on her left hand.

Watching her, Joy began to worry that all was not well in the Carter castle. Kay had nine years invested in this marriage, and she'd always seemed relatively happy. Except for the times she complained about her husband's tight fist in all matters financial.

But every man had his faults. A woman couldn't just give up on hers because they didn't see eye to eye on one or two things.

"Don't worry, honey, he'll appreciate you by the time Christmas is over," Sharon predicted. "That's what this strike is for, to open our men's eyes."

"I'll drink to that," Laura cracked, and hoisted her cup of cider in salute.

Joy saw Carol and Jerri exchange a wise woman glance, and she couldn't help feeling petty and trivial.

"I know you think this is silly," she said to Carol later that evening as the women made their way out of the knitting shop.

"I do think it's beneath you," Carol said, "and I don't really understand why you're doing it."

"Menopause-induced insanity," Joy suggested. Carol gave her a look that said, "Be serious," and she shrugged. "I don't know. I guess my marriage isn't as perfect as yours was. Maybe I want to make it into something more before it's too late." She sighed. "You'd think after so many years of marriage a couple would have all their differences worked out."

"Oh, I don't know," Carol said. "You're always two different people."

"Even when you're different, you still have to live together. I thought I could, somehow, push us onto some middle ground where we could both share more of the holiday experience. Bob hates so much of what I love."

"And vice versa?" Carol suggested.

The three little words hit Joy like a rock-hard snowball. They were on the street now, next to her car. If she'd come alone, she'd have jumped in and driven away fast. She leaned against the door. "So, you're saying I'm selfish."

"No, not at all. I'm just wondering if you've gotten so locked in to what the season should look like that you can't see other possibilities. Maybe your husband represents those possibilities."

Horrible possibilities, if you asked Joy.

"It's just something to consider," Carol said.

Laura had joined them now, and Carol ended the conversation and gave Joy a hug.

"That looked like a serious talk you two were having," Laura observed once they were in the car. "She's still trying to convince you to end the strike, right? Make you feel guilty?"

"I guess I can't blame her. She doesn't want to see anyone create problems in their marriage."

"Yeah, well, it's easy to tell other people what to do when you're not walking in their Jimmy Choos. She has no idea what our marriages are like. It's not a crime to give your husband a wake-up call, and you don't have to feel guilty. Got it?"

166

Joy nodded. Still, she found herself turning over Carol's words as she turned over the engine. She wasn't the problem, she decided as she and Laura drove away. She'd been paring down her life for years, always containing her personality in smaller and smaller spaces, pruning guest lists, leaving functions early or going alone because Bob didn't want to climb out of his shell. She didn't want to pare down any more. There'd be nothing left of her.

Anyway, Bob was the one in the wrong here. She loved him dearly, but she wanted him to realize that spending time with family and friends was important, especially at the holidays, and that they needed to participate in those gatherings together, as a couple. She wanted him to see what happened when someone simply checked out.

Let the Carols and Jerris of the world shake their heads, but at her house, the strike had to continue, no matter what people thought. And if they thought she was enjoying this they were nuts. Proving a point was sucking all the fun out of her favorite time of year. Picketing was the pits.

"Have you seen the letters to the editor?" Bob asked the next morning, handing Joy the paper. She set aside the recipe clippings she'd been sorting through and took it and began to read.

> Dear Editor,
> Hats off to Joy Robertson for her brave stand.
> It's about time women shook off the shackles of

holiday planning and gave the men something more to do than eating cookies and making a run to the store on Christmas Eve. Count me in.
    Erna Johnson

"I'm surprised you were able to convince your mom to go in on this," Bob said, sounding half-accusing.

"You're not nearly as surprised as me," Joy said. "I didn't recruit her, believe me."

"She could have at least mentioned that men put up the Christmas lights," Bob said in disgust. "I don't know a single woman who does that. You've opened Pandora's box," he added in a voice of doom.

Joy envisioned all manner of cackling, little gremlins hopping out of a big, beribboned box. She could see them rushing in front doors and hopping down chimneys, all the while screeching, "Joy Robertson sent us. Ha, ha, ha, ha." Don't be ridiculous, she told herself. "I refuse to feel guilty," she said, more for her benefit than Bob's. She peeled off her sweater and turned her attention back to the paper.

The letters-to-the-editor page was crammed. It seemed everyone in Holly had an opinion about the strike.

Dear Editor,
I'm positively inspired by this strike. These women are brave and Joy Robertson is a genius.
    Susan Steinham Johnson

168

Cute, Suki. Had everyone in her family written to the paper?

> *Dear Editor,*
> *A strike at this time of the year hardly matches Holly's wonderful Christmas spirit, and I'm sorry to see the paper encouraging it with so much publicity.*
> *Sincerely,*
> *Beth Samuelson*

Big shock that the owner of The Pantry, a popular kitchen shop in town, would be down on the strike. Every year Beth Samuelson gave classes on how to make the perfect gingerbread house, then displayed her students' art work in her store window. She also sold a ton of gingerbread house — building materials. No ulterior motive in that letter, huh, Beth?

> *Dear Editor,*
> *My wife has joined the strike and now I'm in charge. How about getting your food editor to put some Cookies for Dummies recipes in the paper this weekend?*
> *Glen Fredericks*

Poor Glen. Joy almost felt sorry for the guy. Almost.

> *Dear Editor,*
> *Is the Herald having trouble finding real news? Is that why they have to print this kind of tripe?*

Husbands work hard enough all day trying to make a living without having to come home and find out they've been put in charge of Christmas.
    Jack Carter

Uh-oh, thought Joy.

Dear Editor,
    I'm glad my wife is on strike. This is the first Christmas in years she hasn't pestered me about getting the lights up. Keep it up, ladies.
    Pete Benedict

Joy felt slightly sick. This was all becoming a nightmare.

The phone rang, making her start.

Bob, who had been hovering nearby, grabbed it. "Hi, Mom. Yeah, she's right here," he said and handed over the cordless. "I'll leave you and your mother to talk about me in peace," he sniped, then left.

Meanwhile, Mom was teasing, "Is this my inspiring daughter?"

"That's me," Joy said, "the inspirer of tripe."

"That's one grump," Erna said, easily dismissing Jack Carter. "Sounds like his wife needs to go on strike permanently."

The last thing Joy wanted was to be responsible for the failure of someone's marriage. "Geez, Mom. Don't even say things like that. Anyway, he's not the only one who's not impressed."

"Oh, big surprise about Beth," scoffed Erna. "Everything in her place is overpriced, anyway. Any woman with half a brain is going to join you."

"So you made it sound in your letter to the editor. A little over the top, wasn't it?"

"I didn't think so."

"How does Dad feel about this, by the way?"

"He's not happy, believe me. He's off at the store buying cookies right now."

Joy couldn't help smiling. "If you thought joining the strike was going to give you an excuse to pull out Dad's sweet tooth, I guess you thought wrong."

"I guess," her mom agreed. "And speaking of sweets, does this mean you're not going to host the cookie exchange this year?"

Disappointment settled in Joy's stomach like a heavy sauce. She was on strike and that meant no baking, and no baking meant no family cookie exchange. She'd been hosting it at her house for the last ten years. "Probably not," she said miserably. Phone to her ear, she went to her baking cupboard and shook out a handful of chocolate chips. She popped them in her mouth, then slumped back down at the table.

"Oh, that's a shame," said her mom.

"That's an understatement," Joy said and started drawing a Snidely Whiplash mustache on the picture of Bob she'd found in the paper.

"Well, we can do it here this year, or at Lonnie's. And nobody will tell on you if you sneak over for a little while."

171

"Thanks," Joy said, "but that would probably be considered crossing the picket line." She tried to imagine the cookie exchange at someone else's house. She couldn't.

You have to sacrifice for the cause, she reminded herself. And no sacrifice was too great to give Bob a George Bailey — style epiphany. She flashed on an image of Bob running down Main Street calling, "Merry Christmas everyone!" and smiled. For that, she could give up a cookie exchange. For that, she could give up a lot of things.

"Sweetie, are you sure you want to do this? I mean you've had your fun. Why not call off the strike now and get back to normal?"

Bob normal? No way. "Did Bob pay you to say that?" Joy teased.

"Of course not, and I'm with you one hundred percent."

"Good. I'd hate to have my own mother deserting the cause, especially after she'd written a letter to the editor."

"I'm no deserter. Well, sweetie, I'd better let you go. I'm sure you're going to have lots of people calling. Anyway, I want to get a few things done before I officially start my strike."

"Like what?"

"I'm decorating the tree today and there's no way I'm letting your father near it."

"With me one hundred percent, huh?"

"All right, ninety-nine percent, and the other one percent needs to get busy. Love you, sweetie. Bye."

172

That was Mom. Only on strike one day and already crossing the picket line.

If Joy hadn't been determined to inspire Bob to change, she would have crossed it, too. This was all getting out of hand, and the lack of holiday baking smells in the house and the empty social calendar were beginning to get to her. And, to make matters worse, Rosemary Charles was showing up for another interview later that morning.

This was one Bob, Mr. I'm-Not-Available-for-Comment, had scheduled. What he could possibly have to say Joy couldn't imagine. And she wasn't even sure she wanted to try.

She wished she had something to report. *My husband's caving. Just the prospect of a bleak Christmas is more than he can stand. He finally realizes how much everything we do means to both of us.*

She was beginning to think that would happen the day she found Rudolph and the other reindeer playing on her front lawn. So far, no matter what she said or did, Bob kept his Scrooge armor firmly in place. He'd done nothing but remain holed up in his office with his imaginary friends. So, basically they were going to give Rosemary Charles a nonarticle to go with their nonholiday.

Rosemary arrived promptly at ten with her photographer in tow. Joy tried not to look at the Charlie Brown tree as she led them into the living room where Bob was waiting to hold court.

"How would you say the strike is going so far, Mrs. Robertson?" Rosemary asked, her pen poised over her steno tablet.

Sucky. "I think we're gaining in numbers," Joy said, fishing for something to report.

"Oh, it's definitely growing," the reporter said, and gave her photographer a look that was positively devilish.

Joy wondered what that was about, but the reporter didn't give her a chance to ask. She was already querying Bob, wanting to know if the strike had affected him adversely yet.

"So far so good," he said amiably, filling Joy with a desire to dunk his head in a punchbowl of wassail and give him a swirly. "I just finished sending out Christmas cards," he added.

Joy's jaw dropped. "You did Christmas cards?" The king of bah, humbug?

"I like Christmas cards," he said.

"When?" Had he been up working at midnight? Had elves been addressing the envelopes for him? "I didn't see you working on them."

"Well, they're done," Bob said.

"That's impossible," she informed him. It took her forever to do Christmas cards. It was a huge project, the one thing on her Christmas to-do list she dreaded every year.

"It's a cinch when you do e-cards," Bob said.

"E-cards," Joy echoed. Oh, she had to have misheard.

"Very efficient," Rosemary Charles said diplomatically.

"Very tacky," said Joy. Never mind that she hated writing Christmas cards, never mind that Bob's way

174

was more efficient. It was sick and wrong and . . . cheating.

"May I quote you on that?" asked Rosemary.

"You sure may," Joy said, glaring at Bob.

Bob shrugged. "Just because it's technology it's tacky?"

Rosemary was scribbling frantically now.

"Well, yes," Joy said. "What thought goes into sending a Christmas card over the Internet? That's so impersonal. Where's the connection? Did you get that?" she asked the reporter.

Rosemary nodded, smiling like she'd found gold in her Christmas stocking.

"I connected," Bob insisted. "I told everyone we were doing fine and wished them a merry Christmas, which is pretty much what you say in your cards every year. And it took plenty of thought. I had to go to the site, pick the card, type the message, get it sent."

Joy shook her head. "That's pathetic."

"It's efficient," Bob corrected her.

"But everyone on our Christmas list doesn't have e-mail," Joy informed him. *Ha! Got him there.*

"Who?"

"Aunt Evie."

"Who else?"

There had to be more than that. "I don't know right off the top of my head," Joy said. "I'll have to check my address book."

"Let me know who's left and I'll send them a card," Bob promised.

"I will," Joy said, and vowed to give him a list as long as her arm, even if she had to lift names from the phone book.

"Okay, how about a picture?" Rosemary suggested.

"Of what?" asked her photographer, looking at her like she was nuts.

"Let's get a shot of Mr. Robertson with his computer, sending an e-card, and we'll put Mrs. Robertson in front of him, reading a traditional card. Have you got a pretty one?" she asked Joy.

Her mother had already sent hers out, and this year's was gorgeous. "I sure do," Joy said. This would be a great picture. Joy would be looking at something beautiful while Bob sat with his cold, tacky technology. Joy liked it.

After they had posed for the picture, Rosemary turned to Bob. "Now I'd love to hear about that plan you said you had to help the husbands of the strikers."

So that was why Rosemary Charles was here. And what plan was she talking about? Whatever it was, it was news to Joy. What was Bob up to now?

"I thought your editor might like a list of suggestions for the men on how to survive the strike. I'd be happy to provide one."

Rosemary Charles nodded slowly. "I'm sure my editor would go for that. How soon could you e-mail it to me?"

"Right away," Bob said, looking disgustingly self-satisfied. He probably had it done already, had probably written it while his e-mail cards were going out.

176

Next to him, Joy smiled politely. The only way she'd been able to dredge up that smile was by envisioning her husband out in the garage, tied to a chair with strings of Christmas lights and being forced to listen to Alvin and the Chipmunks singing "Christmas Don't Be Late" over and over and over again.

"Real cute, Bob," she said to him after Rosemary Charles and her sidekick were out the door.

He held out both hands in a typical male don't-blame-me gesture. "The men need help."

"The men need to shape up."

"Maybe my suggestions will help them," Bob said.

"Maybe you should just worry about your suggestions helping you," Joy snapped. She left him to think that over and shut herself in the bedroom with the phone.

"We have complications," she said as soon as Sharon answered the phone. "Bob is dishing out advice for the men now. It's going to be in the paper."

"Well, bless his heart. Isn't he just the clever one?"

"Too clever." Now Bob not only was deliberately missing her point, he was publicly declaring war.

"Don't worry, sugar," Sharon soothed. "A man writing advice on how to do Christmas is like a rooster trying to give a hen lessons on how to lay an egg. We're fine."

"I sure hope so," Joy said, but she was having serious doubts.

"The chicks are gonna lose this one," Rick Daniels predicted as he and Rosemary drove back to the paper.

177

"It's still early in the game. I've got faith in the women," Rosemary said.

"Gee, I wonder why."

Rosemary gave him a playful punch in the arm. "Not just because we're all women."

"Sure."

"No, seriously. I think the strikers have got a point. Women bring something to special occasions that just wouldn't be there if the guys were in charge."

"Yeah. Extra work."

She frowned at him. "How'd you get to be such a cynic? You're not even married."

"I'm not a cynic," he said. "I'm a realist."

"No, you're a cynic. And, mark my words, before the women are done these guys are going to have a whole different outlook."

"Even Robertson?"

"Even Robertson."

"Wanna bet on that?" he said.

"Okay. Why not? What should we bet?"

"Loser buys the winner dinner at one of those all-you-can-eat places."

"A cheap restaurant. Boy, I can see you really believe in putting your money where your mouth is," Rosemary taunted.

"Okay. Fine. Loser buys the winner dinner at —"

"Chez Louie's."

Rick turned to stare at her, bug eyed. "Chez Louie's! You don't get out of that place for under fifty bucks a person."

"Like I said, you really believe in putting your money —"

He cut her off. "Okay, okay. Chez Louie's it is. So, when do we decide who won and who lost?"

Rosemary considered. "Christmas Day. The strike will be over then and we'll know who won."

"Okay. So, if she gives up."

"If he gives in."

"He won't."

"It's not over till it's over," Rosemary said.

Rick was grinning. "Man, I'm gonna enjoy my dinner at Chez Louie's. Let's do it New Year's Eve."

"New Year's Eve? What if someone has a date?"

The look Rick gave Rosemary sent a zing all the way from her chest to her panty hose. "They break it."

CHAPTER
TWELVE

Glen wound up working late on Friday. Naturally, this had to happen on the day of the big party. Friday night for a party, now there was a winning idea. Laura could have picked a Saturday, but no, she had to pick a night at the end of a long workweek, a night when some people often had to work late. Real considerate. But he had his game plan in place. No problem. He could do this.

His secretary, Kathleen, had poked her head in his office door before abandoning him. "See you later," she said. "I'd offer to bring something tonight, but Laura says you've got it all under control."

"I do," Glen assured her. "Piece of cake." He was running late, but it wouldn't take that long to swing by the store and get party fixings.

There was nothing to this party stuff. At the Town and Country he grabbed a supply of Hale's Ale, some Bud, a couple bottles of white wine, a case of pop, and half a dozen bags of various kinds of chips. There. That should do it.

He came home, laden with grocery bags and announced, "Okay, we're set."

"Good job, babe," Laura commended him as he stowed the beer and wine in the fridge. "Hurry up and eat. You've got to get the kids in bed and everything set out before the company comes."

Glen stopped in the middle of emptying a bag and looked at her. "Wait a minute. Why can't you put the kids to bed?"

"I want to come to the party," Amy said.

"No, baby, this is a grown-up party," Laura told her.

"Girls can come to grown-up parties," Amy suggested.

"Not this one," Laura said firmly, and hauled Tyler's hand out of his mashed potatoes. To Glen she said, "I'm not putting the kids to bed because I'm you. You never clean up dinner or put the kids to bed before a party."

"I sure as hell do."

"You come and kiss them good night after I've given them their bath."

"And I clear the table," Glen reminded her. "That's something." He wasn't a total bum.

"Okay," Laura said. "I'll clear the table. But I'm not loading the dishwasher."

"Geez, you're hard."

"I'm not hard, I'm on strike. So be glad I'm even clearing the table."

"And what are you going to be doing while I'm getting the kids in bed and doing the dishes?"

She smiled at him. "Getting ready. I wonder if there's a game on TV I can watch while I'm waiting for the company."

"Ha, ha. Hey, go ahead. I can handle this," Glen said in his double-dog-dare voice.

"I know you can," she said as she put a pile of plates in the sink. "Well, I think I'll go take a bath."

She patted his cheek as she went by. She might as well have said, "Neener, neener, neener." He almost growled in response.

Look at that cute butt, he thought as she left the room. When it came to bodies, his wife's was perfect — a nice small package, curved in all the right places, and she had a smile that a man would do anything to win. And what was hidden inside all that great packaging? A real sick puppy who loved to see a guy squirm.

Stay in the game, urged Glen's inner coach, bringing him back to the moment at hand.

Right. Stay in the game. Keep your eye on the goal. He sprang into action and dished up his dinner from the stove, wolfing it down like he was in some kind of speed-eating contest. A guy shouldn't have to hurry through his dinner like this. But, if he wanted to get everything done and prove to his wife that he could handle whatever she threw at him, he would. Heck, at this point to prove to Laura that he could handle this holiday stuff, he'd eat ground glass.

"I want to come to the party," Amy said again, as he put his dish in the sink.

"Yeah, I know, but you've got to go to bed." Glen heaved a heavy sigh. He was really draggin' his wagon, and right about now, going to bed along with the kids sounded pretty good.

He hurried the kids upstairs and into their jammies. Laura usually gave them a bath before bed, but, hey, a kid didn't need a bath every night, and especially not this night.

"Okay, guys. Into bed," he said. "Mommy will come hear you say your prayers." *If she can spare the time in between her bubble bath and painting her nails.*

He found Laura in the master bathroom, standing in front of the mirror looking totally hot. She'd put on perfume. Oh, man, it smelled good and it made him think of sex. Perfume and sex went together like milk and Christmas cookies. She was wearing his favorite slinky, black dress and putting on a kick-ass red lipstick. Her hair was all down and sexy. She looked like just what he wanted for Christmas. She set down the lipstick, then pulled a bottle of red nail polish out of one of the drawers and began shaking it. Red, his favorite color.

Glen developed instant amnesia and all his earlier irritation slipped away. He came up behind her and put his arms around her. "Let's have a quick party of our own before everybody gets here."

She looked at him in the mirror and gave him a flirty little smile that really raised his hopes, then said, "You have too much to do." Then she slipped away, saying, "I'm going to go kiss the kids. You'd better hurry up and change."

"You're cruel. You know that?" he called after her.

"Yes, I am," she called back. "Be a good boy and get dressed, and if you're lucky I'll chain you to the bed later and get out my whip."

"You're already whipping me pretty damned good," Glen muttered. He climbed into his jeans, then grabbed a polo shirt and ran downstairs to party central.

The kitchen clock assured him he had twenty minutes before the guests came. He heaved a sigh of relief. Good. He was going to make it. He went out to the garage for the big bucket they always put the drinks in. Oh, yeah. Ice. He looked in the spare freezer in the garage for the party ice. Nothing.

He hauled the bucket in and set it on the work island in the kitchen, then went and called upstairs, "Hey, baby, where's the party ice?"

"You didn't pick any up?" she called back down.

"Don't we have any?" Laura always got ice for the parties. Except he was Laura now. Oh, boy.

"Not unless you got some."

Well, okay. He'd make a quick run to the 7-Eleven and still be back in time. He piled the bags of chips on the island next to the bucket with no ice. The dinner remains were still on the stove and the dirty dishes sat in the sink. Who cared? It made the place look lived in.

He grabbed his car keys, pulled a coat from the closet, and rushed out the door. The clock on the minivan dash told him he had fifteen minutes before the first guests arrived. Laura would come down and see the messy kitchen, see him not there, and give him a bad time when he got back. And if so much as one single party guest sneaked in before him, she'd really give him a bad time. "Not gonna happen," he vowed, and squealed away from the curb.

184

It had started to snow since he got home, and cars were cautiously tracking along a slippery sheet of white. It didn't bother Glen, though. He could drive in anything. And right now he needed to drive fast.

The cop got him half a block from the 7-Eleven. Glen swore. Now he'd never make it back in time. He slumped in the front seat, a beaten man.

The officer came up to the window and Glen let it down. "Sir, could I see your license and registration?"

Glen obliged. He hated to think how much this ticket was going to cost. This was turning out to be an expensive party.

"Do you know how fast you were going, sir?" the cop asked.

Sadly, he did. "Too fast."

"You were doing forty in a thirty-mile zone, and the streets are slippery. Is there some emergency?"

"Party ice."

"Party ice?" The officer's polite smile leveled into a straight, narrow line.

"My wife's on strike for Christmas," Glen blurted. "I'm doing everything. Last night I burned cookies. I'm in charge of the party tonight. I forgot the ice. Everyone will be there any minute. I've got mashed potatoes and green beans on the stove and dishes in the sink and I didn't give the kids a bath and she's painting her nails." Glen took a deep breath. "Just give me the ticket. I deserve it."

But the cop was now looking at him like he'd confessed to losing his job.

"I'm going to give you a warning this time, sir. But you need to get the lead out of your foot, especially on a night like this."

"Oh, man, thanks," Glen breathed. "I really appreciate it."

The officer nodded. "My wife's on strike, too."

CHAPTER
THIRTEEN

Mac and his wife, Tiffany, were already there when Glen got back to the house. Mac was eating out of one of the chip bags, and Laura and Tif were leaning against the kitchen counter, giggling together about something. Him, Glen decided, since they stopped their yuck-it-up fest at the sight of him.

"I see you got the ice okay," Laura observed.

"No problemo."

"I guess you've got everything under control, then." If that was supposed to be an observation on how well he was coping, it hadn't come out right. It sounded more like a taunt.

"Of course I do," Glen said. "You women make such a big deal out of having a party. Some chips, some beer, and some party ice, and you're set. Nothing to it."

"So, where's the booze?" Mac greeted him.

"It's coming," Glen said. He ripped open the ice bag and dumped its contents into the bucket. "Go get the beer and wine out of the fridge and put 'em in there."

"What do I look like, the maid?" Mac joked.

"You're too ugly," Glen retorted. He let Mac fill the drinks bucket while he started pulling bowls out of the cupboard. It only took a couple of minutes to empty chips into them and set them on the dining room table. Everything was under control again. Ha! Score one for the guys.

In the kitchen he could hear Tiffany saying to Laura, "Maybe I should have brought something."

"No," Laura said. "Glen's got it covered. You heard him. Hey, baby," she called, "don't forget to put out your Christmas cookies."

Was she kidding? There were maybe three he hadn't burned.

Mac was in the doorway now. "You made cookies?" He stared at Glen like Glen had just admitted to having a sex change.

"Don't be an idiot. A lot of guys bake, you know," Glen informed him. "Most of the famous chefs in the world are men."

Mac just shook his head like Glen had somehow failed him.

The doorbell rang. "I'll get it," Glen said, glad to get away from Mac and his sexist views on cooking.

Roger strolled in with his wife and handed over a bottle of wine. If only he'd brought cookies.

Laura came out and greeted them and took their coats. They were still talking when more guests arrived. Within minutes the house was packed, and everyone seemed hungry. They drifted out toward the dining room table like so many ants to a picnic. Glen saw that the chip bowls were already rapidly emptying. Great. The night was just starting and the food supply was already dwindling. How much food did Laura buy for a party, anyway? Obviously, more than he had. And, of

188

course, the women all usually brought stuff: plates with candies and appetizers and homemade caramel corn. The eats department was really suffering without those extras he'd always taken for granted. Was every woman in Holly on strike, for crying out loud?

"I brought some food," Glen's pal, Mort, said, holding out a crockpot full of cocktail sausages drowning in barbecue sauce.

Thank God, Glen thought. He was so grateful he almost hugged the guy.

Mort eyed the table. "You got plates?"

Laura usually had little plates and holiday napkins. Both of which they'd need to eat Mort's sausages. Oh, boy. Glen hurried to the kitchen and began searching the cupboards. Where the hell did she keep those plates? The pantry, of course.

But the pantry was empty. Wasn't there some old nursery rhyme about that? *Old Mother Hubbard went to the cupboard to get her poor husband some plates.*

Glen stopped himself. He was cracking up. "Laura!"

She leaned into the pantry, a smile on her face, one eyebrow cocked. "You bellowed?"

"Where are the paper plates?"

"You didn't get any?"

"I thought we had some."

She lifted a shoulder and gave him a mock sympathetic look. "Sorry. We're out."

"Yeah, I'll bet. You probably hid 'em someplace."

She didn't deny or confirm. Instead, she said, "Guess you'll have to use real ones." She shook her head. "That'll be a mess to clean up."

"And I can tell you feel real bad about it."

She just smiled and wandered off.

"You won't win," he called after her.

No response.

He dragged a bunch of little plates and saucers from the cupboard to the dining room table. Two of the chip bowls were now almost empty. Mac had probably single-handedly emptied one. What was it about tall, skinny guys, anyway? They all ate like pigs.

"Laura said you made some cookies," one of the women said to Glen. "Are we going to get to try them?"

She was looking at him innocently, like she really wanted to sample his baking. Yeah, right. She was probably one of the strikers, waiting for a chance to gloat.

"I don't have too many left."

Laura had drifted within earshot now. "I'll get them," she offered.

Suddenly she wanted to help? He believed that like he believed in Santa. This was a setup.

"Hey, I've got it covered. I'll get 'em."

Laura's cookies were always perfect, the frosting smooth and decorations looking like something out of a bakery. Looking at his burned messes, wavy with lopsided frosting and haphazard sprinkles, he wished he'd taken a little more time on the dumb things. Better yet, he wished he'd picked up some boxed cookies at the store.

He suddenly had a brainstorm. He ditched the plate with his cookies in the cupboard, then went over to Mac and pulled him aside.

"What?" Mac looked irritated.

"You gotta help me," Glen said in an under voice.

"I'm not bakin' any cookies, dude."

Glen looked over his shoulder to make sure no one had heard, then dragged Mac farther away from the other partiers. "You don't need to. Just slip out and go down to your place and steal some of your wife's."

Mac looked at him in shock.

"She did bake, didn't she? Oh, shit. She's on strike, too."

"Yeah, but her mom felt sorry and sent a bunch over. Just for the kids. I'm supposed to stay out of them," Mac added miserably.

"Well, what are you, whipped?"

"Look who's talking. Your wife started this thing."

"And yours is in on it. Now, we can't let 'em win, can we?"

"Well, no."

"Okay, then. I need you to sneak over to your place and get some cookies. You don't have to take all of them."

Now Mac looked perturbed. "I don't want to miss the party. And besides, Tif'll get pissed."

"She's not gonna know, pinhead. Only take a few. If she notices some are missing you can blame it on the kids. Or the babysitter. And it's gonna take you all of ten minutes to run one block. If I don't get some more good stuff on the table there won't be any party. Come on now, help me. I'm dying here."

Mac frowned and came up with a reluctant, "All right."

"Thanks, man. I owe you." Glen looked around to make sure no women had drifted over to eavesdrop. "Put a bunch in a paper bag so nobody sees what you've got. Then I'll put them on the plate with mine."

Mac nodded and started for the door.

Glen grabbed him by the arm and hissed, "And don't break 'em."

Mac made a face but went to do what he was told.

"Hey, we're a little sparse on food out here," Rog called from the eats table.

"I'm working on it already," Glen called back. "Have another beer." Geez, what did Rog think this was, anyway, a restaurant?

People were busy talking. No one noticed when Mac returned and did a behind-the-back hand-off to Glen, who then ducked into the pantry and started the cookie transfer. Oh, this was good. There was some kind of brownie-looking thing with green frosting, a layered cookie with a thin coat of chocolate on top, and those little round ones with the powdered sugar that looked like snowballs. Perfect.

He brushed the powdered sugar off the brownies, then went and set the plate out on the dining room table. The guests fell on it, snatching cookies like they were trapped in the desert with nothing to eat but cactus and tumble-weeds.

"You made these?" asked Mort, holding up a frosted brownie.

"What can I say?" Glen answered and tried to look humble. And honest.

192

"I can't believe you made these," said Kathleen, narrowing her eyes at him. Why had Laura invited her, anyway? Bad enough to have her torturing him every day at the office.

"Oh, I have a recipe like this!" cried Tiffany. "It was my mom's. And I make these snowballs, too. And the fudge meltaways."

"What an interesting coincidence," Laura said, eyeing Glen. "Glen must have baked these after I was asleep last night, because I sure didn't see him making them any other time. I only saw him burning cookies."

All eyes turned on Glen. His face felt like a burning cookie, but he braved it out. "I'm a fast learner. Hey, who's for a game of Ping-Pong? I've got the table set up in the garage."

Half the guys jumped on the offer and Glen ducked out after them. Laura could have all the suspicions she wanted, but she couldn't prove anything. And Mac wouldn't talk. He was an accomplice.

They were just getting started when the door to the garage opened and Rog stepped through it. "Those cookies are great. I hope you've got more."

"Don't tell me you ate them all already," Glen said, panic gripping him. How many cookies did they have over at Mac's? And how many more could they steal without Tif noticing?

Rog scowled and replied with an affronted, "No. But I didn't know there was a limit."

"Look, those are all I've got and they have to last."

Rog shook his head. "Man, I hope your wife never goes on strike again. The food supply tonight sucks."

Oh, no. Nothing at his party was going to suck. "Well, we can fix that," Glen said. "What do you want? You guys cover for me and I'll make a food run."

"Works for me. What you've got now won't last another half an hour," Mac said.

"But nobody tells Laura," Glen cautioned. "I'll let her think I've had it stashed somewhere all along."

"You're the man," Mac approved, and they high-fived each other.

"Get some more cookies," said Mort. "And some eggnog," he added.

"I like those little quiche things," Rog said. The other guys looked at him like he'd just donned a frilly apron. "What?" he said, his voice defensive.

"I don't even know where to find those," Glen told him. "Be reasonable."

"Okay, pickled herring."

A general moan filled the garage. "That's totally gross," said Jer.

"How about those little frozen pizzas?" Mort suggested.

"Now, that sounds like real food," Mac approved.

"Okay. Minipizzas, eggnog, and cookies." Glen felt in his pants pocket. The car keys were still there. Good. He could slip out the garage door and Laura wouldn't be any the wiser. With all the talking the women were doing in the house she'd never hear the door go up.

He punched the button for the automatic door opener and it began its noisy ascent. They all froze, like spies in enemy territory, fearing they'd been heard.

"Don't tell Laura? Your garage door is so loud we won't have to," Rog said after it was up.

"If she comes out tell her we opened it 'cause we were getting hot," Glen said.

"That'll work great until she notices you're not here," Rog retorted.

Glen scratched his head and thought a moment. "Tell her . . . I'm out back smoking a cigar with Mac." He grabbed Mac by the arm and hauled him toward the car.

"Hey, what are you doing?" Mac protested. He held up his Ping-Pong paddle. "I just started a game, in case you didn't notice."

Glen snatched the paddle out of his hand and tossed it to Mort. "You can finish when we get back. Meanwhile, I need you to come with me. That way she'll believe Rog about the cigars."

Mac let out a snort of disgust. "First you send me home for cookies, now you're dragging me to the store. I'm sure having fun at this party so far."

"I'll buy more chips," Glen promised, and pushed him into the minivan.

Glen drove like his grandmother to the 7-Eleven, but once they got there, he sped up and down the aisles like a contestant on *The Amazing Race*.

"You have to have set some kind of record in there," Mac said approvingly as they tossed the bags in the mini-van. 'Now, if you can not drive like an old woman on the way home."

Glen stuck a finger in Mac's face. "I don't drive like a woman."

Mac raised his eyebrows. "Yeah?"

"Get in," Glen growled. He stomped to the driver's side and got in, then stomped on the gas.

That might have been a mistake.

They'd only gone a block when it happened. "Uh-oh," said Mac. "Looks like you're busted, dude."

CHAPTER
FOURTEEN

"May I see your driver's license and registration? Again," the cop added.

"Again?" Mac echoed.

"Don't ask," Glen said as he pulled out his license. "How far over the speed limit was I this time?" he asked miserably.

"Only five," said the cop, "but I'm going to have to write you a ticket this time."

Glen nodded, and the cop returned to his patrol car.

"Boy, this is fun," Mac grumbled, slumping against the door.

"What are you griping about? You didn't get the ticket," said Glen.

The cop returned with Glen's license and registration and an early Christmas present from the police department. "Maybe you should forget the party ice from now on," he suggested.

"It was food this time," Glen said with a sigh.

"Boil some eggs," suggested the officer.

"Hey, good idea," Mac said.

Glen glared at him. "Shut up."

Mac gave an apologetic shrug. "Okay, no eggs." He glanced at his watch as Glen pulled out (nice and slow). "Man, we've been gone over half an hour. Are we gonna actually spend any time at this party?"

If they hadn't had a cop right behind them, Glen would have popped him one. "We are having fun," he said between gritted teeth. "This is the best party we've ever had. Got it?"

"Yeah, right," muttered Mac. "Want me to wake you up now?"

"It looks like this strike is working pretty well for you," one of the women observed to Laura.

She took another cookie off the plate. "It's been the first Christmas in years that I've actually had time to enjoy myself a little. I've got to hand it to Joy. She's a genius."

"Where is she?" asked Tiffany. "I thought maybe she'd be here to sign autographs," she added, and the other women giggled.

Laura gave her gum a snap. "She wanted to come, but since she's on strike her husband's in charge of the social calendar and he didn't want to go out."

"She should have come without him," said Tiffany and some others echoed their agreement.

"Yeah, she should have," Laura said. "Poor Joy. I hope she's managing to have fun, whatever they're doing."

Joy wished she'd never looked out the window at the Frederickses' house down the street and seen all the cars parked along the curb and the windows strung with Christmas lights framing the revelers inside. It had left her feeling sour. Bob had decided a nice, quiet evening at home would be much better than their suffering through a noisy gathering of relative strangers. Then he'd had the nerve to tell her he was only doing what she did every season — making social decisions without consulting him.

That wasn't true. Well, okay, so she did the neighborhood party without asking his majesty's permission. They'd been hosting it for years. It had become a tradition. Since when did you have to consult someone over a tradition?

She crossed her arms in front of her and glared at the TV. Nicolas Cage was busy becoming a family man. She loved this movie, loved Nicolas Cage. But if she had to choose between Nick and a real, live party . . .

What were they doing over there right now? Exchanging recipes? Stealing silly white elephant presents back and forth from each other?

"This isn't my life," Nicolas was saying. "It's just a glimpse."

Joy shot a glance at Bob, slumped next to her, happy in Escape Land. She hoped this wasn't a glimpse of her future.

Bob didn't have to ask to know Joy wasn't happy about his decision to avoid the Frederickses' party. He could feel irritation coming off her in waves.

Well, he'd gotten what he'd wanted, a nice quiet evening at home. There was only one problem: the quiet was lacking serenity. It felt more like the calm before the storm.

An olive branch might be nice about now. He paused the movie. "Want some popcorn?"

She shook her head and said, "No, thanks." Very polite words in the very polite tone of voice she always used to let him know she was not happy. Wrong-size olive branch. Of course, she was hoping like crazy he'd give in even at this late date and say, "What the heck. Let's just pop in for a little while." But if he did that, it would be all over for him. No, this was his chance to make a statement and he didn't dare lose it.

"I bet you'll change your mind if I make some," he said, and went to the kitchen to build up his emotional resistance.

It didn't quite feel like their kitchen this year. Usually by now Joy had baked up a storm and it was full of containers of fancy cookies to raid. He had to admit, it felt a little odd to find it goody free. Popcorn is just as good as cookies, he told himself. He pulled a microwave bag out of the junk food cupboard and started it popping.

As he stood in front of the microwave watching the bag expand, he found himself wondering how Fredericks was doing over at his place. What kind of food were they having over there? Poor guy. He was going crazy trying to outdo his wife. Of course, the secret was to keep it simple, show the woman a party didn't have to be a big production. A person could have a perfectly good time with just a small number of friends. That was something Joy needed to learn.

Hmmm. Maybe he should give her a demonstration.

Fortified with popcorn and a new plan he went back into the living room. He offered her the bowl. "Sure you don't want some?"

She shook her head.

Poor Joy. Going on strike from a good time didn't agree with her. Well, she'd be feeling better soon. And maybe he'd actually be able to enjoy himself, too. There would be a novel experience. Bob smiled to himself as he started the movie.

"There's nothing worse than a gloater," she said grumpily.

"Maybe I wasn't gloating. Maybe I was planning something nice."

She frowned at him. "And maybe I'll tell Santa you've been a good boy this year."

"The year's not over yet," he said.

The only response he got was an irritable "Humph."

"You and Bob are becoming quite the local celebrities," Joy's mom said the next morning.

Joy propped the phone receiver between her ear and shoulder and went back to sorting socks. "Being a celebrity isn't all it's cracked up to be."

"Well, there's one quick way to get out of the limelight."

Joy knew exactly what her mother was suggesting. "I'm not ending the strike." That would send the wrong kind of message to Bob.

"Joy, what is going on? What's the real reason behind this strike of yours?"

Empty nest panic. Joy slumped back on the family room couch. The morning paper lay in front of her on the coffee table, open to the Living section, which was full of updates on the strike.

She sighed. "I thought, somehow, if I didn't do anything Bob would see how flat the holidays are without the events and people we love. I just wanted to teach him a lesson so he'd be more . . . there."

"I'm sure you've proved your point by now."

"Not really," Joy said glumly.

"Bob's never going to be as social as you. You know that. He's a quiet man."

"I know, but what bothers me is he's getting quieter every year. Well, except to me. To me he complains."

"Oh, come on, now. You're exaggerating."

"No, I'm not. Every year he pulls a little farther away, and complains a little more. It was different when the kids were little. He tried harder. Now they're grown and it's just the two of us and . . ." She stumbled to a stop, unable to articulate her fears for the future. A vision of Mrs. Anderson, her friend's lonely mother, popped into Joy's mind, dressed up like the Ghost of Christmas Future.

There was a moment of silence on the other end of the line; then her mother said, "Honey, marriage is about compromise. You know that."

"I think I've compromised enough."

"He's probably compromised a little, too."

"Whose side are you on?"

"I'm on both your sides, and I hope by the time you're done with all this you'll both have learned something."

"What's that supposed to mean?" Joy demanded. "What am I supposed to learn?"

"How should I know? I'm just your mom, not your shrink. But I'm sure you'll learn something in all of this. You're a smart woman."

Too smart for my own good, Joy decided as she said good-bye to her mom and hung up. Was Mom right? Was Joy being unfair, expecting Bob to be something he wasn't? If she just gave up the fight and let them drift where would they end up?

She picked up the paper and scowled at it. They'd added a sidebar to this latest article — Bob Robertson's suggestions for surviving the strike. Joy ground her teeth and read.

1. *Relax. This strike is nothing to get bent out of shape over, just a friendly competition between the sexes. Enjoy it and play to win.*

Just a friendly competition? Had he really managed to convince himself that was all this was about? She'd been too easy on him, too nice. That had to change.

2. *Eliminate. You don't have to do everything she does. No one in his right mind would do everything she does. Show her how to take life easier.*

Bob's idea of taking life easier: Sit in front of the TV and watch holiday specials and old movies. Well, that certainly made the holidays merry and bright. Maybe he could invite the Grinch over to join him.

> 3. *Take shortcuts. Shop the Internet. With great sites like the one I used (UShopTillIDrop.com) you're done in an hour.*

So impersonal.
Send e-mail Christmas greetings.
So tacky.
Buy the Christmas cookies. No one can tell the difference, anyway.
So rude! Now she knew the real value he placed on her baking skills.
Have your Christmas party catered.
He should have added, "Call my wife. She's got nothing else going this month."

> 4. *Hire scabs. You can hire struggling college students to decorate and run errands. Don't let your wife brainwash you into thinking you have to do everything yourself.*

Or you could do it yourself and have the world's ugliest Christmas tree.

> 5. *Keep your sense of humor. This won't last forever. Chances are your wife will either get*

frustrated or go through baking withdrawals
and end the strike before Christmas anyway.

How condescending! How obnoxious! How very Bob of him!

He'd even had the nerve to offer cooking advice.

Bob Robertson's Easy Bake Christmas cookies

Take two halves of a graham cracker. Put canned frosting on one half and dump on colored sprinkles. Top with the other half of the graham cracker. Do this until you run out of frosting. Kids love these.

He should know. Their children had loved that treat when Joy was first letting them play in the kitchen. (Only she'd made the frosting from scratch.) How completely tacky of him to use her kindergarten cookie recipe and pass it off as his own. Bob Robertson, Recipe Raider.

She was just beginning to crumple the paper into a ball for the trash when he came into the room.

"What are you doing?" He snatched it from her and began to smooth out the wrinkles. "I want to save that."

"Are you going to put it in your trophy case along with your college tennis cup and your mystery writer award?"

"I might."

Joy frowned at him. "You should be ashamed of yourself."

He went to the kitchen and dug a couple of cookies out of a bag he'd bought at the store. "I don't see why. You didn't think it was good?"

"Oh, it was quite the masterpiece. I don't know what I liked best — the part where you stole my recipe or where you insulted my baking."

Bob sat down opposite her on the couch. "I didn't insult your baking."

"No one can tell the difference between home baked and store bought? If that isn't an insult, I don't know what is."

He frowned and set aside the last of his second cookie. "You know I didn't mean that. It was just for the article."

"Everyone who knows us knows I'm a caterer. They'll think you meant me."

"And they'll also think I consider you a great cook because I suggested hiring a caterer."

"That's why that was in there?" How stupid did he think she was?

He shrugged. "Just trying to be nice."

"You're not trying to be nice. You're not taking any of this seriously. I was really trying to prove a point and you're making a joke out of all of it." Joy's voice was turning wobbly on her now and she could feel tears rising to the surface. They came so easily these days. She dumped the socks in the laundry basket, then headed for the laundry room.

"Come on, hon, don't cry. Maybe I'm trying to prove a point, too," Bob called after her.

Oh, how like him to try and turn the tables! She whirled around. "What? That you can be a complete beast when you want to be? Well, you're doing a really good job of it."

He was being deliberately mulish, refusing to see the point of why she was doing this, refusing to care about her feelings or their future together. No, worse than that, he was mocking her.

Forget the laundry, she decided. She grabbed her purse and car keys and cell phone and marched for the front door.

Bob fell in step behind her. "Come on, now. Don't go away mad."

"Too late for that," she shot back and yanked open the front door.

"Where are you going, to your mother's?"

"No. You're turning me into a chocoholic and right now I need a good stiff mocha if I'm going to make it through the morning."

Glen woke up only slightly hung over. Laura's side of the bed was empty. No surprise there. It was always empty the day after a party. She hated to let the house stay dirty and usually had all the party remains picked up and the dishes washed by the time he surfaced.

Not today, though. Glen made his way through a living room littered with glasses and beer cans and napkins and plates with bits of cookie on them. The coffee table was covered with chip crumbs. The kitchen was no better. Bottles and cans sat everywhere, and the dishes from dinner were still in the sink.

Laura was already dressed and sitting at the kitchen table, reading the paper. She smiled at him. "It's about time you got up. I was just about to come in and wake you."

He leaned over and kissed her and caught a whiff of leftover perfume. "Yeah? I can go back to bed," he offered, and took a nip of her ear.

She wiggled away. "You snooze, you lose. Anyway, I'm leaving in a few minutes to meet Joy."

"You guys planning to picket somebody?"

"We might picket you if you don't watch it," she teased.

"Ha, ha." Glen looked over to the family room where the kids sat huddled in blankets, watching Saturday morning cartoons. "I don't suppose you're taking the kids."

She gave him a condescending wife look. "What do you think?"

He scratched the back of his neck. "I think I'm stuck."

"Maybe they'll help you clean. Also, you need to bake more cookies. And no cheating this time," she added, shaking a playful finger at him.

"Cheating!" He tried to look innocent.

"You heard me. Oh, and you should probably start on Amy's costumes. Don't forget, her school program is this week."

This holiday thing was like being in the ring with Evander Hollyfield. You barely survived one hit when another one came at you from out of nowhere.

208

"Where's the Excedrin?" Glen moaned, and plopped down at the table.

Laura poured him a cup of coffee. "Here. This will make you feel better." She looked at her watch. "Oops, gotta go. I'm sure you'll have the house looking great by the time I come back." She gave him a peck on the cheek, then was gone, leaving only a hint of perfume behind for comfort.

"Thanks," he muttered, and pulled the paper across the table.

The Living section had another blurb on the strike. Glen looked at it and frowned. He hoped Laura hadn't made some secret arrangement to bring that reporter and her photographer over to chronicle this after-party mess. If they showed up, he wouldn't answer the door.

That problem solved, he began to read the story. It looked like Bob Robertson had a good handle on this strike thing. Glen checked out Bob's cookie recipe. Now, there was a recipe he could handle. They'd go to the store and get some graham crackers and frosting after he got the house cleaned up. But what about the costumes? Bob's words came back to him. *Hire scabs.*

Glen called his mother. "Mom, I need help."

CHAPTER
FIFTEEN

Laura and Joy sat sipping mochas at a table in the Winter Wonderland Café that had been set up downtown alongside the small outdoor skating rink the Rotary Club had created for the Hollydays celebration. Laura studied Joy as she watched sweater-clad skaters gliding by in rhythm to the canned holiday music and let out a long, frosty breath.

"This feels good," Joy said. "I needed to cool off."

"Somehow, I get the feeling you're not talking about hot flashes."

Joy frowned. "No, Bob flashes. Nothing's going the way I thought it would. I really wanted to make a point, you know. And instead of taking me seriously, what does he do? He appoints himself the leader of the opposition. I've already gone through two bags of Hershey's Chocolate Mint Kisses. At this rate, by January first I'll be the New Year's Blimp." She sighed and looked out at the skaters. "They make it look so easy, don't they?" A woman practicing some fancy move at the center of the rink miscalculated and went down. Joy winced. "Youch."

"Don't give up," Laura said. "This was a good idea."

"Well, I'm glad it seems to be working for you, anyway," Joy said. "And thanks for meeting me."

"Any time. Just remember what Sharon says: You have to stay strong."

"Sharon is not married to a criminal mastermind. It doesn't matter how strong I stay. Bob will just outsmart me at every turn." Her cell phone rang and she pulled it out of her purse. "Great, it's Mr. Mastermind himself." To Bob she said, "I'm still on a chocolate bender. Don't expect me home for a while."

Laura couldn't help smiling. If Bob was calling Joy on her cell, she had obviously managed to make him feel guilty. And that meant she was having more success than she realized.

Joy's eyes widened. "You're what?"

"He's what?" Laura pumped.

"You won't believe it," Joy told her. "I don't even believe it. Does this have anything to do with our discussion this morning?" she asked Bob. Her eyes began to twinkle. "You were already planning it, huh? No, no objections. I think that's great. So, why are you doing this?" she added suspiciously. Then she made a face, filling Laura to the bursting point with curiosity over what was being said on the other end of the conversation. "Well, I'll just sit at your feet and learn then. See you in a little bit."

"Okay, what's going on?" Laura demanded as Joy snapped her phone shut.

"Bob has decided to throw a party tonight," Joy said with a triumphant smirk.

"You're kidding."

211

"He said he's been planning it for a while and wanted to surprise me."

Laura nodded sagely. "A long while. Like since this morning."

"Probably. Anyway, he's going to demonstrate how to plan a simple but great party."

"What does that mean?"

Joy shrugged. "Your guess is as good as mine."

"At least you'll have a great dress to wear to it." Laura pointed to the shopping bag at Joy's feet.

"I hope it doesn't turn out to be a waste of a perfectly good dress," Joy said, and reached for her mug of hot chocolate.

"You never know. He might pull it off. Glen did."

"There's just one difference between your husband and mine," Joy said. "Glen likes parties."

"Yeah," Laura said, "and the messier the better. I'm hoping last night cured him."

"Could we transplant his brain into Bob? Please?"

Laura gave her an encouraging smile. "Poor Joy. But don't give up. Tonight might turn out to be fun. You seem to have a good time wherever you go. And who knows? Maybe it will even turn Bob into a party animal."

Joy gave her half a smile. "The only thing that would do that is hypnosis. But you're right. I'm sure it will be fun. Maybe. At least it will be better than nothing."

"Party on," Laura said, and saluted Joy with her mug.

212

Poor Joy, Laura thought later as she walked to her car. It must be hard to live with a husband who was such a party pooper. Maybe she should be a little more grateful for the fact that Glen was a social guy. And pretty darned mellow, too. He'd really risen to the impromptu party challenge, even if he did cheat on the cookies. In fact, so far he'd been a pretty good sport about having to do everything. And he wasn't trying to sabotage her at every turn like Bob was doing with Joy. Yes, she could have done worse.

All the way home she hummed with the radio, thinking of the little surprises she'd gotten to put under the tree just in case Glen screwed up and needed bailing out at the last minute. And she knew he'd love the little extra something she'd picked up at Femme Fatale.

But when she entered the living room, her smile flew South for the winter. The room was just as she'd left it. Oh, she was going to kill him!

She walked into the kitchen and got hit with the smell of burned toast. Glen had managed to take care of the dirty dishes from the night before, but new dishes had stepped in to take their place. The kitchen table was scattered with broken pieces of graham crackers and drops of dried frosting and frosting-coated knives. There was even frosting on the floor. In the middle of the table sat a plate of graham cracker sandwiches filled to overflowing with frosting. Glen had obviously read Bob's piece in the paper. So, when did the scabs arrive to clean this disaster?

Laura picked up a piece of paper covered in Glen's scrawl. "Don't worry, babe. I'll clean up the mess when I get back. We're at Mom's having a costume fitting."

So, he'd suckered his mom into helping him. That was fine with Laura. She didn't care as long as the job got done. And, speaking of jobs, Glen had better get home pretty soon and clean this place up. No way was she cooking dinner in a disaster kitchen.

She wandered into the family room. And that was when she saw the Santa pictures lying on the coffee table. She picked one up and stared at it. There were the kids in pajamas with the price tags sticking out. They wore deer antlers on their heads, crooked, of course, and Tyler was crying and red faced. Santa didn't look too happy, himself. He looked like a man who had just caught a whiff of dead skunk. *Cute. Really cute.* So, this was the "Night Before Christmas" theme Glen had said he went with? More like the *Nightmare Before Christmas*. Just who were they supposed to send these to?

She dropped the picture back on the coffee table in disgust. How hard was it to get a red dress and a red bow tie and put the kids on Santa's lap, for heaven's sake?

And what *had* he been doing all day that he managed to avoid cleaning the house? He could have cleaned before he went to his mother's. He was probably secretly hoping the mess would drive Laura so nuts that she'd give in and do it. Yeah, right. In his dreams.

Her earlier mellow mood vanished. No way was she going to stay here and look at this pigpen. She put away

214

her surprises — Glen wouldn't be seeing anything from Femme Fatale tonight, not in the mood she was in now — then set the Christmas PEZ candy dispensers she'd brought home for the kids on the kitchen counter. They'd find them eventually in all the mess. She got her purse and headed for the front door.

She got there just as Glen and the kids were coming in. Tyler immediately reached for her and Glen handed him over and gave her a kiss on the cheek. "Hey, babe."

"Mommy!" Amy cried. "I'm going to be an angel."

"You already are, doll baby," Laura told her, and bent to give her a kiss.

Glen held up a pizza box. "Got dinner."

"And a pigsty to eat it in. What did you do all day?"

He looked affronted. "Hey, I've never asked you that."

"You've never had to. The house never looked like this."

"Well, I'll have you know I've been busy. We got cookies made and then we went to Mom's. And don't worry. I'm gonna clean the kitchen."

"You've got that right. Meanwhile, maybe I'll go someplace where I don't have to look at this or think about those awful Santa pictures."

Glen's earnest expression melted into uh-oh wariness. "Oh. You saw those. Well, I can explain."

Laura held up a hand. "Please don't. I am getting out of here and going to a movie." She reached for the door.

"Awe, come on, babe," he protested.

"I want to come," said Amy.

215

"Sweetie, you've been out all day," Laura told her. But so had she, and she hadn't spent any time with the kids. "All right," she decided. "We'll all go to a movie. We'll go watch *Frosty the Snowman* up in Mommy's bed. How does that sound?"

"Yay!" cried Amy, and ran up the stairs.

"Yay!" Tyler echoed, and followed her.

Laura plucked the pizza box out of Glen's hands and started up after them.

"Hey, what about me?" he called after her.

"There are graham cracker cookies in the kitchen," she said, and kept walking. "You can nosh on those while you're cleaning up. If you're lucky, we'll save you a piece of pizza."

Bob was in the process of microwaving frozen chimichangas when Joy got home. "I made dinner."

It was a nice gesture. He was good at thoughtful gestures like that. Funny how she was so good at forgetting the things he did right.

"Thanks," she said, guilt making her words stiff as meringue.

He studied her hopefully. "You still mad at me?"

They were having a party tonight. He was making some effort. And her hormones had settled down. "No."

He grinned. "Good."

The microwave dinged and he pulled out dinner. "So, what did you get? Is that a Barnes and Noble bag I see?"

216

"No snooping," Joy warned. "Not all of us did our Christmas shopping on the Internet."

"Unlike some people in this household, I don't snoop," Bob countered.

"I think I'll wrap it after we eat and put it under the tree. I hate having a tree up with no presents under it."

"There'll be more soon enough," Bob predicted. "I ordered mine in plenty of time. No muss, no fuss."

And no people, Joy thought, but she kept the thought to herself. There would be plenty of people in the house tonight. That, in and of itself, was a big step for Bob.

She stowed her purchases and washed up, then joined him at the dinner table. In addition to chimichangas, he'd filled two glasses with water — a real feast. Hopefully, they'd be eating better at the party.

"So, are you all ready for tonight?" she asked.

He nodded. "As soon as I finish eating I'll run over to the store and pick up the party trays."

Grocery store deli platters. Ugh. Oh, well. What did she care? "So, you never told me who all is coming." Their best friends, Ben and Marcy, were out of town, but there were still the book club members and the neighbors.

"Let's see," Bob said, rubbing his chin, "we've got Don and Darla."

"Pendergast?"

Bob nodded.

"Your bookkeeper and his wife."

"What's wrong with them?"

"Nothing, I'm sure. It's just that we hardly know them."

"Don's a nice guy. And he saved us twelve thousand in income tax last year."

"You sent him a case of wine. He's been thanked."

"I thought it might be nice to have them over."

Joy nodded thoughtfully. Okay, there was nothing wrong with expanding their circle of friends. "Why not? Who else do we have coming?"

"Harold and Linda."

Bob's critique partner and his wife. Harold wrote fantasy novels, and in the summer he and Linda got dressed up in costumes and attended medieval fairs so Harold could throw axes at chunks of log and run around with a crossbow.

They had never done anything with Harold and Linda as couples. Joy tried to look on the bright side. Maybe Linda would have some cool medieval food recipes, hopefully some that didn't involve baking blackbirds in a pie or roasting a whole pig.

"So, who else?" Surely Bob had invited someone she knew.

"Lyle."

"Your publicist?"

"He's in town. I thought it would be nice to include him."

"Sure," Joy agreed, smiling. "The more the merrier. Anyone else?"

"That's it."

Joy's smile died. "That's it? None of the neighbors?"

"Karen Doolittle's got the neighborhood party this year."

"I didn't hear anything about it. How do you know?"

"Because I delegated that job to her when I ran into her at Hollywood Heaven."

"Nice of you."

"I thought so. Anyway, it's time for someone else to take a turn having his home invaded."

That was the definition you'd find in Bob's dictionary under the word "hospitality," Joy mused. It was a miracle they were having anyone over. Baby steps, she told herself, baby steps. Be glad he got inspired to do something.

While he was out picking up his party supplies Joy wrapped her present for him, a thick tome full of philosophical observations on the writing life, and put it under the tree. Then she put on her new dress. It was Christmas red with a scooped neck, trimmed with red sequins. Just seeing herself in it put her in a party mood. Okay, this wouldn't be a typical Joy party, with lots of friends and a holiday table filled with goodies, but it would probably be fun.

Bob returned with party platters and eggnog. He smiled at the sight of Joy in her new dress. "Wow, you look great. Did you buy that today?"

She nodded.

"Let's call everyone and tell them not to come and we can have a two-person party instead."

She pointed to the headlights outside the window. "Too late. I think our first guests are here."

"Wow, they're early."

"I guess they can't wait to see what a Bob Robertson party looks like," Joy quipped. "I'll get it."

"Thanks." He set the platters on the dining table, then went in search of the punch bowl while Joy answered the door.

There, in all their glory, stood Harold and Linda Bradbury. Harold was sporting a blue velvet cap with a feather in it. A matching velvet cloak hung over his beefy torso, and his legs were encased in some sort of leggings. He looked like Henry the Eighth without the turkey leg. Next to him stood Linda, equally large in a black velvet cape over a royal blue gown. She wore a headdress that made her look like the Queen of Hearts, freshly escaped from Wonderland.

"We're here," Harold announced. " 'Let the games begin.' "

Well, at least he'd said the word "games." Joy hoped he hadn't brought his axe with him.

"Come on in," she said. "May I take your, uh, coats?"

They stepped inside and Harold removed his cape with a flourish. "Thank you, my lady."

"You're welcome . . . Lord Harold," she said, and took Linda's cloak. "Bob is just getting the food set out."

"Ah, food. I'm famished," Harold declared.

Wasting away to a shadow, Joy thought, as she hung the capes in the coat closet.

Harold and Linda went to hover by the table and watch Bob work. "You've done a great job, old man," Harold congratulated him.

220

"Of course, I'd have been glad to bring something," Linda put in. "I'm not on strike. I like to eat too much to do that," she added, patting her rounded middle. "I make a wonderful moose mincemeat pie. It's the hit of the medieval fair every year. Isn't it, Har?"

"Oh, yes," he agreed, nodding his head.

"Har tells me you're doing everything," she said to Bob. "I could give you some recipes."

And what did Linda think Bob, the most kitchen-challenged man in town, would do with them? "I'm still doing the cooking. Bob's just in charge of Christmas this year," Joy said as she went to answer the door.

This time it was the Pendergasts. Don Pendergast was a tall, thin man with a thin mouth, and his wife, Darla, was short and plump. She looked around as she stepped inside the house as if wondering what she was doing at the Robertsons'. Well, that made two of them, Joy thought.

Unlike the Bradburys, the Pendergasts had dressed in slacks and sweaters in muted colors knitted in a pattern of trees. Darla regarded Linda, who was sailing out to the living room in full medieval regalia with a plate of rolled meat and cheese like she was an alien invader.

"Well," Joy said after she'd settled the Pendergasts in the living room with some eggnog, "it's nice to get to meet the wife of my husband's genius bookkeeper. Are you good with numbers, too, Darla?"

Darla shook her head. "Oh, not really," she said in a quiet voice.

"So, what is your specialty?"

"Specialty?" Darla repeated.

"I mean, what are you good at?"

Darla thought a moment. "Well, I . . ." She stuttered to a stop and looked like she was going to cry.

Joy tried another tack. "What do you enjoy doing?"

"I like tropical fish."

Come to think of it, Darla's voice reminded Joy of a tropical fish tank: soft and burbling — the kind of voice that could put you to sleep. Just like the subject of tropical fish. Joy nodded, trying to look interested.

"And I like to read," Darla added.

Oh, good. Common ground. "Me, too," Joy said. "What do you like to read?"

"Nonfiction."

Would it be too much to hope that Darla enjoyed cookbooks? Joy nodded encouragingly.

"I'm especially fond of true crime," she said quietly. "Serial killers."

Joy kept her smile pasted on and nodded. *Serial killers, how cozy.* "I'm sure you and my husband will have a lot to talk about then, since he writes murder mysteries."

"I'm not fond of mysteries," Darla said, frowning and shaking her head.

Okay.

"I'm with you. When you've read one mystery, you've read them all," Linda said with a flick of her pudgy hand. "You should try fantasy. Now, there's a genre worth reading. My husband's work is brilliant."

222

Well, that took care of Bob in one sentence, Joy thought, and tried to make her smile look genuine. It was getting harder by the second.

Harold joined them, his plate piled high, and sprawled on the couch. "Now, this is my idea of a good time. Good food, good conversation, good friends."

Good friends? Oh, please, dear God, no.

Bob came up to him with a plate of the Christmas bonbons. "You might like these. I made them with my daughter."

"Oh, how sweet!" Linda exclaimed, digging in.

Bob beamed. "It's a Christmas tradition."

Really? Since when did being forced once to do something with his daughter qualify as a tradition? Bob was becoming a legend in his own mind.

"Joy usually does it," he added, picking up on her not so good vibrations.

"Of course, you didn't this year because of the strike." Linda leveled a how-could-you? look at Joy.

"The strike is exposing Bob to all kinds of new experiences that he's missed out on all these years," Joy said in her own defense, "including this party."

"And you're doing a bang-up job, old man," Harold boomed. "I'll have another of those candies. Great stuff."

Harold was expanding on the delights of good food when their last guest made his appearance. Lyle Forsythe was younger than the rest of them, a nice-looking man in his late thirties, wearing jeans and a sweater under a leather jacket. He offered Joy a box of

Godiva chocolates, giving her false hope that the evening wouldn't be a total wash.

But, sadly, he didn't stay more than an hour, claiming yet another party to attend. Joy was tempted to ask if she could go with him.

Bob's soirée hadn't exactly been swinging so far. The food was abysmal: dried-out veggies and dip from a plastic container, cold cuts and cheese — big deal — and store-bought cookies. The only highlight was the big jar of truffles Bob had purchased at Costco. Conversation had been no better than the food, just a dull road of tax deductions and family holiday plans, with a quick, interesting detour instigated by Lyle into brainstorming how Joy could turn her catering experiences into a book. But Linda had cut that short when she got inspired with an idea for a book of her own and hijacked the conversation.

And that was when Lyle had remembered his other social obligation. He was backing toward the door like a hunted man even as Linda was still talking. She flung her final words at him as he bolted for freedom. "I'll keep you posted on my progress with *Life in the Kingdom*."

With Lyle gone it was back to the six of them, and the party lost what little shine it had. Harold waxed eloquent over the joys of crossbow competition while the Pendergasts sat in a stupor.

Joy was going to lose her mind. They needed a diversion, something to do to breathe life into the evening. She looked at Bob. "So, what have you got planned for us?"

224

"Planned?" He gave her a quizzical look.

"Entertainment, fun and games?" she said lightly.

"Oh, not games," protested Darla in a weak voice. She looked to her husband as if she might need him to protect her from some kind of attack.

"We don't have to do anything but talk," Bob assured her, and Joy sank back against her seat. Not more conversation with these people, please.

The polite expression still on his face, he looked expectantly at Joy, like she should somehow turn this into a successful evening.

Was he crazy? Superman himself couldn't rescue this flat affair. Anyway, it was Bob's party. It was up to him to save the evening. She looked expectantly back at him.

He cleared his throat and asked the Pendergasts, "So, do you have family coming over for Christmas?"

"We're actually going to have a quiet Christmas this year," said Don.

This year? Joy was willing to bet every year at the Pendergasts was a quiet Christmas. There were probably mortuaries noisier than their house.

"I think people go overboard too much at the holidays," added Darla, her expression prim.

It took Joy a moment to recover from her shock. Other than her terrified reaction to the prospect of doing something fun, this was the first time all evening Darla had actually offered an unsolicited opinion. And it wasn't a very welcome one. "But it's such a wonderful time of year," Joy protested.

Darla shrugged. "It's all become so commercial. And people get so silly this time of year."

This from a woman with trees on her sweater. "Well, I think a little silliness is good," Joy said. "They say laughter is the best medicine. And you really don't have to spend a lot of money to enjoy the season."

"Oh, we don't," put in Don.

"Anyway, we're not too into parties and other frivolous things," Darla added, helping herself to another one of Bob's bonbons.

She was sure enjoying those frivolous bonbons. Joy smiled on, wishing all the while she could kick the woman.

"We're just as happy staying home reading a good book," Darla continued.

"Well, that is an option," Joy agreed. *Why didn't you?*

"Of course, it's always nice to get to know a good client better," Don said, coming along behind his wife to do cleanup.

His words weren't quite enough to sweep the uncomfortable silence out of the room.

"I know some card tricks," Harold offered. "Got a deck, Bob?"

Bob produced a deck and Harold did a tolerable trick. Okay, Joy thought hopefully. The evening was picking up. She encouraged Harold to do some more. He did. Several more. By the eighth trick Joy felt her eyes glazing over.

"Should we be going?" Darla finally asked her husband.

Joy always begged her guests to stay longer. Tonight she kept her mouth shut. But as soon as they were gone, she intended to open it and give Bob an earful.

CHAPTER
SIXTEEN

"Good time, old man," Harold told Bob as he and Linda walked out the door after the Pendergasts.

"We'll do it again next year," Bob promised.

We? We who? Joy stared at her husband. He was grinning.

He was insane.

"That was fun," Bob said after he shut the door on their guests.

Joy gaped at him. He had to be joking. That was the most boring, awful party they'd ever had. "That's your definition of fun?"

"Like Harold said, good food, good conversation, good friends."

"Good food?"

"Well, not as good as yours," Bob amended.

"And good friends of whom?"

"Of mine."

"You are not good friends with your accountant," Joy said, disgusted.

"We're friends," Bob insisted.

"You can't want to be good friends with any of those people. Harold may be a great writer, but he and Linda are just too self-centered and weird. And if you thought

228

it was good conversation listening to them drone on about life in the 'kingdom' I'm going to have you declared legally insane. I thought I was going to throw up when Linda started talking about the big search for the fairest maiden. I mean, a kingdom, Bob? It's a bunch of people who all go camping together and sell Robin Hood outfits to the tourists."

"It's a bunch of people who enjoy exploring history. That's no stranger than grown-ups getting together and acting out titles of books and songs."

"You can't compare playing charades at a party to dressing up in fake suits of armor and shooting arrows at each other," Joy argued. "What normal person does that sort of thing?"

"Normal people will do lots of strange things for fun," Bob said, "like chase each other with cans of whipped cream."

"Well, at least my family doesn't dress up in costumes to do it," Joy retorted.

"Only because they haven't thought of it."

He could be right. She decided to steer them in a different direction. "Look, I'm not saying Harold and Linda aren't nice. But how can you connect with people like that? I tried, but I couldn't. And the Pendergasts aren't any better. There was no real interaction with any of them, certainly no laughter. Oh, except when Harold laughed at his own witty remarks. That's not my idea of a party."

Bob's gentle smile fell away and he looked at Joy soberly. "Now you know how I feel." He picked up an empty platter and took it out to the kitchen, leaving Joy standing speechless in the living room.

He didn't belabor the point. He didn't need to. She got the message loud and clear. And his words gave her plenty to think about as she lay in bed that night. She vacillated between guilt that she made him attend things he hated and irritation that he hated the important things she wanted him to be a part of. And it really irritated her that he'd had the nerve to put her family in the same category as the Bradburys.

The whole night had been a bitter pill to swallow. And she really choked on it when she thought about what life would be like if they lived it according to Bob Robertson's specifications, the man whose theme song could have been the Beach Boys' "In My Room." So, why had he bothered to throw a party at all?

She found her answer when she walked by the Charlie Brown tree in the morning. Of course, once more Bob was on a passive-aggressive rampage. *Bob Humbug strikes back*. She ground her molars. Well, Bob Humbug had just earned a lifetime supply of coal for his Christmas stocking.

Joy was grim-faced and tight-lipped Sunday morning, a sure sign that she wanted to talk. But Bob didn't want to talk. All they'd been doing lately was talking. And all that yakking had taken them in so many circles he was getting dizzy.

Much of their married life had been a dance, one that was perfect when they were moving together. But often, when he just wanted to slow-dance, she had to speed them up and pull them into some wild hip-hop that left him confused and breathless. He loved his wife dearly, but why was she always trying to change the steps? Or maybe it wasn't that she was trying to change the steps. She'd always preferred fast steps. In fact, her very liveliness was what had attracted him to her in the first place. Was it her fault he couldn't keep up?

Bob frowned. After all these years, you'd think she'd understand him. But maybe men and women never really understood each other. They just pretended they did. Or maybe they understood more than they liked to let on. Maybe they just didn't care.

That seemed more likely. Okay, so last night had been a little lacking in luster. At least they'd had a party. He'd tried, but what had his wife cared? He'd gone to the trouble of hosting a party and all she'd done was complain, just like she accused him of doing. There was no pleasing her. He went to take a shower and found her pantyhose dangling from the showerhead.

Dangling pantyhose, wifely silent treatment — Bob suddenly felt smothered in estrogen. He needed to get out, needed to breathe. He bagged the shower and pulled on some jeans and an old sweatshirt, then went to announce his departure from the henhouse.

He found Joy standing out on the back porch in the freezing cold, talking on the cordless. "He did it out of spite," she was saying.

He did not. He tapped her on the shoulder and she jumped and turned. It was hard to tell if the flush on her face was embarrassment or a hot flash. He sure couldn't tell anything from her expression. She always had a smile and a kiss for him, but not this morning. She looked at him with a face devoid of emotion. No anger, but no love, either.

"Who are you talking to?" he asked.

"My mother." She might as well have added, "So there."

It was definitely a good idea to leave. "I'm going to the hardware store," Bob said. "I'll be back in a couple of hours."

"Fine," she said in a dull tone of voice that made her sound like a character from *Invasion of the Body Snatchers*.

Great, he thought as he got in the car. He was already coping with Menopause Joy, now he had to deal with Alien Invader Joy. When would the real Joy, the carefree, happy one, come back? Was his life ever going to be good again?

Everywhere Bob looked as he drove downtown he saw Christmas cute. Who had come up with the idea of garlanding and lighting everything? Surely not a man.

He couldn't find parking close to Hank's so he had to walk. He passed the florist shop with its window filled with displays of frilly holiday arrangements. What would life look like in a world without women? Would everything be plain and utilitarian, black and white, colorless? The door opened as a customer came out, and a gentle snatch of laughter slipped out on the woman's heels. He thought of all the laughs he and Joy had shared over the years.

He ducked into the bakery and the aroma of gingerbread and yeasty rolls danced up his nose. The frosted biscotti caught his eye, and he ordered one and a cup of coffee. Joy always made biscotti for him this time of year. The girl behind the counter handed over the bakery special and he took a bite. It wasn't as good as Joy's and he wound up tossing it in the garbage.

Wait a minute. What was he getting all sentimental over? It was only biscotti. He left the bakery and picked up his pace, marching past the jewelry store and the women's clothing boutique and straight into Hank's Hardware.

No gingerbread smell here. It smelled like sweat and lumber. He could hear the shoop-shoop of the paint mixer, and the voices of the sports commentators on Hank's TV, warming up for the day's game.

He saw Pete Benedict, the guy with the baseball cap, over in the aisle with the Christmas lights. He had three boys with him, and the littlest one was bouncing up and down like he had springs on the bottom of his feet.

Not sure how he'd be greeted, Bob ducked down the nearest aisle and started to check out the drill bits. But he could hear the other man and his kids.

"Come on, Dad. Hurry up."

"Don't worry," Pete said. "There'll be plenty of trees left. And plenty of time to surprise Mom."

He sounded okay, almost happy even. Well, good. At least somebody was sailing through the strike.

By Sunday night Joy and Bob had made up. They always did. But they had postponed negotiations and the strike was still on. And Joy was still wondering how they would smoothly navigate their golden years when she went to meet with the Stitch 'N Bitchers Monday night.

Laura had come straight from work, and she was already there, showing the others her children's picture with Santa when Joy walked over to their table.

Sharon took it and cooed, "Bless their little hearts. That is absolutely priceless."

"Is that what you call it?" Laura said with a scowl.

Kay peered over Sharon's shoulder. "Oh, my gosh. That looks like something that should get passed around the Internet."

"Thanks," Laura said with a frown. "That makes me feel so much better."

"It really is cute in a perverse sort of way," Sharon assured her. "Reminds me a little of Norman Rockwell."

"Norman Rockwell on drugs," Laura sneered. "What a disaster."

"Oh, honey, people will love this," Sharon said. "The kids are just plain adorable. And at least they got new jammies," she added with a frown. "Pete says the boys don't care about getting new ones for Christmas Eve so he's not bothering." She shook her head. "Nothing's getting done right. My tree is a terror. It's full of tinsel rats' nests, and they put every toy car the boys ever owned in its branches. And, naturally, they're entering the thing in the *Herald*'s decorating contest."

"Well, obviously they're happy with it," Laura said.

"Oh, they're happy all right. They're turning my house into a horror," Sharon said in disgust. "I swear, every day I go to work at the flower shop it's like

234

getting a sabbatical from hell. The whole house is filled with those awful singing trees and snoring Santas. The worst is the reindeer that sings 'Grandma Got Run Over by a Reindeer.' I know my mama will love that when she comes out to visit. And I can just imagine what she'll say when we have turkey ordered from Town and Country and stuffing mix out of a box instead of Grandma Patrick's recipe for cornbread stuffing. I can tell you, that will be about as welcome as a skunk at a lawn party."

"Eew, gross," said Kay.

"That is my life," Sharon said, deadpan. "Gross. But that's enough of my misery. Tell us about Glen's party, Laura."

Laura's expression turned impish. "Let's just say that Glen is on a steep learning curve." Her delight suddenly got swallowed by concern. "Although I've got to admit I'm beginning to feel sorry for him. He actually fell asleep at the computer yesterday, ordering Christmas presents."

"Oh, boo-hoo," said Kay, rolling her eyes. "Shopping the Internet is so hard."

"Thanks to the Bob Robertson article he had a step-by-step tutorial," Sharon added. "And a recipe for cookies."

"Which he made," said Laura. "The kitchen looked like Florida at the peak of hurricane season. Did Bob think that up all by himself?" she asked Joy.

"You've got to be kidding. It was something I did when the kids were really little. He must have found it in my kid recipes file."

235

"And passed it off as his own? That's lower than a snake's belly," Sharon said in disgust.

"It's plagiary. Sue him," Kay joked.

"No," Laura said. "Hit him where it really hurts. Don't have sex with him."

"Honey, you should never withhold sex as punishment," Sharon said, sounding like Dr. Laura. "Unless he really deserves it," she added with a guffaw.

"I should make my husband pay for sex. That would be one way to get money out of him," Kay said, and everyone giggled, everyone but Carol.

Joy realized they were being insensitive and decided it was time to turn the subject. Except it would be easier to turn a Carnival cruise ship with a rowboat. She couldn't ask how everyone's week had been; that would only bring up more talk about the strike and everyone's husbands. Questions about shopping and baking were equally out since the husbands were now in charge of that. This was one instance where it would be nice to be more like Bob, who was a verbal gunslinger, able to draw the right words faster than you could say dictionary.

"You know, I'm beginning to think I should . . ." Laura stopped and bit her lip.

"If you say 'end the strike,' I'm going to smack you," Kay told her. "The whole idea is to get him to really get how much you have to do so that next year you won't be pulling the load alone."

"She's right," said Sharon miserably. "If you cave now and bail him out you'll be back to doing everything faster than my dog can say bone. We have to stay strong." She smiled at Joy. "You don't see our fearless leader talking about ending the strike, do you?"

Their fearless leader should never have started this in the first place. What had she been thinking, anyway? She had to have been under the influence of hormones. "Oh, let's talk about something else," she begged.

"Good idea," Carol said in a crisp voice. "Maybe someone could ask where Jerri is."

Everyone grew quiet; then Sharon said in a small voice, "She's usually here by now. I wonder if she's all right."

"No, she's not all right," Carol snapped.

CHAPTER
SEVENTEEN

"I talked to Joe today," Carol said. "Jerri's starting more chemo. By Christmas she won't be able to see anybody, including her kids, for fear of infection. Her morale's in the toilet, she's only done a little decorating, and she hasn't got either the strength or the taste to bake. Her husband's trying to do all the holiday things she loves and keep up the house, go to work, and take care of her. He's doing it all, just like yours would do if you needed them to." Carol looked around the table, pinning each of them with her angry glare. "You should all be bitch-slapped."

She gathered her yarn into her knitting bag and stood.

"Where are you going?" Laura asked.

"Someplace where the air smells better," Carol said, and left them staring at each other.

Joy felt like she should be wearing a T-shirt that said MRS. GRINCH. She looked at her fellow strikers. Laura was biting her lip and staring at her lap. Kay's eyes were just about to overflow with a major tear spill and Sharon didn't look far behind her.

Debbie closed her cash register and came over to the table. "What's going on?"

238

"We just got bitch-slapped," Sharon said.

"And we deserved it," Kay added, then brought Debbie up to speed.

"Oh, no," Debbie said. "Of all the rotten timing."

"She wasn't even on strike and her husband is doing everything," Sharon muttered.

"I feel like poop on a stick," said Laura.

"You know," Joy said thoughtfully. "There's nothing that says we have to be on strike from helping a friend."

Sharon looked at her. "Are you suggesting what I think you are?"

"Why not?"

"I could decorate for someone who might appreciate it," Sharon said, excited.

"I'll help you," Laura offered.

"I've been dying to bake," Joy said. "We could make a real party of it and do our gift exchange."

"Well, if you do, let me know," said Debbie, "and I'll send along a gift certificate for her."

"A party, great idea. When should we do it?" Laura asked, and everyone looked at Joy.

"I'll call Carol," she said, and they all looked relieved. "She can find out a good time for us to come when Jerri won't be too tired."

Conversation took a turn to higher ground the rest of the evening as the women discussed plans for injecting Jerri with Christmas spirit. Joy planned to bring frosted sugar cookies as well as a big pot of veggie soup to the work party, and Laura offered to supply salad and rolls to go with the soup. Sharon volunteered to bring several boxes of her best decorations and Kay said she'd take care of the shopping if Jerri's husband would give her a list of names, ages, and sizes.

"Ask Carol if she'll go with me," she said to Joy. "She knows Jerri best and would have a better idea what her family would like. And while we're out," she added thoughtfully, "maybe I'll see if I can talk Carol into a Christmas makeover."

Sharon nodded. "Good idea. That poor gal looks like human leftovers."

"She probably feels like it," Joy said. "She's been through a lot, and the last two years can't have been easy."

"Still, I think she needs to rejoin the human race," Sharon said.

"Maybe she's not ready," Joy suggested.

"Maybe it's time we helped her get ready," Kay said, a determined glint in her eye.

Good luck in your mission, Joy thought. Getting people to change was no easy feat. Her situation with Bob was proof of that.

She came home to find him in the family room, camped out in front of the TV, a remake of *A Christmas Carol* providing background noise while he fiddled with a crossword puzzle.

"How was your knitting club?" he asked.

"Jerri's going through more chemo, so we're going to go over to her place and Christmas it up."

He took off his reading glasses and cocked an eyebrow at her. "No strike at Jerri's, huh?"

"No need for a strike at Jerri's," she retorted.

"No need for a strike here, either."

240

"Because you've seen the light?"

"You mean the light at the end of the tunnel?"

Joy kicked off her shoes, then plopped down on the couch next to him and playfully burrowed her toes under his thigh. "That doesn't sound like a man who's gotten a new attitude for Christmas."

"I like my old attitude just fine. No need for a new one," he said, slipping a hand up her pant leg.

"You are so irritating," Joy said in disgust. "I'm beginning to think you're completely unteachable."

"What is it I'm supposed to learn again?"

"That is so not funny. You know all I want is for you to try and appreciate the time we spend with the people who are important in our lives. I mean, really. Is it too much to ask you to step outside your comfort zone just for special occasions so I don't have to feel like I'm experiencing them alone?"

Bob rubbed his forehead. He looked like he was in a headache commercial.

Joy pushed on. "You beg off from as many social gatherings as you can, and when you do come to one you stay on the sidelines. And then you want to leave early. I've cut back a lot over the years just to make you happy. I would just like you to give up a little, too, especially this time of year."

"Joy, your definition of a little is a lot."

Now she was in the headache commercial, too. He was hopeless.

They both sat silent, staring at the TV while Ebenezer Scrooge made Bob Cratchet's life miserable over a piece of coal.

Finally Bob sighed and gave Joy that sorry little-boy look that always melted her heart. "So, do you want to poison me and go find yourself a Mr. Fezziwig?"

She shifted position and cuddled up next to him. "No, I just want you to get in touch with your inner Fezziwig. I know he's in there somewhere because every once in a while I get glimpses of him. You're a fun guy. It seems like a waste that so few people know it." When he was with her or the kids or one of their small circle of close friends, he was a completely different man. Maybe that was what had kept her hanging in there all these years. She knew the real Bob, the one he hid from most people. "You hide your light under a bushel." Why, oh why couldn't she get it into his head that he didn't have to do that?

"I like it under the bushel. It's safe."

And that was Bob in a nutshell — shy, afraid to put himself too out there in a group of people for fear of looking stupid. Maybe that was why he was a writer; because he could control every situation, edit his words, avoid missteps. But he missed out on so much holding himself apart from people. Others missed out, too.

"What are you thinking?" he asked warily.

"About how wonderful you can be when you want to. I wish you'd let more people see it. That's why I started this whole strike thing, you know."

"Joy," he murmured. "Can we just, for one evening, forget the strike, knock off negotiations?" He touched his lips to her neck and sent a warm shiver through her. "Can't we just remember that we love each other?"

242

Well, even strikers had to take a break once in a while.

Later, after they had rejoined Ebenezer Scrooge on his journey, she realized how very like a rerun their marriage was. Don't bother to tune in, you've seen it all before. Bob and Joy disagree. Bob outmaneuvers Joy. Joy caves.

She watched while Bob Cratchet persuaded his wife to toast the first Grinch in history. Mrs. Cratchet caved. Joy's jaw set into determined lines. *Note to self: No caving this Christmas, no matter what.*

Tuesday afternoon Bob came home from a run to the library to find Joy in the kitchen baking.

"Is the strike over?" he asked hopefully.

She shook her head. "No. These cookies aren't for us. I just got off the phone with Carol. This is the night the Stitch 'N Bitchers are going over to Jerri's to get her ready for Christmas. These are a morale boost."

Bob eyed the cut-out Santas cooling on the cookie rack. "It would be a nice morale boost if you left a few of those behind."

"You know I can't do that. Anyway, the extras are going to the nursing home for their Christmas party."

"I've had enough. I don't want to play anymore," he said, reaching for a cookie.

Joy gave his hand a playful slap. "You're stuck. Didn't you read the paper?"

"Only the headlines and the sports page."

"Well, you might want to look at the letters to the editor. You're the new guru of Christmas, savior of all those inept, uncooperative, insensitive husbands whose wives are on strike. You're a hit. If you give in now every man in the city will hate you."

Bob slipped behind her and put his arms around her. "How will my wife feel if I give in?"

She looked over her shoulder at him. "Are you telling me that you are a changed man, that you'll go to my family's at Christmas and really participate?"

"I'll try."

Joy frowned and went back to rolling out dough. "That's a cop-out and we both know it. No, I think I like things just like they are. Anyway, it's for your own protection."

"Bah, humbug," he said grumpily.

"That's Bob Humbug," Joy corrected him.

"I feel like I'm following a general through some big military campaign," Carol complained as she trailed Kay out of yet another shop.

"When it comes to shopping, a woman should always have a plan," Kay said.

Giant candy canes grew up along the street and white twinkle lights clothed trees otherwise stripped for winter. Every other corner hosted a bell-ringing Santa presiding over a donation pot for a good cause. Whether the people they passed on the street were businesspeople or leisurely shoppers, everyone seemed to be wearing a smile for the holidays. The local bank had set up a carousel not far from the ice rink, and it was doing a brisk business this weekday afternoon. Small children in winter coats and stocking hats

244

bobbed up and down on prancing wooden horses, while their mothers stood next to them, making sure no young rider got thrown. A calliope rendition of "Santa Claus Is Coming to Town" rode the air.

"Isn't this great?" Kay said as they strolled by a storefront window painted with dancing elves and snowflakes. She took a deep breath of frosty air. "I love this time of year."

"It is nice," Carol said, but Kay could tell she was just being polite. What had Carol been like before the hard bumps on life's road had bruised her? She had laugh lines around her eyes, so she must have been fun.

"So, what will you do?" Kay asked.

Carol shrugged. "I'm not exactly sure yet."

It was mid-December and Carol wasn't sure? That was just too depressing. Whether Jack shopped or not, Kay knew that his kids would be with them and the day would have a form and a purpose. What would it be like to get up to a holiday of nothing? There would be life at her house, plenty of it. Maybe even a scene or two, not exactly an ideal situation for inviting a friend. Still . . .

"How about coming over and spending the day with us?" she suggested.

Carol smiled and shook her head. "You don't need strangers hanging around your house on Christmas Day."

"You're not a stranger. And, anyway, I might need protection in case Jack goes nuts. Or a witness."

"You'll be fine."

"But will you?"

"Don't worry about me. I'll find something to do. Oh, here's our store," she added, and turned into Sweet Home, a popular home decor shop.

Kay took the hint and followed her in, leaving the subject outside where Carol had dropped it.

They picked up a cut-glass Mikasa cookie platter to cheer up Jerri, then proceeded to His and Hers, an upscale clothing boutique Kay knew was running a big Christmas sale.

"Jerri's going to love that plate. It's gorgeous," Carol said as they walked.

Kay stopped in front of the boutique window and pointed to a mannequin all decked out in winter white wool pants and a Christmas red sweater, a silk scarf wrapped around her neck. "Speaking of gorgeous. Look at that. You'd look great in that outfit."

"You think so?" Carol said politely.

"I know so."

"Well, let's get Joe's present. That's what we're here for."

It didn't take Kay long to pick out a shirt and tie that would go great with Joe's dark coloring. "Can you wrap it?" she asked the clerk.

"Sure," the woman said.

"And while she's doing that, let's see what we can find to deck ourselves out," Kay suggested.

Carol looked at her watch. "Oh, I should get going."

"Where do you have to be?" Kay pressed. Carol hesitated just long enough for Kay to push home her advantage. "Oh, come on. I'm dying to see you in that red sweater."

246

Carol looked dubious. "I haven't worn red in ages."

"So I've seen," said Kay, and led the way to a rack of sweaters on sale.

An hour later they emerged from the store, laden with bags. "I shouldn't have bought so much," Carol said.

"Oh, no," Kay said sternly. "No buyer's remorse. When was the last time you bought new clothes?"

"I can't remember."

"Then you certainly didn't buy too much. Why don't you wear your new sweater to Jerri's tonight?"

"We'll see," Carol said, and Kay knew what that meant. She gave a mental sigh. Now she understood the meaning of that old saying about leading a horse to water but not being able to make it drink.

Well, maybe Carol would change her mind. Maybe she'd take out the sweater when she got home and something magical would happen. You never knew. They didn't call this the season of miracles for nothing.

CHAPTER
EIGHTEEN

Carol was actually relieved when she and Kay parted. Kay was like an overload of holiday joy, and she left Carol feeling drained. But not so drained that she was ready to pass up stopping by Ariel's house and dropping off the plastic tea set she'd gotten for Chloe during the afternoon shopping extravaganza. She'd had it wrapped right at the store, and its wrapping paper, covered with snowmen, was sure to put some holiday promise under Ariel's tree. After that, she'd back off, before they all became too attached to each other.

Ariel and Chloe had come to Carol's for hamburgers, then stayed to enjoy an old video of the Peanuts Christmas special that Carol had dug out. She'd watched them go down her front walk toward Ariel's battered car and felt a surge of joy that countered the bittersweet tug on her heart.

That surge, she realized, was becoming addicting. But not so addicting that she wanted to enter much further into a friendship that would only last until Ariel moved back home. And certainly not so addicting that she was going to go be a third wheel at someone's holiday gathering or wear a Christmas red sweater she'd been harassed into buying.

248

It was a little after five when she got to Ariel's and discovered the girl wasn't alone. Darren had dropped by to fix a leaky sink that Ariel's apartment manager had been avoiding for the last week. Of course, she should have recognized his truck parked at the curb. Dumb.

"How's that for weird? Two visitors in one day," Ariel said. "It's cosmic or something."

Or something, Carol thought. She pushed the present at Ariel. "I really can't stay. I just came to drop this by."

"Can't you just stay for a few minutes?" Ariel pleaded. "Chloe will want to see you."

Just then Chloe came rushing up, no longer shy, arms outstretched, calling her name.

So, of course, Carol had to pick her up. Was there anything in the world that felt as wonderful as having a child in your arms?

"Come on in," Ariel said. "Have dinner. I've got Hamburger Helper. There's plenty."

Ariel had already shut the door behind them and was moving Carol into the small living room, which was furnished with thrift store bargains. The huge tree they had decorated dwarfed the room. Memory rushed Carol and clutched her heart at the sight of her ornaments hanging on it.

"You're good to go," Darren said, walking into the room, wiping his hands on a towel. He stopped at the sight of Carol, still holding Chloe. "Well, hi."

Her heart suffered an assault of a different kind and kicked into high speed. "Hi."

"I just asked Carol to stay for dinner. Can you stay, too?" Ariel asked him.

He looked at Carol and smiled. "Sure. I've got no plans."

"I can't stay too long," Carol said. "I'm going over to a friend's tonight."

Darren looked disappointed.

"You're not going for dinner, are you?" Ariel asked.

"No."

"Then you've got to eat somewhere. It may as well be here. Want Carol to stay for dinner?" she asked her daughter.

Chloe's head bobbed up and down and she hugged Carol's neck.

"There you go. You have to stay." Ariel slipped the package under the tree. "Sit down and I'll make us some tea. You like it plain, with no sugar, Carol. Right?"

Carol nodded. Chloe squirmed to get down, then followed her mother out of the room, leaving Carol to perch on the edge of the worn, plaid couch.

Darren took the other end and smiled at her. "So, were you out shopping today?" he asked, nodding at the package under the tree.

"I got a few things."

"Getting ready for a big Christmas, then?"

"No, probably a quiet one. Most of the shopping I was doing today was for a friend who's going through chemo."

"You're a good friend," Darren observed.

"Oh, not just me. Several of us are teaming up to help her get through the holidays."

250

"You're not one of the women who are on strike?"

Carol shook her head. "No, not me."

"So, what are you doing for Christmas?" he asked.

Why did everyone keep asking her that? "My plans are still up in the air," she answered. "How about you?"

"My son and his wife will probably come by later Christmas Day." He shook his head. "They've got to hang out with her family, then see my ex and her new husband, then me. I think they're eating two Christmas dinners."

"No dinner at your house?" Carol teased.

"I'm not much of a cook. I'll probably have a TV dinner. Turkey, of course," he added with a smile.

A TV dinner — how sad was that?

"I never was much of a cook," he added quickly as if that explained his pathetic dinner plans.

Just then Ariel returned with mugs of tea. "You guys talking about Christmas?"

Carol nodded. "What are you going to do?"

Ariel gave a half shrug. "My mom was going to fly me out for the holidays but I told her to save her money. She can't really afford to, and I'll be moving home after I finish school, anyway." Chloe climbed up in her lap, and Ariel hugged her. "So, it's just us this Christmas."

At least you have an "us," Carol thought. And Darren had his son. Well, she had George the cat.

"I guess I'd better start dinner if you have to be someplace," Ariel said, and got up.

The last thing Carol wanted was to be left on the couch with Darren. She might as well have been a teenage girl again, awkward and uncomfortable. "I'll help you," she offered, and got up, too.

"Me, too," he said. "I'm not much in the kitchen but I set a mean table."

So she and Ariel worked companionably in the kitchen, preparing dinner, while Darren set the table. Dinner conversation was light, covering favorite TV shows, books, and movies, but Carol still found herself glad when the table was cleared and the dishes were washed. The way Darren kept looking at her, she was sure he was poised on the edge of some social invitation she wasn't ready for. Well, part of her was ready. Her body was practically whining for her to get her head together.

"I'm sorry to eat and run," she told Ariel. "But I've got to get going. My friend's expecting me."

Ariel nodded and plucked Chloe from her seat.

Ariel and Darren both wound up walking with her to the front door. "Say 'bye,'" Ariel instructed Chloe, who laid her head on her mother's shoulder and murmured, "Bye."

It felt a little like being a family, only without the parting hugs and kisses. Family, Carol thought wistfully as she went to her car. It was such an emotion-packed word, one easily taken for granted until life set a fuse to it.

You are not going there, she told herself firmly. Inside her car she flipped on the heat and turned the radio up full blast to drive away the despondent thoughts.

252

Several cars were already parked outside Jerri's house when Carol pulled up, and she realized she was the last to arrive.

The door flew open almost as soon as she rang the doorbell. There stood Kay in her new Christmas finery. "You made it. Here, give me your coat. Are you wearing your sweater?"

"No, sorry." Carol shed her coat and Kay took it, looking disappointed. The general had failed in her mission. "I didn't have time to change," Carol said. "I came here straight from somewhere else."

"Somewhere else?" Kay teased. "Hey girls," she called. "We're not number one on Carol's social calendar."

"I don't even have a social calendar," Carol said, walking into the living room where Jerri lay on the couch, covered with a blanket.

A candle burned on the coffee table, filling the room with the scent of bayberry, and a fire roared in the gas fireplace. The house felt like an Arizona summer.

"Joe said she gets cold easily," Kay whispered.

Jerri looked so frail lying on the couch. A plate of Joy's Christmas cookies sat ignored on the coffee table in front of her. Chemo had already taken away her taste for sweets.

Her husband perched in a chair next to her like he was guarding her. Guard duty was clearly wearing him out. He'd lost weight even since Carol last saw him; his body seemed to hang on his tall skeleton like a suit in a closet. His swarthy face looked drawn and he had circles under his eyes.

"Hi, Joe," Carol said, and he smiled and nodded a hello.

"Thanks for organizing this," he said. "You guys are . . ." He stopped, choked up.

"We're fabulous, we know," Sharon said from where she and Joy stood at the mantelpiece, draping it with gold netting, holly, and glittering pears and apples. Joy's face was flushed. Her sweater lay discarded on a nearby chair and she was holding netting with one hand and fanning herself with another. Poor Joy. This wasn't the place to be if your hormones were misfiring.

Carol didn't bother to offer to help with the decorating. The others had everything well in hand. Instead, she went to the couch where Jerri lay and perched at her feet, giving her leg a gentle pat. "How are you doing?"

"Great," Jerri said, beaming. "Laura's in the kitchen heating soup. Thanks to you and Kay we've got presents under the tree for when the kids come Friday, and the house will be decorated. I'll even have cookies to serve." Her eyes filled with tears. "You guys are the best."

"What are friends for?" Carol said.

"I hear you're the mastermind behind this."

Carol gave a one-shouldered shrug. "They were getting too obsessed with this strike. They needed to snap out of it."

She looked over to where Sharon and Joy were chatting. Kay was fussing with the Christmas tree decorations. She'd heard. She just rolled her eyes and kept working.

254

"Are you sure you're going to feel up to having the kids over this Friday?" Carol asked Jerri. She looked at Joe, who shrugged as if to say, "What could I do?"

"Pretty soon I won't be able to see anybody because my immune system will be in bad shape, so it's Friday or not at all. I don't want to go through the holidays without seeing my family."

Carol nodded her understanding and gave Jerri's leg another pat.

"Anyone want a sample of Joy's veggie soup?" Laura called from the kitchen.

"I'll pass," Joy called.

Joe rubbed his hands together and smiled. "Homemade soup, *querida*. Doesn't that sound great?"

Jerri shook her head. "I'm not hungry right now."

"You can't try a little?" he urged.

"Maybe later. You go have some, though. You need to keep up your strength."

He nodded, then disappeared into the kitchen.

"How about you?" Jerri asked Carol. "Have you made plans for Christmas yet?"

"Oh, I have plenty of time for that," Carol said evasively. She pretended to be absorbed with watching Sharon and Joy, but she could feel Jerri's gaze on her. "What?"

"Maybe someone else here needs to snap out of it."

"What's that supposed to mean?" That had been the wrong thing to say because now Jerri would feel free to explain.

"I don't think our friends here are the only ones on strike for Christmas."

Carol suddenly felt like a bug under a microscope. "Oh, don't be silly. Just because I didn't want to bother with putting up a tree."

"Kay said you bought a new Christmas sweater today. Why aren't you wearing it?"

"I didn't have time to change. I was out somewhere and got delayed."

"And what are you going to do on Christmas Day, sit home and watch *It's a Wonderful Life* on TV?"

"Good idea. I love that movie."

"Even George Bailey rejoined the land of the living," Jerri said gently. "Do you think Ray would want to see you like this? Do you think he wants you as dead as he is?"

Carol felt her friend's words like a sharp razor across tender skin. If anyone else had talked to her like that she'd have turned and walked away, but you didn't turn your back on a friend undergoing chemotherapy. Carol squirmed, looking for a way to change the subject.

Jerri pressed on. "Life's too short. Do you really want to live it in a way that you'll regret farther down the road when it's too late to change?"

Kay had drifted over to a nearby chair now. "Amen to that, sister. The time to make changes is now."

"Nobody expects you to go out dancing," Jerri added. "But maybe you could do something . . ."

Kay nodded toward the baby grand in the corner of Jerri's living room. "I know a good place to start. How about playing some Christmas songs for us? I know you play."

256

Carol was hardly in the mood for Christmas songs. She wasn't in the mood to even be here now. "I don't play by ear," she said stiffly.

"I think we've got an old Christmas songbook in the piano bench," Jerri said. "Our daughter always plays them for us. Please," she added. "I'd love to hear some nice music."

Joe was back in the room now, carrying a bowl of soup.

"We've got a book of Christmas music, don't we?" Jerri asked him.

"Sure," he said. He set down the soup and dug the book out of the piano bench.

Carol had no excuse now. Anyway, it would be rude to refuse her friend, especially when they'd come here for the express purpose of bringing Jerri some holiday cheer. And at least if they were singing, Jerri couldn't be lecturing.

She settled at the piano, and propped open the book Joe had found. "What do you want to hear?"

"'Silver Bells,'" Kay requested.

Carol found it and started to play. She was no concert pianist, and her sight-reading skills were a little rusty, but no one seemed to care. They started humming along, and Kay drifted over to stand behind her, reading the words over her shoulder.

She poked Carol in the shoulder. "Sing with me."

Carol obliged, although the saccharine lyrics about happy shoppers almost gagged her.

"That was lovely," Sharon said when they had finished. "You gals should go on the road."

"We could become stars," Kay joked. "I'd be rich, and I'd never have to hear another word about budgets ever again."

"What would you like to hear, Jerri?" Joy asked.

" 'Joy to the World.' "

Carol flipped to it and began to play. Joy left the hearth and came to add a third voice, and then Joe added a new dimension with his baritone.

Halfway through the song the message behind the lyrics hit Carol full force. There was a reason to be glad this holiday season. Hope still remained, and even if she couldn't find her way back to full-fledged joy this season, maybe she could create a small corner of happiness. If she could convince herself it was worth the effort.

She accompanied Joe while he sang "Feliz Navidad" to his wife, making her smile. Then, as Jerri was looking tired, Joy suggested they exchange their Christmas presents. Carol's was from Jerri. Her throat tightened as she opened her gift box and found a hand-decorated photo album and a disposable camera.

"For those great memories you'll soon be making," Jerri said softly.

"Thank you," Carol said. *For everything*.

She felt a warmth, small like a candle flame, stirring inside her when she finally headed home. Maybe Jerri had a point. Maybe it was time to quit worrying about her friends and their strike and look for a way she could end hers.

She'd left only one lamp on, and her entry hall was dark and still, like a mausoleum. Beyond it, the living room lay in equal darkness. No cheery tree greeted her, no candles, no festive decorations. Was this really how she wanted to live the rest of her life? Was this how Ray would have wanted her to live?

George the cat brushed against her leg, making her jump.

She bent and picked him up. "This is no way to live, you know," she informed him. She scratched behind his ear, then put him down and went to the kitchen. He trotted hopefully behind. "No, it's not all about you," she said to him. "You can wait a minute or two."

She pulled the phone directory from one of the kitchen drawers and looked up Darren's phone number. Her heart began to hammer against her chest, threatening to really make her uncomfortable if she didn't stop what she was doing immediately, but she bit her lip and punched in his number anyway. She ignored the urge to hang up when she got his answering machine and forced herself to leave a message. She had to take a deep breath after she hung up, but, in spite of her accelerated heart rate, she realized she felt good. No, not just good, excited.

She dialed Ariel next. "How about joining me for dinner Christmas Eve?"

CHAPTER
NINETEEN

It was Friday. It had been the day from hell at work, and now Glen had to come home, put on his Santa hat, and do more Christmas stuff.

"You're almost through this," he told himself as he pulled into the garage. The house was decorated, the shopping done (thanks to that cool Web site Bob Robertson had suggested), and the cards had all gone out, along with copies of the much-hated Santa pictures.

Actually, Laura had changed her mind about the picture. Now she'd decided it was kind of cute. Mostly he knew she was looking at it as proof of her superiority when it came to managing anything having to do with the family and the holidays. Like he'd ever said she didn't have it together? He'd always known it. Okay, so he'd taken it all for granted. She'd made her point. He wished he could end this thing.

Of course, if he threw in the towel he'd never hear the end of it. He'd said he could handle this, and he would. But only the knowledge that he was almost to the finish line kept him going.

That and a little help from his mom, the scab. She had come through with flying colors on the costumes, producing some weird, brown cloth topped with green felt leaves for Amy's tree costume for the winter concert. And she'd made the necessary white robe and gold tinsel halo that would turn Amy into a perfect angel for the Christmas pageant. She'd even found wings. Lucky for him his mom thought Laura was carrying the strike thing a little too far. It would have been hard, no, impossible to pull off those costumes without Mom's help. But he wasn't admitting that to Laura. Now the tree and the angel outfit sat side by side in giant black, plastic garbage bags in the front hall, ready and waiting for the shows to go on. And the first one would be tonight.

He found Laura and the kids in the family room, watching *Veggie Tales*.

"We have to hit Burger Land tonight," she informed him. "I'm too pooped to cook. We got slammed at work."

"Oh, yeah. Tomorrow's the big Hollydays Fair." He always liked going to that. Laura usually bought Christmas presents at it. No need for that this year, though. Everything was already ordered and on its way.

Still, he supposed they'd all go anyway. It was a big community event. Held on the Green at the center of town, the fair offered every kind of entertainment from Dickens carolers to school choirs and bands. And a guy could find every Christmas junk food known to man. All the local artisans would be present, peddling their wares. And, maybe, if every subscriber to the *Herald* hadn't shopped with Bob Robertson's online personal shopper, they'd even have some customers.

"Well, then," Glen said, "if we're gonna be on time for the school program we'd better get going." He clapped his hands together. "Okay, guys. Let's go get some dinner."

"Beggie tales," Tyler protested as Glen turned off the TV, shutting down Bob the Tomato.

"We've gotta go eat, kid. Otherwise we'll be late for your sister's concert."

"Beggie tales," Tyler repeated, and started to bawl.

There was no reasoning with a two-year-old. Glen scooped him up and followed Laura and Amy to the front door.

Tyler kept crying all the way. He finally simmered down to whimpers when he saw Laura pulling their coats out of the closet.

"Oh, we almost forgot the camera," she said. "Put your coat on, sweetie," she instructed Amy, and hurried off to the spare room that doubled as an office to retrieve the digital. "Can you get the diaper bag?" she called to Glen.

"Got it. Stay right there," he told the kids.

He found the diaper bag hanging on a peg in the laundry room where Laura always kept it along with the spare diapers. Of course, it was empty. The daycare must have used up the last of them.

He sighed. Why was it always such a big production to go anywhere with kids?

He had just reloaded when he heard Amy cry, "Tyler, no! That's mine."

Oh boy, Tyler the Terrible was at it again and that meant trouble. Glen left the laundry room at a fast trot.

262

"Tyler, no!" This was followed by fresh wailing from Tyler. Really not good.

Glen's trot became a gallop and he and Laura both got to the front hall just as Amy shoved her little brother. Tyler tumbled back, his crying accelerating to a screech. He caught a potted plant on his way down and tipped that over, sending dirt everywhere. Amy the aggressor stood clutching a stuffed reindeer.

"Amy!" Laura scolded.

"He took my reindeer," Amy said.

What a mess! Glen set the pot upright again while Laura got a completely bananas Tyler on his feet, all the while soothing, "It's okay. You're all right."

"You need to share with your brother," Glen said to Amy. He had to raise his voice to make himself heard over his son. The kid was going to break his eardrums, he was sure.

"He'd wreck it," she insisted.

"Tyler, stop crying," Glen pleaded. "We're going to Burger Land. I'll get you a Monster Meal."

Tyler was crying too loud to even hear him.

"Come on. Let's get your coat on," Laura said calmly to the howling Tyler, and started stuffing him into his jacket.

How did she manage to stay calm when Tyler was carrying on so hard he looked like his face was going to melt? Listening to that racket fried practically every nerve in Glen's body. He took the Dust Buster out of the corner of the coat closet and set to work vacuuming up the mess. Even that couldn't drown out his son.

Laura picked up Tyler the noise machine. "Okay, let's go. Make sure you get the right costume," she told Glen as she opened the door.

What did he look like, an idiot? "I'm on it," he snapped, and stuffed the Dust Buster back in the closet. He was just getting his keys when the phone rang. He snagged it with one hand while he grabbed a bag with the other. "Hello," he barked into the receiver.

"Hello, sir. I'm Leon from the *Holly Herald.* How are you tonight?"

Fried and half deaf. "Look, I'm headed out the door," Glen said.

"Well, this will only take a minute," Leon assured him. "I'm calling to offer you a free trial subscription to the *Herald.*"

Laura was already buying the paper on a regular basis, thanks to the strike. Once this was over Glen didn't care if he ever saw that rag again. Anyway, he got all his news on the Internet.

"No, thanks," he said.

"How about just the Sunday edition?" Leon pushed.

"Come on, Glen," Laura called from the driveway.

"I'm *in* the damn Sunday edition," Glen snarled, and hung up.

With everyone piled in the minivan, they all took off for Burger Land. Tyler had finally shut up, but it took Glen two burgers and a salad to feel like he was in control of his world again. Tyler spilled ice cream all over himself, but who cared? At least he wasn't crying.

264

"We'd better get going," Laura said after she'd mopped Tyler down. "We don't want our star to be late," she added, smiling at Amy.

"I have a part to say," Amy announced once they were back in the minivan, then launched into her speech. "I am Mother Nature's child, and when it's cold and snowing you can make a fire from me and get warm while I'm glowing."

"Good job," Glen told her. "You'll do great."

At school, Laura took Tyler and went to find seats in the auditorium, leaving Glen to get Amy to her classroom. Mrs. Green, the kindergarten teacher, was in her glory, oohing and aahing over every kid's dopey-looking costume as she helped each one get ready. Two slightly frazzled parent helpers — both dads, big surprise — were helping her get the kids' costumes on over their regular clothes. One guy was trying to pin leaves in his little girl's hair. It gave Glen horrible flashbacks of when he had to get Amy ready for her picture with Santa. The guy saw Glen and glared at him like it was all Glen's fault he was in this room with twenty hyped-up five-year-olds. Right. Like it was Glen who started this thing.

Mrs. Green came up to him and Amy, her dangly Rudolph earrings flashing. "Hello, Amy. Hello, Mr. Fredericks. Did Amy tell you she has a part to say tonight?"

"Oh, yeah," Glen said. "She knows it by heart."

"And she's going to do a very good job," said Mrs. Green. "Aren't you, Amy?" Mrs. Green was the perfect woman to be a kindergarten teacher. She was middle-aged, short and round, and looked like everybody's grandma.

Amy looked adoringly at her and nodded.

She patted Amy's shoulder, then said to Glen, "We're a little behind, so maybe you wouldn't mind staying behind a moment and helping Amy into her costume?"

That was the last thing Glen wanted to do, but how did you say no to Grandma? "Sure, no problem."

Another parent came into the room, kid in tow, and Mrs. Green gave Glen and Amy a final smile and hurried off to usher in the new arrival.

"Well, let's get you ready for your big role," he said to his daughter. He opened the bag and pulled out . . . "What the hell?" Panic rose in him clear up to his eyeballs. "This is your angel costume," he told Amy. What was that doing here? He shoved it back into the bag.

"But, Daddy, I'm a tree," she said, looking at him wide-eyed.

Shit, shit, shit. Where was the tree costume? Back home, of course, in the other bag. What was he going to do? He couldn't put Amy in this. She'd stick out like the Easter Bunny at a Halloween party.

She was biting her lip now and looking around at the other kids in the room. Tree, tree, angel. She was going to be a math genius; even at five she could tell when things weren't adding up.

"Don't panic," Glen said to both of them. "It'll be okay."

266

No, it wouldn't. This was a disaster. His kid would be a laughingstock. He thought fast, calculating the time it would take to get from school to home and back again. They were here fifteen minutes early. It would take almost ten of those fifteen minutes to get out of here and to the house. But these things never started on time. Then the principal would give a welcome speech. That would take at least five minutes. He could do it. He had to.

Kneeling in front of Amy, he took both her arms. "Daddy's going to run home and get your tree costume, so don't worry. Okay?"

She nodded, a world of trust in those big eyes. "Okay."

He turned and bolted for the door. Going out of the room he almost knocked over Mac, who was delivering his son.

"Whoa, dude. What's the hurry?"

"I've gotta get home," Glen called over his shoulder. "We got the wrong costume."

"You'll never make it back in time," Mac called after him.

Oh, yes, he would. He was in the minivan in less than two minutes. He took it slow going out of the parking lot, not wanting to run down a kid, but once he was on the road, he floored it. He had to get back with that costume.

His cell phone rang and he pulled it out of his coat pocket and checked the number. Laura. If she thought he was going to take her call so she could rag on him she was nuts. He dropped the phone back in his pocket and pressed down harder on the gas pedal.

He made it home in record time, snagged the bag, and dashed back to the minivan. You can do this, he told himself and screeched away from the curb. Just a few more minutes . . .

He was almost to the school when he heard the police siren. *Shit, shit, shit!*

Rosemary Charles had noticed that Glen Fredericks wasn't seated in the school auditorium with his wife like the rest of the men. She'd elbowed Rick and pointed to where Laura Fredericks sat. A tall, skinny guy with hair like Weird Al was leaning over the chick's shoulder, whispering something in her ear.

"Something's gone wrong," Rosemary said.

That was obvious. Laura Fredericks looked ready to go ballistic. She shot up from her seat like she'd gotten an electric shock to the butt and scooted down the row of people, trampling several sets of feet in the process, then raced out of the auditorium.

"Okay, I smell something juicy," Rosemary said. "Be right back." Then she was off across the auditorium and talking to the tall, wild-haired guy and his wife. She nodded sympathetically, but she was wearing her reporter's-scoop smile when she came back to Rick. "Oh, this is good. Fredericks brought the wrong costume and he's gone home to get the right one."

Rick frowned at her. "And you're hoping like hell he screws up and doesn't get back in time so his kid will be scarred for life."

Rosemary frowned back. "I don't want his kid scarred for life."

"But you want him to not make it back. That's kind of sick, isn't it?"

Rosemary smiled. "His little girl will be okay, trust me. Teachers are always prepared for this sort of emergency. And it's Fredericks's suffering I'm interested in. It's great for the story. So, I need you to go hang out in the parking lot and get a picture of him coming in."

"I'm surprised you don't want a picture of the kid in her underwear," Rick grumbled.

"Just go, will you?"

He was here on assignment. He had to. But he didn't like it. And as he lurked in a dark corner of the parking lot, hunched inside his coat, he felt like some sort of traitor to his sex.

The cold air tickled the back of his neck with icy fingers, and he pulled his coat collar tighter around his neck. This was a total waste of his talent. Some photographers got pictures of people digging through the ruins of war, or of runners breaking through the tape for a gold medal. What was he getting? Pictures of pathetic Christmas trees and even more pathetic men who couldn't even find the right costume for their kids' Christmas program. This was dumb, if you asked him. But no one had.

In the distance he heard a police siren. Probably the one big thing that would ever happen in Holly was taking place right now and here he was, hanging around the elementary school parking lot, missing out.

But wait. The siren was getting closer.

Suddenly he saw a minivan blowing up the street, a patrol car in hot pursuit. Who did the clown think he was, O. J. Simpson? Was he ever going to stop? Wait a minute. That minivan looked familiar. Forgetting all about feeling like a traitor, Rick took off across the parking lot. This picture wouldn't exactly measure up to Olympic gold, but it was as close to gold as he was going to come here in Holly.

"Officer, I can explain," Glen started to say to the angry cop approaching his window. And then he recognized that square jaw and the thin lips. "Oh, no."

The thin lips got even thinner and pulled down into a frown. "What was it this time, Mr. Fredericks? Did you run out of eggnog?"

"I got the wrong costume for the school program. My little girl's gonna be the only one who's not wearing leaves. They're starting any minute." The cop didn't look like he believed Glen. "I've got it right here," Glen rushed on and started to reach for the bag next to him.

"Keep your hands where I can see them," barked the cop.

"Oh, man, look. I'm not lying. And you know I'm not a criminal. You already ran my license twice, for God's sake. You can check my story for yourself if you don't believe me. The bag's right there."

"I'm going to ask you to please step out of the car, sir." Hand on his gun, the officer stepped back.

As Glen got out he caught sight of that damned photographer from the *Herald*, across the street,

270

snapping pictures. "Great. This is just great," he muttered.

The officer leaned into the car and snagged the bag. He opened it and looked inside, then tossed the bag back on the seat with a disgusted frown.

"Okay, can I please go to the school now?" Glen pleaded.

"As soon as I give you a ticket. Please get back in the car. I'll need your license and driver's registration."

"Oh, come on!" Glen cried. "The program's going to start. I promised my kid."

"The sooner you get that information for me the sooner you can go."

"Oh, man. How about a little sympathy here?" Glen begged as he dug out his license. "You've got kids. What would you have done if you were me?"

"Checked the bag before I left home."

Glen handed over his license and registration, then swore under his breath as Barney Fife went back to his patrol car. He drummed the wheel while the cop did his thing. His heart was thumping like he was racing down a football field. *Come on, come on, come on!* He was starting to sweat now. He looked at his watch. Okay, the program had started. If the cop gave him his ticket in the next sixty seconds, then if he made it into the parking lot in under a minute, if he ran down the hall . . . he'd still be almost fifteen minutes late. *Please don't have started on time.*

The officer came back with yet another present from the Holly P.D. "You might want to remember that I'm right behind you when you pull out."

271

"Thanks," Glen said between clenched teeth. This was police brutality. Or something. He was going to report this guy.

He pulled out. Slowly. Went down the street. One mile under the limit. Signaled. Turned into the school parking lot. And parked his car in a load zone.

He grabbed the bag with the costume and bolted into the school. Down the hall, turn the corner, past the principal's office, down one more hall, heart pumping, lungs stinging. There was Mrs. Green's room.

And no one was in it.

"Noooo," Glen bellowed, and collapsed on a little desk. The thing crumpled under his weight and tipped him on his butt. It was the final straw. He lifted his eyes heavenward and roared, "Why me?"

But deep down, he knew. This was like some huge, cosmic plot to ruin him. God was punishing him. First he'd taken his wife for granted, then, only last week he'd . . . He had to get to confession. He'd go tomorrow, he resolved. If he lived through tonight.

He picked up both himself and the desk, then left the room for the auditorium, where Laura would be waiting to kill him.

CHAPTER
TWENTY

The kindergarten class was just filing off the stage when Glen made his way down a row of irritated parents, muttering, "'Scuze me."

Laura frowned up at him. "Why didn't you answer your cell?" she hissed as he fell onto the seat next to her.

"I was kind of busy," he hissed back. He looked at the departing forest of trees. "Where's Amy? Did she get to go on?"

"That's what I was trying to call you about. Mrs. Green had an extra costume that she keeps for emergencies. You didn't need to leave."

He'd risked heart failure, broken the sound barrier, gotten another ticket, and sent his car insurance rates through the roof for nothing. And he'd missed seeing Amy make her speech. He crossed his arms in front of him and began to quietly turn the air blue.

"Glen." Laura glared at him.

He shut up, polite on the outside, cursing on the inside.

"Hey, sorry you missed seeing your kid," Mac said to him after the program was over. "At least your wife got pictures of it." He stuck his cell phone in Glen's face, showing Glen a picture of his son. It was impossible to tell whether or not the kid in the picture was Mac's. Mostly it looked like a brown cardboard tower with legs under it.

They collected Amy, who, like all the other kids, was already bouncing in anticipation of cookies and punch. "Did you see me, Daddy?"

Laura was looking at him in disgust. He felt like the world's biggest doof. "You were great," he said. No lie there. He was sure she was.

They ate cookies and drank gross red punch with the other parents for a while. But then Tyler managed to dump punch all over another kid and it was time to go.

They found the minivan right where Glen had left it. No ticket, thank God. Maybe he just wouldn't tell Laura about the one he got tonight. She'd find out soon enough, and she already had plenty to get on him about. And she was gearing up for it. He could tell by the way she was snapping her gum. He climbed in behind the wheel and braced for the assault.

Sure enough. "Glen, I thought you checked the bag."

Was every woman given a lifetime supply of salt at birth to rub in a guy's wounds? "Don't start with me," he warned as they drove out of the parking lot.

"It's probably going be in the paper, you know. Rosemary Charles and the photographer were here tonight."

"I know," Glen said between gritted teeth. That would be front page news. And tomorrow she'd have something to say about that, too. Like he needed her telling him he'd screwed up. Like he couldn't see that

274

for himself. Like he didn't already feel rotten. Like this wasn't all her fault in the first place, her and her damned strike. He kept his gaze straight ahead. If he even so much as looked at Laura right now he knew his head would pop off.

"I should have checked the bag."

Because, of course, she knew her dumb shit husband would screw up? Okay. That was it. He screeched the minivan to a curbside halt and turned to face his wife. "Hey, I'm doing the best I can." He stabbed a finger at her. "You want things to go the way you want them? You end this dumb-ass strike of yours. Otherwise, you take what you get."

Laura blinked, then clamped her lips tightly together. From the back seat Amy softly said, "Daddy?"

Great. Now he was like George Bailey in *It's a Wonderful Life*, having a complete meltdown. "It's okay, baby girl. Daddy and Mommy are just having a little talk," he said calmly, and put them back on the road.

Next to him, Laura looked ready to pop like a string of Christmas lights. Merry Christmas, Glen thought glumly.

They completed the trip home in silence. Glen broke it as they walked in the door. "I'll put Amy to bed."

"Fine." Laura bit off the word like it was his head and walked away with Tyler.

He put Amy in her princess jammies, then supervised the tooth-brushing ritual. He almost cried when she said her prayers asking God to bless Daddy. Daddy didn't exactly deserve blessing right now.

Glen tucked her in and stayed on his knees by the bed. It was so small, covered with pink blankets and pillows and stuffed animals. Kneeling there he felt big and clumsy. And dumb — a big, dumb doof.

"Daddy's sorry he blew it and you didn't get to wear the tree costume Grammy made for you tonight," he said miserably.

She smiled at him, such details unimportant. "I liked being a holly bush."

"I think Santa's going to have to bring you something special for doing such a good job saying your part. What do you think?"

"I just want my Shopping Babe doll Santa promised," she said sleepily and snuggled into her pillow.

"Then I know you'll get it. I love you, baby girl," he whispered and kissed her forehead. That was one thing he wouldn't screw up, anyway.

Laura was still in with Tyler when Glen came out of Amy's room, so he went downstairs and hid out in the family room, aiming his remote at the TV like a gun and flipping channels. She never came downstairs and he didn't go up. When he finally went to bed, she was turned with her back to his side. He doubted she was asleep, but he didn't ask. Instead, he just slipped into bed and lay with his back to hers. He didn't like lying facing this way. It felt unnatural. So, what else was new? His whole life felt unnatural.

Horrible dreams chased him through the night. In one he was in stocks in the Green, wearing nothing but a pair of red long johns. Everyone he knew had gathered there to throw snowballs at him, and Laura stood at the head of the line, stuffing a rock inside her snowball. Right in back of her stood his mom, who scolded, "I went to all that trouble to make costumes for you and look what you did!" And then he was out of the stocks and floating alone on an ice floe somewhere in the Arctic. All he had was his burned Christmas cookies. He kept hollering for Laura, and his voice got hoarser and weaker. Finally he lay down on the ice floe. "Just let me die."

The words were still on his lips when he woke up. And the bed was empty.

He pulled on socks and jeans, grabbed a T-shirt, and went downstairs, anxious to negotiate a truce. They'd never before gone to bed mad. This had to get fixed.

The kids were in the family room, doing their Saturday morning cartoon ritual, and Laura was in the kitchen, on the phone, probably talking to that reporter from the *Herald*. She glared at him, effectively zapping his desire to make up. She'd thrown him in the deep end of the pool and now she was acting like it was his fault he couldn't swim.

If he stayed here one more minute, he was going to . . . Okay, time to leave, right now. He stormed out of the kitchen, grabbed his coat and car keys, and went out the door.

It was snowing outside and it looked like it was going to stick, a sure guarantee to bring out all the bad drivers. The way things were going it would be just his luck to run off the road and hit somebody's tree. He got in the mini-van. Destination: church.

He drove by the Green on his way and saw there was already a good crowd collecting for the Hollydays arts and crafts fair. It looked like one of the school PTOs had set up a booth to sell Krispy Kreme doughnuts again this year, and they were already doing a brisk business. Couples strolled among the booths, holding hands. Some men were alone, wandering aimlessly like they were lost — obviously the guys who hadn't used Bob's Internet shopper. Thank God he'd at least done that right, Glen thought. Amy would have her Shopping Babe doll.

The memory of the previous night's debacle jumped on him like a mugger, making him feel almost sick.

Ten minutes later he was at church, in the confessional with Father Thomas. "Bless me, Father, for I have sinned. It's been two weeks since my last confession."

Glen began to go down the list. "I've taken the Lord's name in vain, I've had impure thoughts. And I wanted to kill my wife."

There was a long silence on the other side of the screen.

Glen suddenly wished he were a Protestant. They didn't have to do this stuff. "Just for a second, though," he rushed on. "I mean, it was one of those thoughts that goes through a guy's head when he's going nuts, just one of those I-could-kill-that-woman kind of thoughts. I wasn't really going to." He wasn't making it better trying to explain. No matter how he said it, it still sounded bad. Anyway, how could you explain to a man who didn't have a wife how insane women could make

278

a guy? Glen gave up. "I can't take it, Father," he said. "This strike is making me crazy. I'm a guy. I'm not wired to do all this woman stuff."

"But you committed yourself to go along with it. You promised to do everything on your wife's list. Isn't that what I read in the paper?"

Whose side was Father Thomas on, anyway? Glen frowned. "Look, Father, I know I shouldn't have had that thought. I love my wife. I really do, and I'm not planning on bumping her off. Just give me my penance, okay?" A million Hail Marys ought to do it. He'd go find a nice, quiet bowling alley to say them and stay away all day.

"Go home and do everything your wife asks you with a smile," Father Thomas instructed him.

Glen almost fell off the seat. "What?"

"I think that will be penance enough," said Father, and shut the window.

A sleepless night, two cups of coffee, and one good talk with her mother had helped Laura see that she'd been wrong. Of course it wasn't fair to blame Glen for an honest mistake, one she could have fixed by just taking a sneak peak in that bag, and it had been both mean and stupid to keep harping on it. Yes, she'd started this strike because she wanted to prove a point, but she sure hadn't wanted to prove it at her child's expense. And if it hadn't been for Mrs. Green, Amy would have paid the price. Somehow, when Laura went on strike, she'd seen it as really involving only her and Glen. She'd been wrong and that mess the night before was as much her fault as his. No, more. She was a rotten mother, a rotten wife, and a rotten person.

She dumped the morning edition of the *Herald* with its incriminating picture of Glen and the cop in the garbage — someone would wave it in his face before the weekend was over, but it wasn't going to be her — then left the kids in the family room playing under the blanket tent she'd made them and wandered into the living room to watch by the window for him. While she waited, she studied the tree he'd decorated with them. He hadn't done a half-bad job. In fact, if she were honest, she'd have to admit he'd done a pretty good job of decorating both the tree and the house. He'd done a pretty good job at most everything she'd dumped on him, especially considering the fact that he'd gone into the whole experience completely clueless.

Which, of course, had been her point when they started this. But whose fault was that, really? Who always picked up the slack, making it easy for Glen to do nothing? She'd ask him to help, but then, when he didn't get around to doing it fast enough, she'd just step in and take over. No wonder Glen thought all the parties and dinners he dumped on her were no big deal. She'd made it no big deal for him. And by being his little holiday enabler, she'd stoked the coals of her own aggravation.

She heard a car door shut and looked out the window to see him coming up the walk. She jumped off the couch and rushed to the front door, ready to tell him she was sorry for putting both Amy and him in such a humiliating situation and that the strike was

280

done. She'd had enough. She got to the front hall just as he came in.

He looked at her sheepishly. "Hey, baby."

She rushed him and threw her arms around him. He was such a big goof, the world's biggest kid, really. And she loved him to death. Her throat tightened, and for a minute she couldn't speak.

"I guess this means you're not pissed anymore, huh?"

"You big goof," she said tenderly.

He grinned. "So, what am I doing today?"

He was ready for more, after last night? "Doing?" she repeated.

"I've got a lot to make up for. I'm ready."

"Well, I'm not. I think we need to end this."

He frowned down at her. "Hey, I can handle it. Anyway, I need to. I'm under orders."

"What are you talking about? Whose orders?"

"God's."

"What?"

Glen frowned. "Don't ask."

Oh, boy. He was cracking up. He looked so determined she didn't have the heart to insult him by telling him she didn't think he could cut it. At least there wasn't much left he could mess up, she told herself. Well, except the shopping, the cooking, Christmas morning. It was a lot to risk. "I don't know," she said.

"I can handle it," he insisted, but she noticed he left off his usual cocky "piece of cake."

"Are you sure?"

"Absolutely. Anything you dish out, I'll eat."

"All right," she said, unable to hide the skepticism in her voice. "You're going to get the full holiday experience." To herself, she added, but from here on, boy, you'll be working with a safety net.

Joy and Carol strolled the Green, visiting the various arts and crafts booths and sipping hot chocolate. Other people passed them, bundled into winter clothes. Joy saw a lot of hand-knit scarves, hats, and mittens, testimony to the women of Holly's new fascination with knitting. Multicolored lights festooned the bandstand at the center of the Green, and a bunch of kids were running around it, laughing and throwing snowballs at each other. All the booths were swathed in red and green bunting. The snowflakes drifting down on the whole scene made Joy think of snow globes.

"I think this snow's going to stick around," Carol said.

"I hope not," said Joy. "We're picking Bobby up at the airport later this afternoon, and I hate driving in the snow."

"Won't Bob be driving?"

"Yes, and that's why I hate driving in the snow."

Carol chuckled. "So, are you excited to see your baby?"

"Oh, yes."

"Did you break down and make cookies for him?"

Joy nodded. "I ran over to Laura's and did it while Bob was out running errands. Now there's a tin of gumdrop cookies under Bobby's bed."

Carol just shook her head. "Aren't you ready to give this up yet?"

"Not yet." Although what good it was doing Joy couldn't say. Bob wasn't even fazed and she was on chocolate overload.

They passed a booth selling homemade cookies that had a long line of men waiting at it. "I wonder if all those men have wives on strike," Carol mused.

"If they do, it's turning out to be a good thing for the cookie business," Joy said. "And good for a story," she added, watching Rosemary Charles approach one of the men in line. As usual, the reporter had her personal Jimmy Olsen in tow. Of course she'd be here covering the fair, looking for strike stories. Interested to hear what the man would have to say, Joy stole a little closer to eaves-drop.

"Sir, I see you found a creative way around the strike," said Rosemary.

He smiled. "Home-baked cookies and I didn't have to bake them. I like it. Between the Hollydays booths and Bob Robertson's advice, we're sailing through the strike."

"May I quote you on that?" Rosemary asked the man.

"Sure," he said.

Goody, thought Joy, more male propaganda. Why had she bothered? Why had any of them bothered?

"Less people this year," Rick observed to Rosemary.

"The women are on strike and a lot of guys shopped the Internet."

"UShopTillIDrop.com? Interesting site."

"It seems a little impersonal," Rosemary said. "Having somebody pick out the presents for the people you care about. I mean, where's the thought in that?"

"Hey, do you really care as long as you get a cool present?" Rick countered.

"What makes a present cool is the fact that someone picked it out specially for you."

Rick shrugged. "Well, I did eBay, so everybody on my list is getting something special."

"Used," Rosemary said in disgust.

"But special."

"Did you get your white elephant gift for the party tonight on eBay?"

"Oh, yeah," Rick said with a grin.

Rosemary looked suspiciously at him. "Geez, what tacky thing are you bringing this year?"

"You'll just have to wait and see," he said. "But I'll give you a hint. It makes gross noises and all the guys are going to fight over it."

"Lovely." Like the setting for the party. Well, what could a girl expect with the men in charge? Rosemary shook her head. "I don't know where we're going to put the presents, since that sports bar probably won't even have a Christmas tree up."

"We can put 'em on a pool table," Rick said.

"Men," she said in disgust. "You put so much thought into things. I hope somebody learns a lesson from this strike."

"Don't hold your breath," Rick said. "And anyway, talk about tacky, that rotten errand you sent me on at

284

the school program probably rates pretty high on the tack-o-meter."

She made a face at him. "That was not tacky, that was news. And didn't I tell you it would be all right? I wouldn't have made a story out of that screwup if I knew their little girl was going to be embarrassed."

"Okay, all-knowing one. How did you know that Teach was going to come through?"

"Easy. Miss Weis."

"Who the heck is that?"

"My kindergarten teacher. She kept spare clothes on hand in case someone wet their pants or fell in a mud puddle. And then there was Mrs. Sonstroem. She kept string cheese and crackers in case someone forgot their lunch. And Miss Hoyle —"

Rick cut her off. "Okay, okay. I get your point."

"You can always count on teachers. They're always prepared." Rosemary gave his arm a playful poke. "And all good reporters know that."

"I think I'm gonna hurl."

They passed a booth peddling hand-beaded jewelry, and Rosemary stopped. One particular necklace using a fat, pink quartz bead as a centerpiece caught her eye and she picked it up. The tag was a little pricey, so she put it back down.

"Everything here is overpriced," Rick said at her elbow.

"You're paying for the artist's time and talent," she told him.

"I guess," he said. "Hey, if we're done I think I'll put my camera away and get some elephant ears. Want one?"

She'd rather have had the pink quartz necklace. She stole a look at Rick. He was standing with his hands shoved in his jacket pocket, his camera dangling from his neck, looking around like he was bored. Mr. Christmas. Whoever ended up with him would wind up just like these other women, frustrated and on strike.

Rosemary suddenly didn't feel all that companionable. "Not right now. I see Kay Carter. I'm going to go talk to her."

"Suit yourself," Rick said and let her go.

As she passed a strolling quartet of carolers dressed in Dickens costumes, she found herself wishing she hadn't committed to going out with Rick on New Year's Eve. He really wasn't her type.

Joy and Bob met their baby at the airport. Bobby was six feet of gorgeous; well muscled, with even features, a strong chin, and heartbreaker blue eyes. His face lit up at the sight of them and he gave them a huge wave. As if they hadn't already spotted him, as if they hadn't both been looking for him since the first passenger from his flight had disembarked.

"Hey, guys," he said cheerfully, stepping out of line. He hugged Joy, then left an arm draped over her while he gave his father's hand a hearty pumping.

Joy smiled up at her son and thought she'd explode with happiness. This was all any mother needed for Christmas. "You look great," she said. He looked so grown up now. Just one year at college and he'd completed the transformation to manhood. Where was that tiny baby she'd rocked during 2:00 A.M. feedings, the little boy who had climbed trees, skinned knees, and sat in her lap whenever he had the chance? It wasn't a new question and she still didn't have an answer. Life went too fast.

"You've shrunk," he told her.

"No, you've grown." And he looked just like his father had when she first met him, right down to the smile.

"Yeah, another inch. Weird, huh?"

"You're just a chip off your old man, a towering presence," Bob joked.

Bobby looked down at him and grinned. "Whatever."

They started toward the baggage claim. "I have to go to Melia's after dinner," he said to Bob. "Can I borrow the car?"

"It's snowing," Joy protested.

"Don't worry, Mom. I haven't forgotten how to drive in the snow," Bobby assured her. "Anyway, Melia will kill me if I don't get over and see Sarah."

They weren't even to the house yet and he was already talking about taking off. This was how it was with grown kids. They came home to visit, but the parents were never at the top of the list. Right after dinner it would be just her and Bob and the TV. Ho, ho, ho, humbug Christmas. Yet again she saw a long line of unsatisfying holidays stretching far into her future and sighed inwardly.

The road was crusted with a thick layer of snow as they wove in and out of airport traffic on their way to the freeway. Bob was skating along, following the car in front of him too closely as always.

"We're toast if that car stops suddenly," she warned.

Bob reached over and gave her a condescending pat on the leg. "It'll be okay."

She shook her head. "We'll be roadkill before Christmas."

"Speaking of Christmas, what's going on, Mom?" Bobby asked. "Melia said you're on some kind of strike. You even made the paper over where I am. What's the deal? I don't get it."

Silence fell like a bomb in the car. At last Bob spoke. "Your mom doesn't think I enjoy the holidays enough. She's on strike so I'll see how much I appreciate what I hate."

Not fair, Joy thought. Bob was twisting this into pro-Bob propaganda and as good as asking their son to take sides.

"What does that mean?" Bobby asked.

"It just means your father's taking care of Christmas this year," Joy said, trying to put a smooth facade over the whole holiday mess.

"Dad in charge of Christmas, huh?"

"It should make things interesting," Joy said, trying to keep her voice light.

"Sounds like a reality show or a sitcom to me," Bobby said, sounding disgusted.

"No TV, just a never-ending newspaper story," Bob said.

288

"That's kind of sick," Bobby said.

Joy wasn't sure if he was referring to her strike or the fact that the paper was following it. "I'm not the only one," she said in her own defense.

"Mass hysteria," Bob cracked.

If their son wasn't with them in this car right now . . . She clamped her lips together and glared out the window. They really were going too fast. Why didn't her husband listen to her?

"Bob, slow down," she commanded.

"Hon, we're fine. Cool it."

He was trying to kill them but he was telling her to cool it. She shut her mouth and did a slow simmer.

Bobby was silent for a moment, then asked, "Um, does this mean we're just going to sit around and do nothing for Christmas?"

"It means we can have a nice, quiet holiday," Bob corrected him.

"We're not going over to Uncle Al's?"

Bobby actually sounded concerned. Joy took hope. Maybe Bob hadn't poisoned their children's minds after all.

Bob's brows knit. "You want to go to Uncle Al's?"

"Well, yeah. I haven't seen anybody since I went away to school."

Bob nodded thoughtfully.

"And what about cookies?" Bobby wanted to know.

"Don't worry. I'll buy some," Bob promised.

"Mom, is he kidding?" Bobby asked, going from sounding concerned to panicked.

Joy smiled over her shoulder at him. "Don't worry, sweetie. It'll be okay," she added, and patted Bob's leg. Bob frowned.

"Who's shopping for presents?"

"I am," Bob said, "and it's already done."

"Cool," Bobby said, sounding impressed.

He was equally impressed when they got home and he saw the Bob Christmas tree. "Holy crap!" he exclaimed, eyes bugging.

"It's up," Bob said. "That's what matters."

Joy just shook her head and went out to the kitchen to heat up the clam chowder she'd made earlier.

She was slicing French bread to go with it when her son came out to the kitchen. "You all squared away?" she asked as he opened the fridge.

He stood there, surveying its contents. "Oh, yeah." He shut the door and rooted around in the pantry, coming out with a lunch-size bag of chips, then leaned against the doorjamb and began to pop chips in his mouth. "So, are you and Dad . . ." He petered to a stop.

"What?" Joy prompted, still slicing.

"Are you guys okay? I mean, you're not having problems, are you?"

"You mean as in about-to-get-divorced-type problems?"

Bobby shrugged. "Well, this strike stuff is a little weird. I thought maybe . . . I don't know."

"We're fine," Joy assured him. "We're just renegotiating our contract, that's all."

"So what happens if you can't renegotiate?"

290

Joy shrugged. "I'll kill him." Bobby made a face and she smiled. "I was just kidding. Don't worry. It will be all right. Just a little different this year."

"A little different," he said in disgust. "What was Dad smoking when he did the tree? And is he really making the cookies?"

Joy stopped on her way to the table with the French bread and lowered her voice. "Check under your bed."

Bobby looked relieved and grinned. "Thanks. At least that's something I know is going to be right this Christmas."

So far it was the only thing.

CHAPTER
TWENTY-ONE

The *Holly Herald*'s staff party was in full swing, and Rosemary Charles had to admit the guys hadn't done a half-bad job planning it. As it turned out, Bruno's Sports Bar did have a tree they could put their white elephant game presents under — a gigantic fiber optics number that sat parked in a corner of the bar. Under it lay a pile of gag gifts. A few were wrapped in Christmas paper or nestled in gift bags, but most (the men's) had come wrapped man-style in brown paper or plastic bags. The newspaper's Web guy, Dustin, had actually used red ribbon to tie his bag shut. But Dustin was new. Next year would probably be another story. The party food consisted of Bruno's buffalo wings and miniburgers, and some bowls of nuts, but there was plenty of beer so nobody seemed to care. Country music kept a steady beat going under the clack of balls on the pool tables and bursts of laughter, and right now some country singer was belting out a number that had Santa driving a 747.

Jonathan Hawkins, their publisher, strolled among the tables, chatting with the reporters and secretaries who weren't bellied up to the bar. Their editor, Walt, was ordering fresh drinks and joking with a cute bartender in a Santa hat. Rick, who was playing pool with Rosemary, Martha, the food editor, and another reporter, stood waiting his turn and stuffing his face with nachos.

"They don't even miss my red velvet cake," Martha lamented to Rosemary as she chalked her cue stick.

Rosemary leaned on hers and watched as Rick set down his nachos and prepared to take his shot. "Oh, well. Your baking skills are wasted on these guys, anyway. Pearls before swine, girl."

Rick sank his ball and positioned himself for another shot.

Martha sighed. "Why do we bother? No one would miss it if we all stopped doing what we do. We just proved it."

Rosemary thought of how her dad rubbed his hands together in anticipation before sitting down to eat Christmas dinner, how he always managed to find where her mom hid the snowball cookies and snarf down every one before anyone else could get a chance. "Oh, I don't know," she said. "I think a lot of guys appreciate it." Then she thought of how pooped her mom always looked by Christmas Day. "But I don't think women need to do as much as they do. And maybe they shouldn't be such martyrs. They should recruit more help."

And speaking of help, those snowball cookies weren't that hard to make. Maybe she'd bake a batch tomorrow and drop some off for her dad. Give Mom a break.

Rick made another shot, smacking a ball into a side pocket.

"You could save some for the rest of us," Rosemary complained.

He walked past her and waggled his eyebrows. "I'm good. What can I say?"

"Something modest?" she suggested.

He ignored her, bending over and setting up for his next shot. He had a nice butt. And great aim. He made that shot, too.

"Beginner's luck," she goaded.

"In pool, there's no such thing as luck," he informed her. "You need a precision eye and a steady hand. And I've got great hands," he added as he sauntered by her.

"And a fat head."

Walt came over and handed Rosemary a bottle of Red Hook. He looked around like a king surveying his kingdom. "Well, we pulled it off." "We" meaning Rick, who had gotten volunteered army-style to find a place for the party. "You women make too big a deal out of everything. Those women didn't need to go on strike. They just needed to delegate."

"You'd have sold a lot less papers if they had," Rosemary teased.

Walt made a face. "Got an answer for everything, don'tcha?"

"Pretty much."

He took a swig of beer. "Well, kid, it's been a fun ride. Nice bit on the smaller turnout at the Hollydays arts and crafts fair, and announcing the winners of this year's tree-decorating contest will make a good twist. After that I think we'll have about milked this thing for all we can. We'll get a picture of the contest winners in the paper Christmas Day and call it quits with that."

"There's still Christmas Day itself," Rosemary reminded him.

He shrugged. "That'll be pretty much of a snooze. Stories about people opening presents don't sell papers. No, I think just about everything interesting that's going to happen during this strike has happened."

She supposed he was right. What else could happen that would be newsworthy between now and Christmas?

"It's sick, that's what it is," Sharon snapped. From the look on her face, Joy decided it was a good thing she'd suggested a Sunday afternoon walk and gotten Sharon out of her house and into the crisp winter air. Otherwise the steam coming out of Sharon's ears might have scalded her husband.

They were on their second lap around Sharon's neighborhood, which had been dubbed Candy Cane Lane because of the extravagant holiday decorating the people all did on their houses.

"I think your tree looks adorable with all those little toy cars and tinsel," Joy said.

"Who'd have thought it would win the tree-decorating contest! He's going to frame the picture," Sharon grumbled. "I'll never live this down."

They walked past a lawn with a huge crèche. "At least Pete's involved now," Joy pointed out.

Sharon sniffed. "Yes, and from now on everything will be messy and sloppy and —"

"And you'll all share the celebration," Joy said, cutting her off. "Isn't that the most important thing? Isn't that what you really wanted? Isn't that why you went on strike in the first place, so you wouldn't have to do it all alone?"

Sharon frowned and kicked at a little mound of snow on the edge of the yard. "I suppose. But now I'm doomed to snoring Santas and singing reindeer all over the house. Honey, that's no improvement."

"Well, you could always confine them to the family room and put out your fancy decorations in the living room," Joy suggested. "Maybe you could put up your own tree in your bedroom. That would be romantic."

A smile grew on Sharon's face. "Now, that idea has possibilities."

"And at least your husband has changed," Joy added, feeling a little jealous. "You've accomplished something with your strike."

Sadly, it was more than she could say. And Christmas was almost here.

Sharon walked back into her house, determined to look on the bright side like Joy had suggested and see how everyone had benefited from her loosening the holiday reins. And then she caught the whiff of burned cookies and followed her nose to the kitchen, where she saw the disaster. Flour dusted the whole work island. Every available counter space was scattered with dirty bowls, measuring cups, and bags of sugar and flour and other baking ingredients. Someone had dropped an egg on the floor and failed to wipe it all up. And that was just the kitchen. All her boys looked like they'd been in a food fight.

"Oh, my stars and little catfishes!" she cried and pressed a hand to her chest. "What is going on here?"

"Hey, Mom," called James. "We're making gingerbread boys."

"Is that what you're making?" she said. "It looks more like a mess to me."

"We'll clean it up," Pete assured her. "Why don't you join us? Oh, yeah, you can't. You're on strike."

His words sounded more like a taunt than a regret, and that irked her.

"Mom, we could use some help. This dough tastes kind of funny," said Pete Junior.

It was all the excuse she needed. "Well, let me see." She shed her coat and gloves and went to take a pinch of the dough. "Did y'all remember to add the sugar?"

"Who was supposed to put in the sugar?" Pete asked, and their middle son, Tommy Joe, blushed and raised a timid hand.

"Well, let's just dump this out and start again," Sharon said.

"You're gonna help us?" asked Pete Junior. "I thought you couldn't do anything."

"Yeah," put in James, "or you'd get a scab."

"I'd be a scab," Sharon corrected him. She looked at Pete.

He was watching her, his eyes asking, "What are you going to say to your kids now?"

That was a hard question. "I guess I can be a scab sometimes, even when there's not a strike," she admitted. Maybe Pete was right. Perhaps she was just a teensy bit of a Yulezilla.

He shook his head and slapped an ear. "Whoa, my hearing must be going. I thought you said —"

"Never mind what you thought I said, Pete Benedict. And this doesn't mean I'm ending the strike. I'm just . . . taking a day off from it to supervise you boys." She started washing her hands. "Okay, now. Let's get all the ingredients lined up here on the counter and we'll put each one away after we've added it. That way you'll know everything is in the bowl that should be."

For the next hour they played together in the kitchen, making not only gingerbread boys but gingerbread trees, pumpkins, and bunnies, and any other shape that James pulled out of Sharon's basket of cookie cutters and fancied. Her oldest son decided to make an anatomically correct gingerbread boy, which got his brothers and his father laughing hysterically. Sharon decided to let it go. Maybe that particular boy would have a sad accident coming off the cookie sheet.

At last they were done and the kitchen was restored to order.

"I'm pooped," Pete declared. "Let's go out for pizza."

"Good idea," Sharon agreed. "I don't want this kitchen all messed up again now that it's clean. Boys, you all go change. We're not taking you out looking like a bunch of ragamuffins."

The boys stampeded out of the kitchen with noisy whoops, leaving Sharon and Pete alone.

He leaned against the counter and pulled her up to him. "I should have taken a picture of you crossing the picket line. I'll bet someone at the *Holly Herald* would have paid big money for that."

"I wasn't really crossing the picket line. I was just keeping you and the boys from demolishing my kitchen."

"Uh-huh." His mouth turned up in a crooked grin. "You miss doing all this, don't you? It's killing you not to be doing it."

She gave his chest a poke. "Let's not talk about me. Let's talk about you. How does it feel to have to finally do something? All these years you've been like a big ol' blister, not showing up until the work's done."

He gave her a slow smile. "Well, Tex, if everything didn't always have to be done exactly your way, maybe you'd get more help."

Pete's statement hit her right between the eyes, making her drop her gaze. It was true. Deep down she knew it. "Don't you dare call me Yulezilla," she said, trying to keep some fire in her voice.

"Things haven't gotten done exactly your way this year and we all survived just fine. Didn't we?"

"I suppose we have," she muttered.

"In fact, I think I've done pretty good so far this season and I should get some kind of reward." He began to rub his hands up and down her back.

"Is that so?" she teased, and slipped her arms around his neck.

299

He was looking at her mouth now. "Yeah, that's so." He gave her a big, juicy kiss and slipped a hand up her sweater.

"Dad! We're ready," said James, bounding into the room.

Sharon pulled away, quickly straightening her sweater. "I guess you'll just have to wait for your reward," she told Pete.

"Don't make me wait too long. All this Christmas stuff is killing me." Before she could say anything he held up a silencing hand. "I know, I know. That's what it's like for you every year. But don't worry. It's going to be different from now on."

She wasn't quite sure she liked the way he said that. "Now, don't you go thinking that just because you got away with tacky decorations all over the house this year that you've set some kind of precedent."

He grinned and sauntered out of the kitchen, humming the redneck version of "The Twelve Days of Christmas."

The man was still a barbarian. And Lord, how she loved him.

It was now December 23, 6:00 P.M., and snowing heavily. Glen had skidded his way through downtown and was halfway home before a lady in an out-of-control SUV finally skated into him and pushed his commuter car into a ditch. He plodded the rest of the way home through six inches of snow, ruining his shoes and freezing his butt off. His only consolation was that Laura had called him on his cell earlier to report that she'd made it home okay. That was one less thing to worry about.

And Glen had plenty to worry about these days, like where all the stuff he'd ordered through that on-line shopper was. Bad enough he still had to figure out everything to buy for the big Christmas Eve turkey dinner and how to cook all that crap (naturally, he'd missed the deadline for ordering the precooked turkey with all the trimmings from Town and Country by one day), but to have to worry about the presents arriving on top of it, it was too much to ask a guy.

The stuff should have been here by now. He'd used the Contact Us option on the Web site earlier in the day and had only gotten a form reply telling him that his merchandise was on the way and would be delivered in five to ten working days — the same thing it had said six days before.

Glen turned the corner to his street, dread chilling him more than the icy snowflakes slipping past his coat collar. He'd ordered everything from that site, from Laura's gift to the kids' presents from Santa. All he needed was some nasty hiccup with the delivery. He picked up his pace, anxious to get home and see if there was a pile of Fed Ex packages in the front hall.

Some of the neighbor kids were racing back and forth across the lawns, having a snowball fight. One of them came darting past him and whoever was after the kid landed a zinger on the back of Glen's head, zapping him with cold and rattling his overworked brain.

"Sorry, Mr. Fredericks," called the kid with the bad aim. "I was trying to get John."

"No problem," Glen muttered. "Hit me again. I can take it. Hell, I'm just a human punching bag these days anyway."

The streetlights cast glitter on the snow-covered shrubs and houses, making the neighborhood look like it belonged in a Robert Kincaid painting. Glen's yard sported a lopsided snowman with a carrot nose and a couple of branches for arms. The kids had obviously been out having fun. At least someone was having fun this season.

He opened the front door and looked for a pile of packages. Nothing. Hope began to leak out of him. Maybe Laura had put them under the tree for him. Ha! In his dreams. He looked in the living room anyway. No packages under the tree. The last bit of hope rushed out, leaving him feeling like a deflated balloon.

Laura came around the corner. "Oh, I didn't hear you come in."

"No packages?" he asked.

She shook her head solemnly.

"I don't understand it. I ordered in plenty of time."

"You might want to do some shopping tomorrow, babe," Laura said. "It doesn't look like they're coming."

At least she had the consideration not to gloat. Still, this sucked. Was he the only guy this was happening to? "I wonder if Bob Robertson got his," he mused.

After dinner he decided to call and see. He got only the answering machine. "Uh, Bob. This is Glen Fredericks. My wife is striking with yours. I shopped that personal shopper site you recommended in your article, and none of my stuff has come yet. I'm just wondering if you got yours."

He hung up, feeling unsatisfied. What had he been expecting Robertson to do, anyway? It looked like tomorrow he'd be at the mall, doing the last minute race for presents.

Bob stood listening to Fredericks's message and feeling once again that miserable ache in his gut like he'd been sucker-punched. This was the third call he'd gotten in two days. It didn't take a Sherlock Holmes to deduce that something was very wrong here in Holly. He went into his office and shut the door, then booted up his computer. He typed in the Web site address for U Shop Till I Drop again, determined to make something happen. He'd e-mail them one last time, threaten to call the authorities if they didn't come through. It was probably already too late to get his presents or anybody else's, but it made him feel better to try.

The computer screen blinked, then brought him up a big, empty, white page, telling him that the page couldn't be located.

What? He went back and tried again. He had to have typed the address incorrectly, had to have made a mistake. The same empty page greeted him, and he knew he'd made a mistake all right, and it had nothing to do with what he had or hadn't typed. He'd been conned, and so had half the men in Holly.

He dropped his head into his hands. "I'm a dead man."

CHAPTER
TWENTY-TWO

A knock on his office door made Bob jump.

Joy poked her head around the door. "That was Sharon Benedict. She said Pete's been trying to access the site where you guys did your shopping and it's not coming up."

Sharon knew. Joy knew. That meant soon all the women would know, and all their men would lynch him. If only he hadn't gotten cocky and offered to write that piece for the paper. If only he'd done some shopping somewhere else. If only he had more time. If only the earth would open up and swallow him.

"Bob?" Joy prompted.

He nodded his head. "I know. I just tried it. I think it's a scam."

"Oh, no," she said, horrified.

"Oh, yes. Every man in Holly is going to be out tomorrow looking for presents, including me. I'll be lucky if I come home alive."

He braced for her to rub it in, to say something like he deserved this. But, bless her, she didn't. Instead she came to him, draped her arms over his shoulders, and kissed the top of his head. "My poor guy. I'm sorry."

304

He shrugged like it was no big deal that he'd played Pied Piper to every man in Holly and led them all into shopping ruin. "Can you get me Benedict's number?" he asked. "Also, give me the Frederickses' number. I'd better give Glen the bad news."

She nodded and left the room. A couple of minutes later she was back. "This isn't your fault," she told him. Who was she kidding? Not him.

It was no fun making the calls.

"What are you going to do about it?" Pete wanted to know.

Like he was the Lone Ranger or something and he was supposed to go track down these crooks? "I'll call the cops first thing in the morning to report it. But it's Internet fraud and there's probably nothing they can do."

"Well, somebody must handle that stuff," Pete said. "The FBI, the CIA."

"Whoever handles it, they won't be able to get our presents for us in time. Every man in town who used that site is going to have to hit the stores, so if you know anybody who did, spread the word. And tell them to keep an eye on their credit card statements."

"You think these guys could be involved in identity theft or something?" Pete asked.

"I don't know. At the least they could try and have fun with our credit card numbers."

"This sucks," Pete said before he hung up.

There was an understatement. Who knew what horrible fallout they'd have to deal with from this Internet debacle? And then there was the shopping.

Bob hated crowds. He always got his present for Joy well before Christmas. Now he'd be out there with all the other last-minute losers, scrambling for something to put under the tree for not only his immediate family, but the in-laws and friends they exchanged presents with. And he'd have to get something for his folks and his brother's family, get it all in the mail, then call and tell everyone the presents would be arriving late. All this because he'd had to be the world's biggest know-it-all. Well, he'd lost that title. Now he was the world's biggest sucker.

And that wasn't even the worst of it. The worst was that he was going to lose the whole day, valuable time that he needed to finish up the surprise he'd dreamed up for Joy a couple of days ago. It was the perfect present, something that would mean a lot to her, and it was costing him something to do it. Now, with this latest development, he wasn't sure he'd be able to finish on time. In fact, he wasn't sure he'd live to do it. A sudden vision of an angry mob of disappointed male shoppers pouncing on him made Bob shudder.

Never mind that, he told himself. *Do this all one step at a time and take first things first. Get to work on Joy's present.* Maybe if he stayed up all night he might get it done in time.

The all-nighter lasted until some time before midnight, when Bob fell asleep in his office. He woke up with his head on his desk at two. Two in the morning and he wasn't done. The day ahead loomed before him like a death sentence. He rubbed his stiff neck and stumbled off to bed, hoping he'd be able to finish in the morning.

When he finally woke up he was alone in the bed. The scent of yeast and cinnamon drifted in to him. Joy had already been up baking cinnamon rolls. That meant it was late morning. Oh, no!

He sat up in a panic and looked at the bedside clock. It was 10:00 A.M. already — 10:00 A.M. Christmas Eve day, and he had a daunting to-do list. He had to call the cops and confess he'd been suckered, then he had to rush out and shop, a misadventure that would be followed by a frantic effort to finish Joy's present. He looked out the bedroom window. The streets were an icy, snowy mess. That made the morning complete.

He fumbled into sweats and his favorite sweatshirt and ran downstairs to find some coffee. He rushed past the tree so fast he almost didn't see the pile of presents under it. Whoa, what was this? He put on the brakes and bent over to look at the tags on the packages.

Some were from their son to each of them, and he found Joy's present to him under there, too. But the rest, the ones for Melia and her family and for Bobby, were signed from Joy and him. It was a miracle.

He hurried on into the kitchen to find Joy and Bobby seated at the table, sharing coffee and cinnamon rolls. The presents were under the tree and Joy was baking again. She was all dolled up in her favorite Christmas sweater and had a pair of goofy-looking Santa earrings dangling from her ears. The old Joy was back. It was as if the past few horrible weeks hadn't happened.

She smiled at Bob and opened her mouth to speak, but Bobby was ahead of her. "Hey Dad, that Web site you shopped at made the news," he said, and held up the paper.

Bob took it and read the headline. PERSONAL SHOPPER RIPS OFF HASSLED HUSBANDS. Back to ugly reality. Rosemary Charles was in fine form today. Who had contacted her, and when? At this point, what did it matter?

He read on. "Men all over Holly are having difficulty contacting the personal shopping site recommended by Bob Robertson, the mystery writer whose wife started the Christmas strike." Bob felt an invisible steel band tightening around his forehead. There he was in black and white, the spoiler of Christmas. "Detective Ben Samuels from the Holly Police Department warns that this site could be a scam. Any readers who have used it should contact their credit card company immediately."

Bob shook his head and dropped the paper on the table. He needed that coffee right now. The phone rang just as he was pouring himself a cup and he looked at it warily. It probably wasn't Santa calling to see if he had been a good boy.

"I wouldn't answer that," Joy warned him. "We've already had six calls from hassled husbands."

"Great," he muttered.

"Don't worry," she said. "I put a message on the answering machine explaining how outraged you are and offering your regrets that so many men, just like you, were taken in. And I said the police are working on it."

"Are they?" Bob asked.

"I got the ball rolling," she said.

Bob leaned over and kissed her cheek. "Thanks, hon. I probably owe you my life for that."

"Oh, and I also offered free copies of your latest book to anyone who sends their mailing address to your Web site. I figured that would smooth most ruffled feathers, and you might pick up some new readers."

Brilliant. Why hadn't he thought of that? "So, is it helping?"

"For the most part."

"What does that mean?"

"Some of the callers want to rip off your head," Bobby elaborated. "I don't know what their problem is, though. It's not like the credit card companies are going to make them pay, since it's fraud."

But their wives were going to make them pay, since it was a major screwup, a screwup for which Bob was responsible. Nobody would forget that. The steel band got tighter. Bob took a fortifying gulp of coffee, scalding his tongue in the process.

"I bet there's going to be a lot of guys running around looking for presents today," Bobby predicted.

"Speaking of presents, where did the ones under the tree come from?" Bob asked as he put a fat cinnamon roll on his plate. "Obviously not from my personal shopper."

"Well, not the one on that Web site, anyway," Joy said.

"You."

"I had a few things tucked away," she said modestly.

She'd saved him. His wife was a true heroine.

"So I guess you don't have to go out after all," Bobby said. "You lucked out, Dad. You can hide out till the storm blows over."

He lucked out the day he married Joy. "But I've still got to get presents for the families," he said, and slumped against the kitchen counter. All those great things he'd ordered wouldn't be arriving on anyone's doorstep.

"I called your mom and your brother and explained," Joy said. "You've got a few days' grace. And I already had something tucked away for Lonnie and Al and Suki and her husband."

"Friends?"

"Done."

"I don't have to go out?"

She shook her head. "All you have to do is get ready for tonight."

Thank God. At least he'd be spared a public beating.

"Speaking of getting ready, I'm going to get a shower," Bobby said, and left the two of them alone.

Bob sat down at the table opposite his wife. "You saved me." It was a funny way to conduct a strike. And, cocky bastard that he'd been, he hadn't deserved saving.

She nodded. "Yep. I did."

"I would have gone out and gotten the presents, you know."

"I know. But there was no need for me to get spiteful about the whole thing. It wasn't like you didn't try, after all."

He took a moment to digest that. It didn't digest well. He took a bite of his cinnamon roll and it was like homecoming for his taste buds. "These are good."

"No, they're fabulous," she corrected him.

"Just like you."

His words didn't have much impact. She simply murmured a polite thank-you and took another sip of her coffee.

The unspoken question hung in the air between them for several minutes. Bob finally voiced it. "So you're no longer on strike?" he asked casually.

She shrugged. "I gave up."

Those words didn't make Bob as happy as they should have. In fact, they pierced deeper than anything she'd said and done so far this season. "So, I'm hopeless, is that it?" *Please don't say yes.*

Her smile was tinged with sadness. He was a disappointment to her. All his earlier anger and resentment had been the feelings of a fool. No man should put that look in his wife's eyes.

"You're not hopeless," she said, "just different. I guess we'll always be two very different people. Anyway, everything doesn't always have to be done my way." Her gaze dropped to her coffee cup. "I've been kind of a brat, expecting you to leave your comfort zone just so I could be happy. I always figured that deep down you really enjoyed the celebrations, that you just needed a nudge. I guess it's hard for me to imagine anyone not wanting to live like my family."

Like everyone would want to be stuck in a never-ending holiday version of *My Big Fat Greek*

Wedding with mobs of people coming and going all the time? What was it about large, loud families that made them think everyone wanted to be just like them? Bob wisely didn't ask. Why his wife thought the way she did didn't really matter. She was who she was and he loved her. And he wanted her to be happy.

"I should be glad you even come to my family's," she continued. "And I'll settle for any kind of party you want. I just don't want us to grow apart. I don't want to experience important events by myself. I don't want you to draw away."

She was regarding him earnestly now, waiting for him to assure her that he wouldn't.

There was nothing he would like better than to pull free of her obstreperous family, to never again have his house full of noisy people during the holidays. If he could he'd whisk her off to a desert island every holiday season where he could have her all to himself, where she would laugh and sparkle for him alone. But the best setting for all that sparkle was a social one. He'd always known it. She lived for her friends, her family, her parties. And this time of year was her time. Anyway, he'd been wrong to be so stubborn and vindictive when she was trying desperately to make a point. She spent eleven months of the year working on making his life good, doing everything from cooking his favorite food to running interference for him at book signings and chatting up the customers. Surely, for one month he could try to do whatever made her happy.

"I'm not going to," he promised, and patted her hand. "Don't give up on me yet. I can be taught." And

312

one thing he'd learned was that having a few holiday traditions was good for the soul. He smiled at the memory of his adventures in the kitchen with Melia, and of how funny Hank and Linda had looked at his party in their crazy costumes.

Now Joy was smiling, too, looking at him with tears in her eyes, and he leaned across the table to kiss her. She met him halfway.

Just then Bobby sauntered back into the kitchen, wearing jeans and a sweater, his hair still damp. "Hey, you two. Get a room."

Bob chuckled and went to pour himself some more coffee. Everything was right with the world again. At least for him. He hoped the other men in Holly were doing okay.

Glen had already gotten into a tug-of-war at Toy Town over the last Shopping Babe doll. She came complete with shopping cart, purse, and charge card, and after the costume screwup at the school concert, getting her was penance he had to do. He'd won, but the goon had actually threatened to sue.

Now he'd nearly gotten into it at Hollyworld with a guy wearing a baseball cap and a kill-you look over the last chick flick DVD on the shelf in the movie section until he realized it was Pete Benedict.

"Go ahead," Glen said, letting go of the prize. It was a consolation prize, anyway. He'd been everywhere looking for the Smoothiccino maker Laura had wanted and he'd come up empty.

"Sorry, man," Pete said. "But I had to come through with something good."

"I don't know," Glen said, scratching his head. "I don't think a movie's gonna do it."

"The movie's part of the package. I'm getting chocolates and bath shit, too."

Another husband of one of the strikers walked by just then, his jaw clenched around an unlit pipe. Jack Carter, Glen remembered. "Sorry," he said. "The bath department's cleaned out. I got the last bottle."

"Try getting a gift certificate to that nail place," Glen advised. "That's what I did."

"You'd better get over there fast," Carter said. "I was there half an hour ago, and it's a zoo." He shook his head. "You wouldn't think it would be so hard to get a few presents, would you? And so expensive. My God, I had no idea."

Pete nodded. "Things go a lot better with my wife in charge."

There was an understatement, thought Glen.

"I better get going," Pete said. Then, clutching the DVD, he hurried off down the aisle.

From two aisles over, Glen could hear raised voices. "Hey, where do you get off reaching over my shoulder?"

"You didn't want it."

"I was looking at it."

"Well, too bad. Piss or get off the pot."

A new shopper had joined Glen on the movie aisle. He saw the empty shelf and burst into tears. Glen decided it was time to go. Anyway, he still had to hit the hardware store and the grocery store.

The hardware store! Maybe, just maybe, Hank would have a Smoothiccino maker.

Don't get your hopes up, Glen told himself. About the only food-related merchandise he'd seen in Hank's were George Foreman grilling machines and barbecues. But it was Christmas, and maybe he'd brought in some extra stuff for his hassled customers whose wives were on strike.

Hank's was a zoo, too, with guys lined up for gift certificates. Glen decided a gift certificate would be great for his father-in-law. But first, the small-appliance aisle.

Hank did have a few more items than usual: a mixer, a blender. And, whoa, what was that? It sure looked like the Smoothiccino machine Laura had been drooling over in that catalog. Glen picked up his pace. Yes, it was. One left.

And then he saw the guy coming from the opposite end of the aisle. Oh, no. He couldn't be. No sense taking any chances. Glen broke into a trot. The guy saw him and bolted for the machine.

"Not that one!" Glen made a flying leap, but he was too late. The other guy was hunched over it, hugging it like a quarterback would a football.

"I saw that first," Glen snarled.

"Get away or I'll call the cops," the guy threatened.

Glen resorted to pleading. "Come on, man. I really need that."

"What? You think I don't? I've looked all over town. I've even been to the mall. This is the last one left anywhere. I'm going to be sleeping on the couch if I don't come home with this." He hauled it off the shelf and hurried away like a troll with treasure.

"Yeah, well I hope it breaks," Glen called after him.

The guy gave him the one-fingered salute and scurried around the end of the aisle.

Glen leaned his head on the shelf and tried to collect himself. Nobody liked to see a grown man cry.

"Okay, shake it off, pull yourself together," he muttered. It wasn't like he'd gotten Laura nothing. He'd get a rain check for the Smoothiccino maker and slip it into the envelope along with the certificate for the nail place and hope that would be good enough. Yeah, right. Who was he kidding?

At least he could get his father-in-law's present here. He joined the long line at the checkout counter. The Smoothiccino maker thief was standing three guys up, clinging to his prize. I hope you choke on the first frappe you drink, Glen thought sourly as Hank rang up the purchase. He gave the guy a dirty look as he passed. The creep pretended not to see.

Finally, Glen reached the counter. "I need a twenty-five dollar gift certificate."

"I'm out," Hank said.

"How can you be out of gift certificates?" Glen demanded.

"You saw the line. All you last-minute idiots cleaned me out."

316

"Whoever heard of being out of gift certificates?" Glen said.

Hank scowled. He grabbed a steno tablet, flipped to a fresh page and started writing. Then he ripped off the paper and pushed it across the counter. "Okay. That'll be twenty-five bucks."

Glen looked at the green, lined paper with its barely legible pencil scrawl. "Oh, yeah. That's impressive."

"It'll work. Do you want it or not?"

"No, and maybe you should stock up for the holidays better. You're out of Smoothiccino makers, too."

Hank glared at him. "Yeah, well I get a lot of demand for those in a hardware store. What do I look like, anyway, Linens and Things? You clowns are lucky I even had one. Go get a hammer. I got plenty of those left."

"My father-in-law has three hammers already. What else have you got?"

Hank threw an arm in the direction of the shelves, stocked with a thinning selection of merchandise. "Go look for yourself."

Like he had time. Glen walked up and down the aisles, trying to make a decision. He couldn't. He hadn't been gifted with the shopping gene, and by now his brain simply refused to work. He finally grabbed some drill bits and marched back to the counter. He spotted a can of nuts and grabbed that, too.

"Big spender," Hank observed.

"Yeah, well, I'd have been a bigger spender if you had any gift certificates left," Glen growled.

He got to the grocery store in time to get the second-to-last turkey in the meat section. The thing was still frozen. How long did it take to cook a frozen turkey, anyway? Hopefully, not more than four hours. That was all he had left until the family arrived. Not for the first time he found himself wishing he hadn't missed the deadline for getting the precooked turkey. He snagged a couple of boxes of instant spuds, some boxed stuffing, and the last two cans of gravy. Then he ended his shopping spree with dinner rolls and frozen peas. His mom had promised to bring cookies, so he was okay for dessert.

The checkout lines were long, mostly guys looking frazzled or ready to punch someone. Glen got behind one with a cart piled high with frozen turkey dinners. Why hadn't he thought of that?

"Good idea," he said to the guy. "Any of those left?"

"I got the last ones," the guy said, and put a protective hand over the pile.

You'd think it was the end of the world, Glen thought, looking around. That was when he saw the guy with six cartons of eggnog in his cart.

Shit. Drinks! Glen pulled out of line and raced to the milk cooler, just as another shopper with a cart full of eggnog was taking the last one. What a hog!

"Hey, do you mind if I have that one?" Glen demanded.

"Sorry, pal," said his fellow shopper. "I'm buying for the neighbors."

Yeah, right, Glen thought bitterly. He settled for a gallon of chocolate milk, then went to the pop aisle. It had been picked nearly clean. He barely beat another frantic shopper to the last bottle of diet grapefruit, then wheeled back to the checkout.

The lines stretched halfway to the North Pole, and they were all moving at the speed of a glacier. He still had to get home, put this turkey in the oven, wrap presents, set the table, then make all the rest of the dinner stuff. *Oh, God, just let me live through tonight. Please. I'll do anything. Anything.*

Finally back home, he hauled the presents up to the bedroom, brought in the groceries, and stuck the turkey in a pan in the oven. Then he went in search of wrapping paper, turning his face from the clock as he passed. The last thing he needed was to be reminded that everyone would arrive in less than three hours.

Bob was at the computer, trying to finish his surprise when Joy stuck her head around the door. "It's time to go."

He was so close. Another hour and he'd have it. "I'm not quite ready. Can we be a little late?"

"I guess," she said, disappointment plain in her voice.

"I just need a little longer."

"Bob, you can write all you want in just a couple of days."

"Not this. It's something I need to finish." He smiled at her over his shoulder.

She sighed and shut the door.

Half an hour later she was back again. "We really need to go."

"Okay," he said, typing frantically. "You and Bobby go ahead. Take your car. I'll meet you there."

"Promise?"

"Absolutely. I'm a changed man. Remember?"

"Okay." Her tone of voice said she was determined to believe him even though the evidence was shaky.

"You won't be sorry," he promised, and returned to his fever pitch writing pace.

"So, where's Dad?" Bobby asked as Joy came down the hall.

"Working."

"Working? On what?"

"On some kind of surprise." She went to the kitchen and fetched the fruit salad, then rejoined her son. "Let's go. Dad will show up later."

Bobby picked up the shopping bag of presents that had been set out to go to Al's and followed her out the door. "Maybe he's going to stay home and hide out so nobody gives him a bad time about the Internet scam."

"If he said he's coming, he'll come," Joy said.

They got to her big brother's front porch just as he threw open the front door. "Ho, ho, ho," he greeted them. He peered around Joy. "Where's Bob?"

"He's coming a little late," she said, and hurried past him.

She had the same response for everyone who asked, and everyone drew his or her own conclusions and dropped the subject.

Except for Joy's sister-in-law, Lonnie. "But what's he doing?"

Joy got busy fussing with a platter of cheese. "I'm not sure. He's working on some kind of surprise."

"A surprise, huh?" Lonnie looked skeptical.

"He'll be here," Joy insisted. But what was taking him so long? She heard a shriek down in the party room that sounded like Melia — probably getting teased by one of her cousins. The party was in full swing and no Bob yet. Joy resisted a sudden urge to grab her cell phone and call him and ask when he was going to get there.

They ate appetizers. Bob didn't show. They ate dinner. Bob still didn't show.

"Maybe he's had a heart attack or something," Melia worried.

"He'd better have at least broken his leg," Lonnie muttered, and put an arm around Joy.

"He'll be here," Joy said. *Come on, Bob. Please.*

The women cleared the tables, and the holiday cookies and candy made their appearance and still no Bob.

Joy sat at a table, drinking coffee with her sisters-in-law. Lonnie pushed a cookie platter toward her. "Come on, Joy. You can't drink coffee without a cookie to go with it."

Joy was having trouble even drinking the coffee. It landed like acid in her stomach. Maybe something had happened. Maybe he'd gotten in a car accident. Maybe she would just get the cell and give him a quick buzz.

"Well, look who's here," cried Susan, smiling.

Joy turned and saw Bob walking through the doorway, a pile of typed pages in his arms. What on earth?

Al came up to Bob and gave him a friendly slap on the back. "We've got plenty of food left."

"What's that?" called one of the nephews. "Your latest book?"

Bob shook his head. "Nope, it's your entertainment for the night."

Susan left the table and went over for a closer look. "What have you got for us?"

"The first annual Johnson murder mystery," Bob told her, and handed her a few papers. "This is your part."

She took the pages and read, "The Cooking of Joy." She grinned over at Joy. "Ha! I like it."

Others had gathered around him now, and Bob began passing out papers.

"Hey," crowed Melia, "I'm Bonita Bon-Bon, the most beautiful woman in Holly."

Al was looking at his. "Big Al Capone?"

Bob shrugged.

"So how does this work?" Al asked.

Joy watched in amazement as Bob explained to everyone what to do. They all had five minutes to find some kind of makeshift costume, then they'd meet again and read through their parts. Everyone had a clue on his or her pages that no one else had. They'd have to pool their clues and use their powers of deduction to find which one of them was the murderer.

With yelps and shrieks everyone scattered, lifting table runners and tree decorations to make their costumes. And Bob stood there in the middle of the chaos, smiling at Joy. Then he said, "Surprise."

And she burst into tears.

CHAPTER
TWENTY-THREE

The house was full of hungry people, and Glen was in the kitchen sweating. He had wrapped the presents that would go home with various guests, using all ten thumbs, but the stuff for Laura and the kids was still on the bed along with a pile of wrapping paper and ribbon, waiting to torture him. Ten minutes ago he'd realized he'd forgotten to get batteries for Tyler's remote control car, and now Scrooge's Ghost of Christmas Future was pointing a bony finger at a vision of Christmas morning and a car that wouldn't run and a crying kid.

Dinner was late, late, late. His mother had offered to help, but Laura had hauled her away, assuring her that Glen had everything under control. Of course, he had nothing under control. He'd managed to burn both the peas and the instant spuds and now the kitchen stank. He had dirty pots and bowls piled in the sink like the leaning tower of Pisa. Meanwhile, everyone was out in the living room yucking it up while he was in here having a nervous breakdown.

His father strolled through the doorway. "Your mother sent me to see how you're doing," Dad said, hooking his hands into his suspenders. Why had his

324

mom sent Dad in here when Dad knew even less than Glen about cooking? That was probably Laura's idea.

"How does it look like I'm doing?" Glen grabbed a potholder and opened the oven to take out the turkey. The pan burned its way through the potholder and he barely got the bird to the stovetop before dropping it with a howl.

His dad shook his head. "You're henpecked."

"Yeah? Well, how come you're in here seeing if I need help instead of Mom?" Glen retorted.

"Because your mother told me to. Looks like you're doing fine, son," his dad added, and left.

"Oh, yeah. I'm doing great," Glen muttered. "I'm in hell."

He slopped the burned potatoes into a bowl, then dished up the burned peas. He had no idea where Laura kept that thing she served gravy in, so he left the canned beef gravy in the pan. He knew enough not to put the hot pan on the table, though. He grabbed the useless potholder and stuck it under the thing. Then he wrestled the turkey onto the serving platter and put that out.

"Okay, guys. Dinner," he called.

The hungry horde charged the table. As soon as Glen's dad had said grace, they fell on the food like Vikings home from a busy day of pillaging.

"Good job, son," his dad approved. He looked around the table. "Where's the rolls? Don't we have any?"

"Of course we've got rolls." Glen rushed back into the kitchen and emptied the bag of rolls into another bowl. He returned and set the bowl in front of his dad.

His mom eyed them critically. "Those don't look like my recipe."

"They're the house special," Glen replied, and couldn't help wondering if Laura had put her up to saying that. Was he really supposed to have made dinner rolls on top of everything else?

He remembered Laura complaining at Thanksgiving about having to make his mom's rolls. At the time he hadn't understood why she'd been complaining. He sure got it now. Laura was right. If Mom wanted her homemade rolls at a family dinner she could make the damn things herself.

His father was attempting to saw into the turkey but not having much luck. "Something's wrong with this bird."

There was nothing wrong with the turkey. Couldn't be. "It's fine, Dad. Just cut it."

"I can't."

Exasperated, Glen got up from his seat and took the carving knife and fork from his father. He almost bent the fork trying to put it in. "What the hell?"

"Oh, my God," said his brother Chuck. "The thing's still frozen on the inside."

"It's been cooking for two and a half hours," Glen said. "How can that be?"

"A turkey takes longer than that. Did you thaw it first?" asked his mother.

"Did you take out the neck and giblets?" asked Laura.

"Um," said Glen.

His cousin Frank burst out laughing, and some of the women giggled.

"I hope you got the rest of Christmas under better control than this," Frank said.

"It's covered," Glen said between clenched teeth.

"He did all the shopping today," Laura added.

"Did you remember to get batteries?" asked Frank's wife.

Tyler chose that moment to spit out his potatoes.

"I don't want my peas," Amy said. "They taste icky."

"That's okay, kid, so does everything else," joked Frank.

Now everyone at the table was staring at Glen, like they expected him to wave a magic wand and fix it all. But he didn't have a clue how to do that and he was too tired to look for one. He'd been going nonstop all month, and he'd used up his last ounce of mental strength getting ready for tonight. Game over.

He threw up his hands. "I can't do this. This is woman stuff."

"It's hard for one person to do alone without any help, isn't it?" Laura said.

Glen fell down on his knees next to her chair. "Make it stop, baby. Please, I give. You win."

She looked down at him, a funny expression on her face. "It was never about winning, you big doof. I just wanted you to understand."

"I understand now," Glen said. He almost added, "Please, God. I want to live again."

"So, from now on, when you get inspired to invite half the world over, will you help me?"

"Yes, yes," Glen said.

"Really help? No just putting a leaf in the table, then going to watch the game?"

"No, never."

"Because I'm not doing this all on my own anymore and letting you wiggle out of helping."

Glen crossed his heart. "No more wiggling."

She smiled down at him. "You promise? We have witnesses, you know."

"Teamwork," Glen promised.

"Oh, that's so sweet," murmured Laura's mother as Laura rewarded Glen with a kiss.

"Henpecked," muttered his dad.

"Leonard, be quiet," said his mom.

"That was all real touching," Chuck said, "but what about the turkey? And the peas and spuds are burned. I hate to say it, bro, but this dinner sucks. This is like prison food or something."

"I don't think cooking is your thing, Glen," one of the women said diplomatically.

Laura got up and picked up the platter with the bad-news turkey. "Don't worry, guys. Mom, Edna, you want to help me?"

Glen's mother and mother-in-law each scooped up bowls of disaster food, and followed Laura out of the dining room. A couple of minutes later they returned, bearing a platter of cold, sliced ham, a big bowl of potato salad, a molded Jell-O fruit salad, and Mom's dinner rolls.

"Plan B," Laura told Glen and kissed the top of his head. "We had it hidden in the extra fridge in the

328

garage for just in case. And we've got Mom's Christmas cookies for dessert. I just couldn't let you keep working without a net, not when you've been trying so hard. It wasn't fair."

Glen sighed in relief. "Thanks, babe."

"Well, it's beginning to look a lot like Christmas," his dad cracked.

"Yeah, but you still need batteries," teased Frank. Maybe Frank wouldn't get invited back next year.

"Don't worry. I bought some," Laura said.

"She saved your bacon," Frank told Glen. Frank was definitely not getting invited back next year.

The turkey and all its trimmings had been consumed, and Carol's old-fashioned figgy pudding had been a hit. Even little Chloe had liked it, licking the sauce from her bowl. Now they all sat in the living room, which was scented by bayberry candles and decorated with a small ceramic tree on the coffee table, watching the gas flames dance over the fake logs in the fireplace and listening to a CD of Christmas music.

Carol looked at Chloe, cuddled in her mother's lap and fighting the heaviness settling on her eyelids. They'd probably be moving in another year. Would she ever see or hear from them again? Maybe not, but that was okay. Maybe it was all right to risk letting people into your life, even if they drifted on out, because the time they were there was so special.

"This sure beats that turkey potpie I had in the freezer," Darren said from his spot on the couch. The way he smiled at Carol told her he wasn't planning on drifting off any time soon.

She wasn't sure how she felt about that. One thing she was sure of, it was nice to have someone here with her right now. She smiled at him and said, "I'm glad you enjoyed it."

She looked back at the fire. Funny, the images you could see in a blazing fire. For a minute there the flames moved in a way that looked like two people dancing.

Rosemary Charles stood at the door of Rick's apartment, stamping snow off her feet and waiting for him to answer the doorbell. She pressed it again. What was taking him so long to answer, anyway? It wasn't like he wasn't expecting her. He'd asked her to stop by on her way to her parents', insisting that he had something important she needed to see. What she needed to see at Rick's Scrooge-in-residence place she couldn't imagine, but she was curious enough to let him lure her over for some hot buttered rum.

She suddenly heard strains of "Grandma Got Run Over By a Reindeer" coming from inside the house. And then Rick opened the door. He was wearing a Santa hat.

She blinked. "What are you doing?"

"Just thought you'd like to see how I celebrate Christmas," he said, and stepped aside for her to enter.

"I got the impression you didn't."

"Well, you got the wrong impression. Want to see my tree?"

"You have a tree?"

"Yeah, I've got a tree."

"Oh, I can hardly wait to see this," she said, following him into the living room. He'd probably decorated it with old Budweiser cans.

But he hadn't. It had old-fashioned tinsel on it and all kinds of those collectible ornaments she saw every year at Hallmark. "This is impressive," she said, moving closer for a better look.

In fact, the whole apartment was impressive. The neutral-colored walls were jazzed up with framed photographs of mountain and sea scenes — Rick's work, obviously. He didn't have a ton of furniture, but what he had was nice: brown leather sofa and love seat, a sturdy coffee table made of cherrywood. It had two steaming mugs sitting on it.

Rick handed one to her.

"How did you manage this?" she said, holding up the mug.

"I'm organized."

"So, tell me about the tree."

"Not much to tell. My mom has gotten me ornaments for Christmas every year since I was born. Of course, she got me other stuff, too," he added, then frowned. "Socks, underwear, pajamas."

"You poor, deprived child," Rosemary teased.

"Well, we could always count on Santa for the cool stuff," Rick said.

"The stuff you got from Santa probably wouldn't be as valuable as these ornaments." She smiled at him. "It's a great tree."

"I don't put one up every year. It's a pain in the ass." He smiled at her. "I just put it up when I'm planning on having really important company."

She felt suddenly fluttery inside and took a sip of her drink. "Well, I've got to say, you have great taste. All except for the music," she added.

"Hey, that's a great song."

She nodded at the tree. "So, was this what you wanted me to see?"

"That and what's under it," he said, moving closer to her.

She looked down and saw a small package wrapped in gold foil. "What's this?"

"Something for you."

"Oh, my gosh. Really?"

He picked it up and gave it to her. "Open it."

She did and her jaw dropped. There was the necklace with the pink quartz she'd admired at the Hollydays Fair. She looked from it to Rick, stunned. He was grinning like an oversized elf.

"You can shut your mouth now," he teased, and lifted a finger to her chin. "Or, come to think of it, you can leave it open."

It was a kiss to remember. He smelled like aftershave and tasted like hot buttered rum.

"So," he murmured after that enticing sample of possible Christmases future. "You got your outfit all picked out for New Year's Eve?"

She grinned up at him. "Who's paying? Who lost the bet?"

He looked over his shoulder at his tree. "Let's call it a draw, but I'll pay."

Joy and Bob and their kids were almost the last to leave the party this year. It was a first.

Al pumped Bob's hand as they walked out the door. "Thanks for doing that, Bob. It was really great. I loved it that you made Lonnie the murderer."

"We'll do it again next year," Bob promised.

Joy could hardly believe her ears. She threaded an arm through Bob's as they made their way down the front walk. "Will we? Really?"

He nodded. "Why not?"

She sighed happily. "That was fun."

He smiled down at her and said, "Yes, it was."

Those were the sweetest words she'd heard in a long time, and, after all they'd been through this season, they felt almost too good to be true. *Note to self: Reward husband properly later.* She tugged on Bob's arm, slowing them down to let the kids go on ahead of them. "Did you mean what you just said? Really?"

He considered a moment. "Yes, I did. And even if I didn't I'd still be there. I love you, hon, crazy family and all."

Al's front door opened to let out a couple other stragglers, and music from his Christmas CD danced out into the cold night air, a choir singing "We Wish You a Merry Christmas."

No need to wish it, Joy thought happily. She had it.

* ★ ★

Glen had done all the dishes after dinner, but he made sure he wasn't alone. He'd bullied his brother and Frank into helping him. Now the kitchen was clean and the family was busy exchanging presents, and Glen found himself wishing he was back in the kitchen, especially when his father-in-law opened his gift.

"Drill bits and nuts," he said. "Interesting combination."

"If you'd been at Hank's today . . ." Glen began.

Laura's dad cut him off with a wave of his hand. "I was. You did better than I did." He lowered his voice and leaned over to Glen. "Your mother-in-law's getting a handwritten gift certificate."

Poor Dad, Glen thought. Although he hadn't done much better for Laura.

"Oh, well. A gift certificate is better than nothing," his father-in-law decided.

Wait a minute. That gave Glen an idea. And it was a great one. He felt so pleased with himself he almost crowed. Santa would be up late tonight, but it would be worth it.

"Say," said his mom. "Isn't it time we left for church?"

Glen looked at his watch. "Whoa, you're right. Hey, everybody, we've got to get going."

"You got the right costume this time?" teased Frank.

"Funny," snapped Glen. Not only was Frank not getting invited back next year, he might not even live to see next year.

Everyone hugged, kissed, then rushed out and piled into cars, and ten minutes later the family was settled in pews for the early Mass, witnessing a new generation of kids celebrating the Christmas story. Watching his daughter sing in the angel choir with his wife seated next to him and his son on his lap made Glen remember why he loved this season so much. And this year he had a new appreciation for all of it. So much effort went into making all the celebrations he loved, effort he'd taken very much for granted. Never again. He was a new man and he was going to prove it to Laura with a grand gesture.

Back home, when it was just them, he got the presents he'd bought earlier wrapped and stashed under the tree while Laura put the kids to bed. Then they filled the kids' stockings together. As it turned out, the stocking stuffers were about the only things that he'd managed not to screw up on. Laura told him it was because he was the world's biggest kid.

"There's nothing wrong with that," he said, suspecting an insult.

"No, there's not," she agreed with a smile. "I think that does it. Let's go to bed."

"You go ahead. I've got a couple more things I need to do," Glen said.

She wrapped her arms around his waist and smiled up at him. "It's over, you big goof. You're done. You can come to bed."

"Not quite." He kissed her. "You go on. I'll be up in a little bit."

She shook her head at him like he was nuts. "Okay."

As soon as she was gone, he slipped into the spare room office and began making his Christmas creation for her, using everything he could find from old stationery to some of the kids' colored craft paper. He got so engrossed in his project he didn't even hear Laura come in until she said his name. Then he about jumped out of his skin.

"What are you doing?" she asked.

He threw an arm over the scattered bits of clipped papers. "Nothing."

"Glen, you've been in here for almost two hours."

Time flew when you were being brilliant. "Really?"

She slipped around him and loosened a rectangle of red construction paper from under his elbow.

"Hey," he protested.

But it was too late. She was already reading it. "Good for one back rub. No expiration date." She gave him a smile that told him he was really onto something, then freed another bit of paper. "Good for one night of dinner and dancing. Dancing, huh? Boy, you're really trying. So how many of those coupons have you made?"

He shrugged. "I don't know. I've lost count."

"And are they all for me?" she asked, her voice teasing.

"Well, they're not for Frank."

She grinned and dropped onto his lap, slipping her arms around his neck. "This is really sweet."

Man, she smelled good. "What I found for you didn't seem good enough," he confessed. "I'm sorry, babe. I'd

336

ordered something really great from that stupid Internet site and —"

She put her fingers to his lips to shut him up. "You already gave me what I wanted for Christmas. You helped. It was all I ever really wanted." She slid off his lap, the flimsy material of her nightgown whispering through his fingers. "Now, why don't you come to bed?" she suggested, her voice silky.

It looked like Glen was going to get something he really wanted for Christmas, too. He followed her out of the room, leaving the coupons on the desk. They'd still be there in the morning.

Merry Christmas to all, he thought with a smile, and to all a good night.

CHAPTER
TWENTY-FOUR

...And a Happy New Year

"The worst was the frozen turkey," Glen said, and proceeded to describe the finishing touch to his disaster dinner. By the time he was done, Bob and Joy's other party guests were nearly in hysterics. "I don't want to be a woman for Christmas ever again," he concluded.

"You won't have to be," Laura assured him, patting his leg. "Just a helpful husband."

"That I can handle. Man, what a nightmare this all was."

"You did do okay with the costume for the Christmas pageant at church," she reminded him.

He rolled his eyes. "Real hard. We were down to one bag."

Pete gestured to Bob's disaster tree. "At least you got the tree right, and that's more than Bob can say."

Bob pointed a warning finger at him. "No fishing for compliments, Martha Stewart. My tree may not have won any contest, but it makes a statement."

"I hope you're not fixing to tell us what it says," Sharon said in disgust.

Whatever it said, it had been the perfect tree to shelter all the funny white elephant gifts the Stitch 'N Bitchers and their husbands had just finished fighting over.

"Well, I have to admit, I was pretty mad when Kay started this," said Jack Carter, who was sitting on the Robertson's couch with an arm around his wife, "but at least I can see now how easy it is to get carried away with shopping."

"He actually spent more this year than I usually do," Kay added.

"So there was something for your children under the tree after all?" Joy asked.

Jack made a face. "Like I was going to let my kids come over and find nothing under the tree." He shook his head at Kay. "Kay exaggerates."

Kay said nothing. She didn't need to. Her smug smile and the new bit of bling-bling on her finger said it all. Her cheapskate husband had learned his lesson.

"Hey, any progress on finding the crooks who ran that Web site?" Glen asked Bob.

Bob shook his head. "Not that I know of. Don't hold your breath about getting any of the merchandise you ordered."

Glen shrugged. "Oh, well. We made out okay anyway. But, let me tell you, I'm sure glad I'm not in charge of the shopping next year." Looking at his wife, he quickly added, "But I'm helping with it. I'm helping with everything."

"It's almost midnight," Joy said, passing around the plate with Bob's bonbons one last time. "Let's break out the champagne."

Bob and Glen disappeared into the kitchen to open bottles and Carol helped Joy set out the glasses.

"I wish Jerri could have been here for this," Carol said.

"Me, too," said Joy. Wouldn't she have loved to see Carol in her new, red sweater, smiling across the room at Darren. He was looking at her like she was blond ginger-bread, and Joy suspected the new year was going to bring serious romance into Carol's life. And she hoped it would bring a complete recovery and perfect health to Jerri's. "Next year she'll be here."

A loud pop proclaimed the champagne ready, and everyone gathered around the dining room table while Joy and Carol poured it.

With the glasses filled, they all looked to Bob for a toast.

He cleared his throat. "Well, here's to our successful negotiations and an end to the strike."

"Amen to that," Glen said heartily. "And here's to Christmas being a lot better next year."

"And maybe a little messier," Sharon added, smiling at her husband.

Joy decided her Christmas couldn't get much better than this one had turned out. Bob had really come through, and for the first time in many years, she had felt like they were a couple at her family's holiday gathering. It had been the perfect Christmas. And tonight's party had been perfect, too. Not too many people, which made Bob happy, but plenty of fun, which was all she needed to rev her batteries for the New Year.

Everyone clinked glasses and guzzled champagne; then, shortly after, the party broke up.

"Hey man, great time," Glen said to Bob as they were leaving.

Bob put an arm around his wife. "We'll do it again next year."

Food Favorites

FROM JOY AND COMPANY TO YOU

For those of you who don't want to go on strike this Christmas, Joy and her friends thought you might enjoy some of their favorite recipes.

Dave's Peppermint Fizz

You can also make this with vanilla ice cream and a drop of red food coloring, if you can't find peppermint ice cream or if you want a more delicate flavor.

2 generous scoops peppermint candy ice cream (or chocolate chip mint)
1 shot peppermint schnapps (you can measure this with a regular liquor shot glass, but Sheila, er, Dave, just uses one of those little espresso shot glasses)
½ cup club soda

Combine all ingredients in blender and blend just until smooth. Serve in a champagne flute or margarita glass and garnish with a small peppermint stick. Pour in just a dab more club soda to add decorative fizz. *Makes 1 drink.*

Joy's Stuffed Phyllo Appetizers

1 box packaged stuffing mix

1 (8-ounce) package cream cheese at room temperature

¼ cup dried cranberries or sultana raisins

½ cup chopped pecans (optional; use if you want some crunch)

4 sheets packaged frozen phyllo dough

16 muffin tins

1. Prepare stuffing on the stovetop according to package directions. After it has set the required number of minutes, cut up the cream cheese and stir it into the stuffing with the cranberries and pecans, if using.

2. Take out 4 sheets of phyllo dough and spread them on a counter, keeping them stacked one on top of each other. Peel back the top three layers and brush the bottom layer lightly with oil or melted butter. Then drop the third layer back over it and brush that. Repeat the process with the second and first layers. Phyllo dough can be intimidating because it tears so easily, but don't worry. A tear here or there won't matter. Cut the stack in quarters and cut each quarter into quarters again. You should now

have 16 small stacks with each stack containing 4 sheets.

3. Take the top 2 sheets from each of your 16 stacks and lay them in a greased muffin tin. Spoon in 1 to 2 soupspoon-size helpings of the stuffing, then top with the remaining sheets and fold them over the bottom so it looks like a little bundle. If the bundles look dry, brush lightly with oil. Bake at 350°F. for about 8 minutes (no longer than 10 — this stuff browns quickly!). *Makes 16 appetizers.*

Joy's Vegetable Soup

(IN LOVING MEMORY OF DON MOYLE)

1 pound short rib or beef shank

Stockpot filled with stock or water

1 (2½-pound) can diced tomatoes

½ cup lentils

2 stalks celery, finely chopped

1 parsnip, finely chopped

1 rutabaga, finely chopped

¼ of a small cabbage, finely chopped

1 onion, finely chopped

2 carrots, finely chopped

2 potatoes, cubed

Parsley, minced

Ketchup

Salt and pepper to taste

Oregano (just a dash)

1. Boil the beef until you can pull the meat off the bones, about 45 minutes. Remove the meat, discard the bone, and when the meat is cool cut it into bite-size pieces. Add tomatoes, lentils, celery, and the other vegetables to broth. Add seasoning and a small amount of parsley, if available. Bring to a slow boil and simmer 2 to 3 hours. Add a couple of shots of ketchup for color and flavor.

2. Return the meat to the soup. Add salt and pepper to taste and a pinch of oregano. *Makes 6 to 8 servings with leftovers to spare. This soup freezes well.*

Sharon's Granny Patrick's Stuffing

(COURTESY OF DUSTIN PATRICK)

1 pan of corn bread (white is preferred, but you can use yellow)
¼ cup butter
½ onion, diced
3 celery stalks, chopped
Salt and pepper to taste
1 tablespoon rubbed sage or to taste
1 can mushrooms, chopped
3 to 4 hard-boiled eggs, cut up
1 can cream of mushroom soup
½ cup chicken broth

1. Crumble corn bread into a large bowl. Melt butter in a large skillet. Saute the onion and celery until onion is tender but not brown. You may add salt and pepper and some of the sage. Add mushrooms to the sauté for the last minute or so. Add the mixture to the corn bread along with the eggs, then start adding sage and stirring. Mix well. Continue adding sage just until you can taste it. Mix in the cream of mushroom soup. Mix in the broth a little at a time until the dressing is very moist but not soupy.

2. Bake at 325° F. for 50 to 60 minutes, or use the mixture to stuff a turkey. If baking separately, stuffing is done when the top is a little crunchy but the inside is still moist. *Makes enough stuffing for a medium-sized (15- to 20-pound) turkey.*

Joy's Christmas Bonbons

(COURTESY OF STACIA SWENSON)

3 boxes powdered sugar
1 can sweetened
    condensed milk
2 sticks margarine
¼ teaspoon each of
3 different extracts, such
    as mint, orange, rum

Food coloring
3 to 4 packages imitation
    milk chocolate chips
    (see note at end)
1 inch paraffin wax

1. Mix powdered sugar with warmed-up milk (heat opened can in a saucepan of boiling water) and margarine until smooth. Separate filling into 3 batches. Flavor and color each batch. Wrap in plastic wrap to prevent air from drying out filling when it's not being worked. Shape each batch into different forms (patties, squares, balls), making them candy-size. Put them on cookie sheets and stick them in the freezer to set until chocolate coating is ready.

2. Melt chocolate and wax together in the top of the double boiler. Chocolate is the right consistency when it pours from the spoon. If too thick, add more wax. Dip the candy forms into the chocolate and set out on foil-lined cookie sheets to cool. Pack them up in gift boxes about the size of powdered sugar boxes and store

in a cool place. *Makes enough for about 6 small gift boxes (about 200 candies). You can use real chocolate chips, but it's much harder to get the chocolate to set up right when making the candies. Be prepared to use more wax.*

Tiffany's Fudge Meltaways

(COURTESY OF RANA FRENCH)

Bottom layer:
½ cup butter
1 (1-ounce) square
   unsweetened chocolate
¼ cup granulated sugar
1 teaspoon vanilla

1 egg, beaten
2 cups graham cracker
   crumbs
1 cup flaked coconut
½ cup chopped walnuts

Frosting:
¼ cup butter
1 tablespoon milk or
   cream

2 cups sifted powdered
   sugar
1 teaspoon vanilla

Topping:
2 (1-ounce) squares unsweetened chocolate (the recipe actually calls for 1½ squares, but Tiff uses 2 to make sure she has enough to spread over the frosting)

1. For the bottom layer, melt ½ cup butter and 1 square of chocolate in a saucepan. Blend sugar, vanilla, egg, graham cracker crumbs, coconut, and walnuts into the butter mixture.

2. Mix well and press into an ungreased baking dish, 9 × 9 × 1¾inches. Refrigerate.

3. For the frosting, mix together the butter, milk, powdered sugar, and vanilla. Spread over the crumb mixture and return to the fridge to chill.

4. After it's set, spread with the melted chocolate. Lightly score the top for easier cutting. Chill again. *Makes 1 dozen squares.*

Sharon's Andes Mint Cookies

(COURTESY OF CAROL SCHMIDT)

This was once a top-secret recipe that Sharon never shared with anyone until Prevention *magazine had the nerve to leak it a couple of seasons ago. So, Sharon sends her apologies to Carol (so does Sheila) for sharing it, but there's really no point in keeping the secret anymore.*

¾ cup butter
1½ cups firmly packed
   dark brown sugar
2 tablespoons water
2 cups (12 ounces)
   semisweet chocolate
   chips
2 eggs

2½ cups flour
1¼ teaspoon baking soda
½ teaspoon salt
2 to 3 boxes Andes crème
   de menthe mints
Chocolate sprinkles
   (optional)

1. In a large, heavy saucepan over low heat, cook butter, sugar, and water until butter is melted. Remove from heat, add the chocolate, and stir until it is completely melted.

2. Pour the mixture into a large mixer bowl and let stand 10 minutes to cool slightly. With mixer at high speed, beat in eggs 1 at a time. Reduce speed to low

and add dry ingredients, beating just until blended. Chill dough 1 hour for easier handling.

3. Preheat oven to 350° F. Line 2 cookie sheets with foil. Roll dough into small (about 1-inch) balls; place them 2 inches apart on cookie sheets. Bake 12 to 13 minutes — no longer (cookies will crisp as they cool). Remove from oven and immediately place a mint over each cookie. Allow it to soften, then swirl over top. If desired, decorate with chocolate sprinkles. Remove from cookie sheets and cool. Frosting will harden once it cools. *Makes about 80. (Each contains 90 calories, but when you eat these with friends the calories only count half as much.)*

Tiffany's Frosted Christmas Brownies

2 sticks butter (salted)
4 ounces (squares)
  unsweetened chocolate
4 eggs
2¼ cups sugar
1 teaspoon peppermint
  extract

1 cup flour
1 (12-ounce) package
  semisweet chocolate
  chips

Frosting:
2 cups powdered sugar
3 tablespoons softened
  butter (salted)
2 tablespoons milk
Green or red food color-
  ing

Crushed peppermint
  candy (about ¾ cup,
  or however much or
  little you want)

1. Melt butter and chocolate over low heat. Cool. Beat eggs with a mixer for a couple of minutes, slowly adding sugar. Add peppermint extract and flour and stir until just combined. Add chocolate chips and chocolate-butter mixture.

2. Pour into greased 9- × 13-inch pan. Bake at 350° F. for 25 to 30 minutes. Cool.

3. For the frosting, combine the sugar, butter, milk, and a drop or two of food coloring. Spread over the brownies. (Note: frosting will thinly cover brownies. If you like more frosting, you may want to double the recipe.) Top with crushed peppermint candy. *Makes a couple dozen or so, depending on what size you cut the brownies.*

Joy's White Chocolate Shortbread

The original shortbread recipe called for 4 cups of flour, but with that you wind up adding extra butter and/or a tablespoon of water to get the dough to hold together, so Joy just starts with less flour. If the dough feels sticky you can always add more flour.

3½ cups flour
2 sticks butter (use the real thing, salted — no substitutes!)

¾ cup sugar
4 (1-ounce) squares white chocolate, melted
Flaked coconut (optional)

1. Mix the flour, butter, and sugar together until it holds in a ball like pie crust, then divide into 3 balls. Turn onto a large ungreased cookie sheet and flatten into circles about ¼ inch thick and 5 inches wide. Poke full of holes with a fork, then cut into pie wedge sections with a sharp knife. (This will make it easier to get the cookies apart once they're baked.) You should get about 6 wedges per circle.

2. Bake at 350° F. for 15 to 20 minutes or until lightly browned. Cut them again after you take them out of the oven and let them cool.

3. Melt white chocolate according to package instructions. Then frost the shortbread from the tip to the middle. If desired, you can top each cookie with a teaspoon of flaked coconut. Let the white chocolate harden completely before storing. *Makes about 18 wedges*.

Joy's Gumdrop Cookies

(IN LOVING MEMORY OF ANNE BATES, WHO DIED WAY TOO YOUNG)

½ cup shortening or margarine
½ cup granulated sugar
½ cup brown sugar
1 egg
1 tablespoon water
1 teaspoon vanilla
1 cup sifted flour
½ teaspoon baking powder

½ teaspoon baking soda
½ teaspoon salt
1½ cups rolled oats
¾ cup gumdrops, cut into small pieces
Approximately 1½ cups flaked coconut (optional)

1. Cream together shortening, sugars, egg, water, and vanilla. Beat until smooth. Sift together flour, baking powder, baking soda, and salt. Add the dry ingredients and the oats to the egg-sugar mixture. Add cut-up gumdrops. Form into 1-inch balls and roll in coconut, if desired.

2. Place on an ungreased cookie sheet and bake the cookies at 350° F. for 12 to 15 minutes. *Makes about 2 dozen. (Joy thinks. It's very hard to get an accurate count when people keep snitching the dough and*

snatching cookies the minute they come off the cookie sheet. She suggests doubling the recipe.)

Tiffany's Snowball Cookies

1 cup butter (can use half shortening)
½ cup powdered sugar, plus additional for rolling cookies in after they are baked

¼ teaspoon salt
1 teaspoon vanilla
2¼ cups flour
½ cup chopped walnuts

Cream butter and sugar. Add salt, vanilla, flour, and walnuts and mix. Roll into 1-inch balls and bake at 350° F. for 8 to 10 minutes or until lightly browned. (Watch these carefully. Don't overbake them.) Cool on rack. After they are cool, roll in powdered sugar. *Makes 2 dozen.*

Joy's Frosted Biscotti

(ADAPTED FROM A RECIPE COURTESY OF SUSAN ABBE)

1 cup pecans, lightly toasted
1 cup dried cranberries
2 eggs
½ cup sugar
½ cup vegetable oil
2 tablespoons grated orange peel
1 teaspoon cinnamon
⅛ teaspoon ground allspice
1¼ teaspoons baking powder
1 teaspoon vanilla
½ teaspoon orange extract
¼ teaspoon salt
2 cups flour
6 (1-ounce) squares white chocolate, melted

1. Toast the pecans by placing them on a lightly greased baking sheet and into a 350° F, oven for about 15 minutes. Stir the pecans at the end of each 5 minutes of baking time. Take from oven and set aside to cool.

2. Place the cranberries in a bowl with hot water to cover and let stand for 10 minutes. Drain and set aside.

3. In a large bowl, combine the eggs, sugar, oil, orange peel, cinnamon, allspice, baking powder, vanilla, orange extract, and salt. Blend. Add the flour, pecans,

and drained cranberries and stir into a stiff dough. Turn out onto a heavily floured surface and knead until smooth, counting your kneading turns. Knead about 20 turns. Add more flour if needed to reduce stickiness.

4. Divide dough in half. Form each half into a 2-inch-diameter log with a slight hump going down the middle. (These actually look a little like mini bread loaves.) Put them on a large cookie sheet greased lightly with cooking spray and bake them at 350° F. for about 30 minutes or until golden brown and firm to the touch. Let cool for 10 minutes. (Make sure you cool them for the full 10 minutes or they won't cut well!)

5. With a spatula, carefully transfer the logs to a cutting surface. Using a serrated knife, cut them on the diagonal into $\frac{1}{2}$-inch-thick slices. Return the slices, cut side down, to the baking sheet. Bake until brown at 350° F. about 20 minutes more. Cool on wire racks. When cool, melt white chocolate slowly in a heavy pan and dip one whole side of each biscotti in the chocolate, scraping off the excess as you remove each from the pan. Return the biscotti to wire racks and let them stand until chocolate is hardened. *Makes 16 to 24.*

Carol's Figgy Pudding

(FORMERLY MRS. MOYLE'S FIGGY PUDDING; IN LOVING MEMORY OF FLORENCE MOYLE)

⅓ teaspoon baking soda (I know. Who uses ⅓ of a teaspoon of anything? My mom. And this recipe is so good I honestly didn't want to tamper with it.)

⅓ teaspoon salt

⅓ teaspoon cinnamon

⅓ teaspoon nutmeg

⅓ teaspoon allspice

½ cup flour

½ cup sugar

⅓ cup each of raisins, candied fruit mix, cut up figs, and dates

⅓ cup grated apple

⅓ cup grated carrot

2 tablespoons melted butter

1 egg, beaten

1 tablespoon lemon juice

1. Sift dry ingredients together and mix with dried fruits. Add grated apple and carrot. Add melted butter and egg and stir in lemon juice.

2. Steam in the top of a medium-size double boiler for about an hour or so. The pudding will remain a little moist, but just be sure the center is a little bit firm. It will firm up a little more when it cools. Wrapped in foil, it will keep well for several weeks in your refrigerator.

3. To serve, heat the pudding in the top of a double boiler. Should be served hot. Makes 6 to 8 servings, depending on how much they eat.

Old-Fashioned Pudding Sauce

1 heaping tablespoon
   softened butter
⅓ cup flour
⅓ cup sugar

Salt
¼ teaspoon nutmeg
2½ cups boiling water
   Lemon juice (optional)

In a small saucepan cream together the butter, flour, and sugar. Add dash of salt and the nutmeg. Pour in a small amount of hot water to make a paste, then slowly add 2 cups boiling water to make a sauce of the desired thickness. If desired, add lemon juice to taste. Serve hot with the Figgy Pudding. *Serves 6 to 8.*

Happy Holidays and Happy Eating!